## PRAISE FOR
### *ALL OF YOU*

"Five words to describe this book (and you'll get this once you read it): hot, sweet, emotional, page-turner, awesome."

—Monica Murphy, *New York Times* and *USA Today* bestselling author of *One Week Girlfriend* and *Second Chance Boyfriend*

"With *All of You*, Christina Lee has crafted a fresh and fascinating twist on the classic love story. At its core, *All of You* is pure NA goodness, full of mistrust and hardened hearts, angst and anguish, hot and steamy scenes, and a satisfying HEA."

—*New York Times* bestselling author Jasinda Wilder

"A one-sitting read simply because I could not put it down. From steamy to sweet and every emotion in between, Christina Lee had me glued to the pages in her unforgettable debut, *All of You*. This is one New Adult you don't want to miss."

—*New York Times* and *USA Today* bestselling author A. L. Jackson

"Bennett stole my heart! If you like hot, sweet, sexy, caring good guys, he'll claim yours too."

—*New York Times* and *USA Today* bestselling author Lauren Blakely

"Steamy, honest, and full of heart, *All of You* kept me glued to the pages and had one of the best heroes I've read all year. A fantastic debut!"

—Roni Loren, national bestselling author of *Not Until You* and the Loving on the Edge series

*continued...*

# ALL OF YOU

## The Between Breaths Series

# CHRISTINA LEE

New American Library

New American Library
Published by the Penguin Group
Penguin Group (USA) LLC, 375 Hudson Street,
New York, New York 10014

USA | Canada | UK | Ireland | Australia | New Zealand | India | South Africa | China
penguin.com
A Penguin Random House Company

Published by New American Library, a division of Penguin Group (USA) LLC.
Previously published in an InterMix edition.

First New American Library Printing, July 2014

 REGISTERED TRADEMARK—MARCA REGISTRADA

LIBRARY OF CONGRESS CATALOGING-IN-PUBLICATION DATA:
Lee, Christina, 1968–
All of you/Christina Lee.
p. cm.
ISBN 978-0-451-46977-9 (pbk.)
1. Nursing students—Fiction.  2. Tattoo artists—Fiction.  I. Title.
PS3612.L325A44 2014
813'.6—dc23          2014000377

Printed in the United States of America
10  9  8  7  6  5  4  3  2  1

Set in Bembo
Designed by Spring Hoteling

To Greg, for allowing me to go first.

That means . . . everything.

# ALL
# OF
# YOU

# CHAPTER ONE

Love was like a loaded gun. You slid your bullet inside the cold metal chamber as a safeguard for the inevitable day that everything went to shit. At the first sign of trouble, you blew your opponent to pieces, long before their finger found the trigger. At least that's what my mother's string of failed relationships taught me.

I downed the warm beer and scanned the frat party from my armchair perch. The low moans drifting from the next couch over awakened a longing inside me. My best friend, Ella, and her boyfriend were going at it again. Our other friend, Rachel, an even bigger player than me, was in the far corner making out with another university jock. And I wasn't about to be the only one leaving empty-handed tonight.

Guys were easy to figure out—at least in the hormonal sense. You needed only to appear helpless or horny, and their pants instantly dropped to their ankles. Except none of the guys here tonight appealed to me. Maybe I'd text Rob for a booty call on my way home. He was always good for one, unless he'd already hooked up with someone else.

My gaze landed on the guy entering the back door through the kitchen. A red baseball cap was slung low on his head and inky black curls escaped beneath it. His arms were muscular, and his charcoal T-shirt hugged his lean chest. He was Grade A Prime Meat and probably knew exactly how to put those full lips to good use.

I watched as he high-fived one of the guys and then propped his forearm against the counter. His smile was magnetic, and I pictured him using it on me in another five minutes, when he sweet-talked me. I stood up and straightened my shirt so that it revealed more of my cleavage—the little I had—and strode toward the keg with my plastic cup.

As I drew nearer, I saw how alarmingly gorgeous this guy really was. The one hand fisted in his pocket tugged at his jeans, revealing a small sliver of a taut stomach. The trail of baby-fine hairs leading downward made heat pool low in my stomach.

I tried catching his eye, but he wasn't going for it.

His friend was a different story, though. He practically growled in my direction.

The friend was cute, too, but paled in comparison to Hot Boy. But maybe his friend was my ticket in. Too bad I wasn't the type to take on both of them—that might be entertaining.

Bile scorched the back of my throat. *Hell, no.* Two meant more testosterone, less power. No telling what might happen, even if I *thought* I was in control. There was a reason I only did one willing guy at a time.

When I stopped at the keg, I overheard Hot Boy telling a friend that he was moving in the morning. Hopefully not out of state. No matter; I only needed him for tonight. His voice was low and gruff, sending a ripple of satisfaction through me.

Hot Boy's friend reached over and grabbed hold of my cup. "Let me help you with that."

Hot Boy looked up and our gazes meshed for the first time. Warm chocolate eyes pinned me to my spot. They raked over me once before flitting away, sending my stomach into a free fall.

He pushed aside the messy bangs hanging in his eyes and resumed his conversation.

I wanted to run my fingers through those unruly curls at the nape of his neck. I made a mental note to do that later, when he was lying on top of me.

His friend handed my cup back, filled to the brim. Hot Boy didn't look my way again.

"Thanks." I clenched my teeth and worked to keep my lips in a neat, straight line.

"So, what's your name?" he asked as he stepped closer. His breath was sour with beer and cigarettes and I knew I could've taken him oh so easily. As simple as the arch of my eyebrow.

But I didn't want him. I wanted Hot Boy. Just for one night.

"My name's Avery," I said, loud enough for Hot Boy to hear.

Hot Boy only paused at the sound of my voice without looking my way. *Damn.* Maybe he had a girlfriend, or maybe he was gay. The pretty boys always were.

"Nice to meet you, Avery. I'm Nate." His friend slid his hand to my hip, and I considered giving up the hunt and taking him upstairs. But for some reason, I just wasn't feeling it.

"I'll be right back." I left him swaying unsteadily on his feet.

I headed back to Ella and Joel, who were still hot and heavy on the couch.

"I'm going to head home," I said, close to her ear.

Ella came up for air. "No prospects tonight?"

"One." I glanced over my shoulder to the kitchen. Hot Boy's friend was still waiting for me. "But I'm not really into it."

"Bitch, you're always into it." Her lips curved into a devilish grin. "Gonna hook up with Rob tonight instead?"

"Maybe." I didn't want to disappoint her. I was ready for a good time most weekends. And, even though she didn't really approve, she was ready for all the gritty details the next day. Ella hadn't gotten me to change my ways in high school, and she wouldn't now. But if I wasn't in the mood, I didn't feel like explaining it to her.

I looked around for Rachel to say good-bye, but she was already somewhere private with jock boy. Ella went back to ramming her tongue into Joel's mouth.

She'd probably felt stranded by Rachel and me too many times to count, so seeing her with Joel actually thawed a corner of my frozen heart. A real live boyfriend was what Ella had always wanted. Someone who *got* her, she'd said. Whatever the hell that meant.

Hopefully Joel would keep treating her right, or he'd have to answer to me. I wasn't opposed to grabbing hold and yanking those balls down hard. My self-defense classes had taught me well.

I decided to give Hot Boy one last shot as I passed by him on my way out the door, luring him with my sexiest voice. Unfortunately that meant passing his friend, too.

"Excuse me." My mouth was close to Hot Boy's ear, my

chest brushing past his arm. He smelled like coconut shampoo. Like warm sand, hot sun, and sex. I wanted to wrap myself inside of his arms, but I kept on moving.

"No problem," he said without even a glance.

Damn. Rejected again. That made me want him twice as much.

Just as my foot crossed onto the landing, I felt a warm hand reach around my waist. I almost fist pumped the air. *Got him.*

I turned to greet Hot Boy, my breaths already fluttery. But the smile slid from my lips and slumped to the floor when I realized it was his friend who'd grabbed me instead.

"Hey, baby, where you going?"

"I'm leaving." I twisted away, hoping to break his embrace.

But he kept in step with me. "How about you hang with me awhile longer?"

"Maybe another time."

His hands frisked around to my stomach, and normally I'd accept that kind of action—initiate it, even—but for some reason I couldn't shake Hot Boy's rejection.

I was more of an emotional train wreck than even *I'd* realized. Despite Ella reminding me almost every fucking day.

And just as I was chastising myself and changing my mind about hooking up with his friend, I heard Hot Boy's low rumble of a voice. "Give it a rest, Nate. She said she was leaving, and I'm pretty sure that means without *you.*"

I blinked in shock. Maybe he'd noticed me after all.

His friend backed away with his hands raised. And then turned to the keg.

Hot Boy gave me a once-over. "You good?"

"Yeah, thanks."

Wait a minute, this was backward. I was thanking Hot Boy for being all chivalrous. And the boys I hooked up with were *so not chivalrous.*

Hot Boy nodded before turning on his heels and heading out of the room, leaving my ego collapsing on the cold, hard tile.

Chivalrous Hot Boy was so not into me.

I walked the two blocks back to my apartment alone.

I tossed and turned, imagining Hot Boy's lips on mine, a fire blazing across my skin.

My cell phone buzzed from the night stand.

**Rob:** You in the mood?

**Me:** Not tonight.

# CHAPTER TWO

stepped out of the shower and slid into my blue scrubs. I had a shift at the nursing home and then a class that evening. I'd gotten my LPN license and was working on my RN degree at the local university, which was only five blocks away and was the exact reason I had chosen this apartment. It was an older building, only five floors, with two apartments on each level. There was one laundry room per floor, and the landlords were pretty cool—a middle-aged married couple with kids. I tried convincing Ella to move in with me last year, but she was saving money by living at home.

And maybe living alone was for the best. The rent was cheap, and I'd become a creature of habit. We'd probably only get on each other's nerves. Besides, she crashed at my place enough.

My phone buzzed from the bathroom counter and I saw it was my mother. She wasn't an early riser, so something must've been up. Maybe she had broken up with her latest asshole and needed consolation. Too bad I wouldn't be giving it to her. Not since she acted like what had happened with Tim four years ago was my fault, blaming it on how I dressed around him.

I told myself I'd never trust her or another man again.

"Mom, I'm going to be late for work."

She was in tears and wanted to use me as her sounding board. No surprise there. I only talked to her to keep tabs on my baby brother, now a senior in high school.

"What happened—did what's-his-name dump you?"

"No, I dumped him. Caught him cheating on me one too many times."

Phone calls with Mom were a sobering reminder of why I didn't get involved with guys. If you remained in charge of your life, they couldn't mess with your head or put their hands on you without your permission. *Not anymore.* Love was only a ridiculous fairy tale that was never satisfying, warm, or safe.

Only I could provide my own security—like a steel cage around my heart.

"Maybe this is a good time for you to take a break from men. Focus on Adam. He doesn't need all of this drama in his life, or he's going to move out when he's eighteen, too." I was always nervous about how my brother would turn out with all those guys traipsing through the house. Would he become an asshole male, too?

I'd had heart-to-hearts with him about how to treat girls despite what he saw going on at home. I hadn't told him about what happened with Tim—at least not the worst part of it. Ella was the only one who knew everything. If you didn't count the people who regularly denied it: Mom and Tim.

"Honey, you're twenty-one. It's high time you found *yourself* a good man."

"I told you. I can take care of myself." Besides, there were no good men out there. Except my brother, who I was hell-bent on saving. He'd been dating the same girl for the last few months, and I warned him about always using protection. The last thing he needed was to support a baby. But he'd told me he'd stick by her if that happened. That he was in love.

I wasn't sure how my brother had come out of that house-hold unscathed. But I was afraid that he was such a good soul, he'd be taken advantage of by someone.

"I know you can. But men are good for some things. I hate to think about you spending your life alone."

And that's when I needed to get off the phone. When my mother was preaching about the virtues of men—even though she herself was some kind of homing device for losers, cheat-ers, and liars. Men who either mooched off her, rent-free, or paid her bills as hush money.

"Okay, Mom, that's my cue. Got to get to work. Talk to you later."

My blond waves were damp and unruly, so I pulled them back in a low ponytail. I trailed mascara over my translucent lashes to help my eyes stand out and so I wouldn't look twelve years old. That way the families of our residents wouldn't think they could boss me around with their crazy-ass requests. I concealed the freckles on the bridge of my nose, and finally dabbed on some pink lip gloss.

Now a twenty-one-year-old woman stared back at me. I had finally developed curves my senior year in high school, but my butt and chest weren't as filled out as I would have liked. My boobs were finally a solid B cup, but the rest of me still looked too boyish.

Not that the men I was with cared about any of that. They were in it for the same thing I was—a quick release of sexual frustration. I could go months without needing it, but my vibrator only did so much. Rob was good for fast relief, but he wouldn't be at my beck and call forever. Sooner or later he'd want something more. Something I couldn't give him.

The sunlight streaming through my window looked so inviting that I decided to walk the three blocks to work today. As I was headed out the front door of my apartment building, a large U-Haul pulled up to the curb. One of the apartments on the fifth floor had been vacant for the last two months, and I'd gotten used to dragging my laundry basket up there, where it was quiet. The other guy who lived on the fifth floor was a pilot and rarely there, so the washer remained unused.

Two guys stepped out of the truck, and as one rounded the corner, I almost tripped over my white, cushy nursing sneakers. He didn't have his red ball cap on today, and his messy hair fell into his warm brown eyes.

*No fucking way.*

He stared at me, a moment of recognition crossing his face. At the party last night, I'd heard him tell his friend he was moving, but never in a million years would I have guessed it was to my apartment building.

My head down, I kept walking, equally embarrassed by my scrubs as by my eagerness last night. Nothing like the prospect of a day spent with geriatrics to sober me right up. Thank goodness the friend with him today wasn't the same one who'd gotten my name and grabbed my waist.

"Hey," he said. I turned and faced him, unsteady in my white nursing sneakers. "You're . . . um . . . do you live here?"

I drank him in with a thirsty gaze, his deep eyes like hot chocolate, drawing me forward for a taste. "Yeah."

"Small world." He extended his fingers toward me. "Bennett. Bennett Reynolds."

His hand squeezed mine. Smooth palms and long fingers. I bit my bottom lip to hold in a sigh. What in the living hell was wrong with me?

Maybe he'd let me get him out of my system. Maybe even tonight.

"Avery Michaels. First floor. Apartment 1A."

"Avery," he said. "I remember."

His eyes darted down to my scrubs and supportive shoes and I felt frumpy. Not at all sexy. Not that he thought I was last night, either, with my tight jeans and low-cut top. "You work at the university hospital?"

"Nope; the nursing home on Hamilton Street." He paused like he was considering what to ask next. His hot cocoa eyes pierced through my layers, inspecting me for any underpinnings of truth. I filled in some of the blanks for him. "I'm taking college courses at Turner State to become an RN. Working on the side helps pay the bills. How about you?"

"Art major at the university. Got a year left. In the meantime, I work at Raw Ink on Vine Street." I was more than familiar with that tattoo parlor. I'd been in the owner's bed a couple months ago. Oliver was skinny, inked up, and just the right amount of bad boy I'd needed for the night.

"You're a tattoo artist?" Holy Mother of God, this man just got hotter. I looked at his arms but saw no telltale signs. "I'd think you'd have more tats on you."

My fingers slid over the back of my ear near the tattoo I'd

gotten when I'd turned eighteen and finally escaped my mother's house. He'd probably think it was amateurish at best.

"Nah, just a couple of well-placed ones." His cheeks pinched into a grin and he looked down at his feet, almost shy about it. His teeth were perfectly white and straight and mesmerizing. "Sometimes less is more, you know?"

And sometimes *more is more*. My eyes roved over his stacked biceps and down the front of his jeans. Having a fuck buddy in the same apartment building could prove to be interesting. Or a disaster.

I needed to reel it the hell in and remind myself that this guy was not interested in me. *Yet*.

"Okay, gotta run," I said. "Good luck moving in."

I eyed his friend, who stood on the grass texting someone. I considered whether he'd be a good prospect as well. "You guys big partiers? This building is on the quiet side."

"Nope. Last night was the extent of the kind of partying I do. And it's only me moving in up there." Bennett was moving in, *alone*. He turned back to the truck. "See you later."

I restrained myself from glancing back more than once to see if he was watching me. He wasn't. Disappointment and indifference waged a war in my chest.

Work was busy that day, between med counts, feedings, and bed changes. Sometimes I felt like a glorified chamber maid. Some of the elderly were downright nasty. Were probably always nasty, even before they became sick.

And then there were gems like Mrs. Jackson. I'd become accustomed to seeing her kind eyes and soft wrinkles every day for the last year. I knew better than to get close to the residents, because I'd said my share of good-byes, usually to empty bed-sheets and untouched trays of food. I wasn't really one to build emotional connections anyway. But Mrs. Jackson had some-how broken through my barrier and befriended me.

If I was being honest, she reminded me of my grandma, who died when I was twelve. Feisty, strong-willed, and never minced words. Total opposite of my mother. No wonder we seemed to understand each other pretty well.

"Is that a smile I see on your face?" she asked as I entered with the extra pillow she'd requested. She could always read me well. I'd just been thinking about Hot Boy living in my building.

"I wasn't smiling," I said, placing the pillow behind her neck. "You're imagining it."

"Mmm-hmmm . . . Then why are your cheeks flushed?"

"Now you're just dreaming," I said, filling her glass with fresh water. "I think the meds are affecting your brain."

"Don't you play with me, girl," she said in her spirited way. The bronze fingers of her good hand reached for my arm. I bet she was a pistol, a force to be reckoned with, in her day. "It looked like you were thinking about a man."

"No way. Never. Boys are stupid."

"Not all of them." It was the same conversation, different day. Mrs. Jackson had a doting husband who had visited her every single afternoon since she'd been admitted after her stroke. He usually had a fresh bouquet of flowers or a Snickers—her favorite candy bar. She may not have had good use of her right arm or leg, but she was still lucid and could appreciate the visits, unlike many of the other patients, who were riddled with de-mentia or Alzheimer's.

"Unfortunately, you got the last remaining good guy in the entire universe," I said, moving toward the door. "There are no more available. Maybe I'll have to steal him from you."

"I may be old and sick, but I'd tackle you to the ground and fight you for him."

"I believe you would, Mrs. Jackson," I said, waving. "I believe you would."

I loved our banter; it was the best part of my day. Mrs. Jackson was in residence because her husband could no longer care for her due to his own medical problems. After her stroke, she'd needed around-the-clock care, which included feeding, changing, medication management, and physical therapy for her weakened limbs.

Her children were grown with lives of their own, and Mrs. Jackson had hinted that she'd never burden them. They visited her once a week and you felt the affection rolling off of them in waves. From snippets of conversations I'd heard, they had all offered to take her into their own homes, but she fought them tooth and nail. Told them they couldn't afford to lose their jobs or provide for all of her needs.

Since her admission, Mrs. Jackson had also had two smaller strokes, called TIAs. Hopefully they wouldn't lead to the big one—the mother of all strokes—anytime soon.

I'd sure as hell miss her around here.

# CHAPTER THREE

hadn't seen Chivalrous Hot Boy Bennett since his move-in day, outside of the one occasion I brought my laundry up to the fifth floor for old times' sake. I heard hammering behind his door. I figured he was affixing something to a wall—maybe a poster of a hot girl with dark hair and dark eyelashes, the exact opposite of me—and I knew going up there in the first place was a bad idea, too stalkerish. So after transferring my clothes to the dryer, I hightailed it out of there, setting a reminder on my phone to check back again in an hour's time.

Except I fell asleep reading my nursing textbook, and by the time I rushed out of the elevator to retrieve my clothes, I spotted Bennett pulling my red lace bra from the dryer.

"Planning on stealing my unmentionables for your private viewing pleasure?"

Bennett froze with my B cup dangling from his fingers, his expression unreadable, except for a twitch in his jaw. If this beautiful man could remain unaffected by sexy lingerie, then all hope for us was lost.

He had on a pair of cut-off khaki shorts, and I scanned down his toned legs to his calves, which were rock hard. He turned toward me, a smirk hanging from his lips. "This belongs to you, huh?"

"It does," I said. I noticed how he took in my shorts and pink heart T-shirt, his eyes lingering on my breasts, as if imagining me in that red lace. "Care to borrow it—or maybe you want to see it on display?"

"Now *that* would be a sight." My cheeks became inflamed. Was Hot Boy's flirting voice finally rearing its sexy head? "Why are you doing your laundry all the way up here?"

"Habit I picked up while your place was vacant. The guy across from you is never home, and the machine on my floor is always broken," I said, smoothing my hands down the front of my shirt. I noticed how his eyes carefully followed my fingers. "Why were you picking through my things?"

And this is where Hot Boy Bennett became flustered. "I . . . uh . . . you . . ." He ruffled his fingers through his hair. "I was waiting to dry my clothes and I figured I'd just move yours aside until you retrieved them."

"Yeah, sorry about that." I inched closer and noticed the stubble on his chin. It made him look more rugged tattoo boy, less clean-cut jock. "I fell asleep reading about the finer points of infectious diseases."

"That *would* be hard to stay awake for. My textbooks aren't much better. Especially the Impressionist period." His eyes scanned up my legs and stomach before landing squarely on my eyes. "I wouldn't take you for a nursing student."

"Really. What kind of student, then?" I leaned against the

washer and inhaled his faint scent of coconut. This one ought to be good. Not sure why his pause made my palms sweat.

"Um, I don't know. A business or marketing major; something more . . ." He trailed off and scratched the back of his neck, looking at the wall behind me.

"More what?" What did Hot Boy really think of me? Maybe I should've just been happy he was thinking of me at all.

"More *aggressive*, cutthroat, I guess."

My face fell. Right there he was telling me he knew I was after him that one night. And somehow I hated what he saw in me. I did *not* go after guys. They went after *me*.

But he thought I was some sort of predator. And that made me want to prove him wrong.

I didn't care about guys. Any of them. And I certainly didn't care what they thought of me. Except for this very instant.

"Nope." I pushed off the washer and moved past him to my clothes, my hip brushing against his stomach, and my knees almost buckled. I hauled my undies and bras out at supersonic speed, wanting to get the hell away from him and how he made me feel. "Guess I've got a soft spot for the sick and vulnerable."

"That's admirable." His voice was velvety soft, almost like a whisper. It rumbled up my spine to my hairline and I almost shivered against it. I didn't say anything in response, because my mouth had trouble forming words.

"So, um, anyway, sorry for touching your stuff," he said, straightening himself. I could feel his body directly behind mine, and the heat rolling off of him. Normally I'd have a seductive or smart-ass retort for his comment, but nothing came.

I left the dryer open and slinked past him to the elevator, pushing the down button a little too aggressively. "Good night." When the rickety doors squeaked closed behind me, I let out the breath I had been holding.

A scraping sound woke me out of a dead sleep. I blinked at the ceiling, trying to get my bearings. The noise was coming from directly outside my bedroom window. Shadows played across the blinds. I saw the outline of a head and shoulders, and my stomach seized up.

Somebody was trying to break in, trying to pry open the glass. My heartbeat thundered in my ears, and my fingers slid like sludge toward my phone on the nightstand.

But the rest of my body was cemented in place. I couldn't move as sheer terror enveloped me and held me captive.

Was this person going to rob me or rape me? My breath shot out in sputtering gasps.

I'd taken self-defense courses three times over the last couple of years and knew how to respond in this type of situation. All I needed to do was reach for my phone and dial 9-1-1, then run like hell out my front door. But for some reason I could not get my body unstuck.

I'd been in a similar heightened state of danger when I was sixteen and had fought back. This was the exact reason I kept my self-defense training sharp, so why wasn't I able to respond now?

Living on the first floor of this apartment building hadn't been my first choice as a female resident, but it was my only choice at the time.

The sound of my window popping and sliding open forced my heart to jam into my throat, and I gagged on my own saliva.

All at once I heard a gruff voice shouting from outside. "What the hell are you doing? Get away from that window. I'm calling the cops."

There was a scuffling sound, a loud clunk, and then heavy grunting. All I could gather is that whoever was at my window had dropped to the ground and started running.

I heard that same voice outside yell, "Son of a bitch! You're not getting away with this!" and then heard panting like he was in pursuit of whoever had been about to break in.

And still I was glued to my bed, my chest painfully throbbing from breathing so damn hard.

Next, there was a voice beneath my window. "Avery, are you in there? Are you okay? It's Bennett. From the fifth floor." I hadn't seen Bennett in a few days. What the hell was he now doing outside my window?

I finally snapped out of it and bolted upright. The relief I felt caused my breaths to slide out of me. "Y-yes, I'm here."

"Someone was trying to break in through your window. I called the police." He paused, breathing hard. I imagined him bent at the waist or leaning against the brick wall. "I'm coming around front. Can you open your door?"

Holy shit. My legs were wobbly and I struggled to stand up. Bennett had run off an intruder. But what the hell had I done to help *myself*? Not a goddamn thing.

I could have been robbed, or raped—or killed, even. So much for taking care of *me*.

Fuck. Fuck. Fuck.

I didn't want to be saved—I wanted to knock that motherfucker out myself.

"Avery?" Now Bennett was at my door, his voice low, his knock gentle.

I stalked to the door completely pissed off at myself. I swung it open and Bennett charged inside, grasping at my shoulders. "Are you okay? Were you awake?"

I wanted to tell him that I wasn't awake so he wouldn't know what a goddamn wuss I truly was. I mean, shit, I could haul ass in my kickboxing class, but I wimped out in a real-life scenario?

"Uh, yeah, the noise at my window woke me up." He was squeezing my shoulders now, all boy-saves-girl, so I backed the hell away from him.

"He ran before I could get to him, but I got a good look at his face and the clothes he was wearing." That's when I heard the siren blaring in the background. Fuck, now the whole goddamn neighborhood would be woken up for this.

"Avery, the police will be here any minute; maybe you should put some more clothes on." I looked down at my skimpy sleep shorts and white tank top—no bra—my nipples standing at attention.

And here was Bennett being a complete gentleman again. Shit.

"Right, thanks." I dashed into my bedroom, grabbed jeans and a black hoodie from my bedroom floor and slipped them on. I headed back to the living room and said, "Better?"

He nodded. "Pretty sure the cops will be able to do their jobs with clear heads now." My whole body heated at his comment. Even in the middle of all of this.

"Bennett, how did you . . . ?" I moved to my bedroom

door and glanced at my partially open widow. "Why were you outside?"

He motioned to the sidewalk beyond our building. "I was walking home from Lou's Bar at the corner of our street and saw him at your window."

"Oh my God," I said. "This is so unreal. Thank you."

Most unreal was how I acted in this situation. Like a fucking damsel in distress.

The lights from the police cruiser blinked eerie shades of red and blue against my apartment walls.

"Guess we should go meet them outside," I said.

Bennett reached for my hand, and I resisted. His eyebrows bunched together, and I felt awful after all he'd done for me. So I let him lead me outside, his hand on the small of my back.

The police were there for a solid hour getting our statements and a description of the suspect from Bennett. Our landlord, Mr. Matthews, showed up, too, and assured me he'd have a locksmith secure all of the first-floor windows in the morning.

Most of the tenants went back to sleep, but Bennett stayed by my side the entire time. He asked the police pertinent questions for me, like how long it would be before I heard anything and how to contact them if I had any more questions. Like he was my flipping spokesman or something. Surprising of all was that I *let* him be.

My head still swirled from shock and anger and, most of all, fear. Especially about falling back to sleep tonight. I'd decided right then and there that I'd be making my bed on the couch, close to the door and the knives in the kitchen.

When all was said and done, Bennett walked me back to my door. "You gonna be okay?"

I didn't want my voice to deceive me, so I just nodded and inserted my key into the lock.

He must have noticed some hesitation. "Avery, are you sure you—"

"Of course!" I snapped at him. "Look, I'm sorry. It's been a long night. Thank you for everything."

"Sure. Good night." He headed toward the elevator and I reluctantly crossed over the threshold to my apartment. I could feel him watching me, so I thrust my door closed and propped my weight against it.

Suddenly my apartment felt different to me. Dimmer. Lurking shadows in the corners. Sinister creaks from the wind.

There was a light tap, and I heard Bennett clear his throat. "Avery?"

I backed away from the door like I hadn't been leaning against it that entire time. I took a deep breath and collected myself, then pulled open the door. "Yeah?"

Bennett's face creased in concern. He held out his hand. "C'mon."

"What . . . where?"

"Up to my place for the night."

"No, I . . ." I sputtered.

He stared at me impassively with his hand still stretched out for the taking.

Was this guy for real?

Going with him would make me look weak.

Who the hell was I kidding? I was spooked from an intruder who had been almost a second away from dropping into my bedroom.

His hand felt warm and protective. He held my fingers the

entire time in the elevator and only broke away to dig out his key and unlock his door.

He gave me a sidelong glance. "Had that happened to my mom or sisters, no way would I have let them sleep there—if that makes you feel any better."

So, he had women in his life that he cared about. My heart melted a little.

He opened his door to dozens of boxes littered everywhere. "Sorry, I haven't truly unpacked yet. Thought I'd get to it this weekend."

He glanced at the couch, where a huge blue bin took up most of the cushion. DVDs were piled on top and spilling over the sides. "Um, listen . . ."

I was about to tell him it was cool, I'd go back downstairs, but then he grabbed hold of my hand and led me to his bedroom. It was the only room in the apartment not filled to the brim with boxes.

A queen bed sat in the center of the room with a black-and-gray-checkered sheet and comforter set. Very understated. Very cozy. Very male.

"You can sleep in my bed."

I blinked back my surprise. Not that I hadn't been in a man's bed before, but this felt so different. Probably because this wasn't under sexual circumstances. This was a caring and concerned gesture.

He motioned to the living room. "I'm going to sleep out here."

"No way, Bennett, I'm not taking your bed." I turned toward the door. "I'll sleep out there."

"Please, don't argue the point." He backed out of the

doorway. "I'll be close to the door, so no worries. Besides, we're up on the fifth floor. Good night."

Something clicked inside my very core. He wasn't interested in me in the same way other men were—at least I didn't think he was—and he wasn't going to take advantage of me. I actually felt safe, even though I wasn't in control. At least not in control for the moment.

"Wait." I looked back at the bed. "Which side do you normally sleep on?"

He pointed to the side nearest the door.

I walked over to the far end of the bed and began unbuttoning my jeans. He gazed at me a second more before shutting the door. I slid out of my jeans and hoodie and slipped inside his sheets. They smelled like him. Coconut, spice, and all boy.

I heard Bennett outside the door sliding boxes around, opening and closing what was maybe the linen closet, and then getting situated. Twenty minutes later I was still awake and feeling restless. I decided on a cold glass of water.

I slid open the bedroom door, tiptoed into the darkened room, and nearly tripped over Bennett. I had assumed he was going to be on the couch, but instead he was on the cold, hard floor. Guilt twisted in my gut.

"So sorry," I muttered. "Just getting a glass of water."

His eyes were open, and his gaze caressed my body. I was back to wearing my white tank top and sleep bottoms, and I could have sworn I saw longing flicker in his eyes.

"The glasses are in the cupboard, left side of the sink."

At least he had unpacked his dishes. I poured a glass and took big gulps of the water, deciding what to do. He was obviously awake and uncomfortable on the floor. He hadn't even attempted to move the boxes off his couch.

I padded back to him and held out my hand much the same way he'd done to me earlier. "C'mon."

"Huh?" He sat up. He didn't have a shirt on, and I tried not to stare at his taut chest and stomach. I didn't quite succeed. I also caught a glimpse of a tattoo on his abdomen, and I made a mental note to ask about it later.

"No questions," I said. He grabbed hold of my hand and I yanked him up and into his room. He was wearing blue boxer briefs, and I averted my eyes from the front of his shorts. "I promise not to bite, and I'll stay on my side of the bed."

He apparently found that amusing, because he shook his head, a grin indenting the side of his cheek. "Are you sure?"

"Absolutely."

He slid into the sheets and sighed, like he was glad to be back in his own bed. I lay down and turned my back to him, my senses heighted and my body on high alert. The tension between us was palpable. But it was different somehow. I didn't want him to paw me or screw me senseless.

Instead, I wanted his arms around me, his chin nuzzling my neck, and his lips kissing me slow and soft. I was pretty sure I could get lost in those lips.

Damn, I wanted him. In a totally different way. A way I hadn't felt since Gavin, my first boyfriend, when I was sixteen years old. Before Tim ruined us. Ruined me.

Maybe I *could* have him. Just to lose myself in. To make me forget.

"You gonna be able to sleep?" Bennett asked in a raspy,

sexy voice that reverberated through my bones. "Are you still thinking about what happened?"

I wasn't, but I said so anyway. "Yeah."

He inched his body toward mine and I immediately felt his heat. His fingers reached out tentatively and I almost arched my back to accept them.

Then he rubbed my shoulder in delicate circles. "Shhh . . . you're safe with me. You can fall asleep."

My entire body tingled, head to toe.

But somehow, after a few minutes, his fingers lulled me into a blissful sleep.

# CHAPTER FOUR

opened my eyes as sunlight flooded Bennett's room, creating slanted lines across his bed. Bennett was no longer next to me, but I heard him tinkering on the other side of the door.

*Did I really just sleep in this guy's bed—because I was afraid to sleep alone?*

Climbing out of the warm sheets, I eased back into my jeans and hoodie. I padded to the bathroom and saw what a wreck I was. My hair was in tangles and my mascara had traveled beneath my eyes. I splashed cold water on my face to wake me up and then used one of Bennett's blue hand towels that hung neatly near the sink. Peeking at some of the toiletries on his counter, I discovered his expensive coconut shampoo. I snapped the top open and took a quick sniff before placing it back where it belonged.

When I emerged from the bathroom, Bennett stood in the living room hold a steaming mug of coffee for me. "This is about all I can offer you this morning. Do you take cream or sugar?"

"Black is fine, and you offered me plenty last night."

"Not a problem," he said, sitting down on the one section of the couch not littered with stuff. He motioned to the chair across the room, one he had cleared for me, and sipped from his mug. He was already showered and dressed. His hair was less unruly when it was wet, and today he wore gray jeans, a black T-shirt, and black motorcycle boots. More like a tattoo artist.

"You work today?" I asked.

"Yeah, Oliver's got me scheduled for a full day of tats." Hearing his boss's name roll off his tongue made me squirm. Oliver ended up wanting more from me than just one evening. Wanted to take me to dinner the next night, and I'd refused. "You know those frat boys—always want those tats in prominent places to show off their school spirit."

"I better let you get to it, then; don't want to keep them waiting," I said. "I've got to get ready for work, too."

"Please, stay and finish your coffee, at least."

I hesitated. "Sure, for another minute, so I don't have to return your cup."

He was watching me, so I looked around like I was taking in the place. Except nothing was unpacked, so I stared at the contents of open boxes. His entire life had been dumped right here in bins in the living room, and somehow it felt too personal, too intimate to be standing in the middle of it all. "So, no roommate, huh?"

"I actually do have someone moving in next month."

"A girlfriend?" I didn't even know why I asked. It was none of my damn business.

"No, no girlfriend. Not yet. I've seen someone a couple of times this past month, but we'll see where that leads." He watched my eyes as if to gauge my reaction. He didn't have to offer me any of that information, but I got the feeling he wanted to. Maybe to give a hint that he wasn't interested. Or that he wasn't attached yet. I wasn't sure which.

"Anyway, my friend will be moving in here next month." He tilted his head. "You know—the one you met at the party?"

I fiddled with the hem of my shirt. "Oh yeah . . . Nate, right?"

Bennett nodded, and then his voice took on a serious tone. "Can I ask you a question, Avery?"

"Sure." I finally sat down across from him on the upholstered chair he'd cleared for me.

"How come . . ." He looked down, breaking eye contact with me. "How come you didn't go for my friend? I mean, besides the fact that he was so blatant. But girls usually fall for that."

Was he asking because he was curious, or because he was interested? Should I go for unabashed honesty here? All at once I stood up and started pacing.

"I don't know." So as to not look so obviously rattled, I strode over to the window to stare at his lackluster view of the parking lot. "Normally, I'd be all for that. I'm a no-strings-attached kind of girl."

As I turned back to look at him, his face showed a flicker of disappointment before he recovered. Now I was the one trying to gauge his reaction.

I decided to continue with my honesty. "But I wasn't interested in *him* that night."

His voice was low and soft. "You weren't?"

"Nope." I looked down, figuring he had gotten my message loud and clear. "Can I ask *you* a question now?"

He propped his foot on the edge of his coffee table. "Go for it."

"How come you told him to back off? I mean, I didn't see you talking to any girls, and it's not like you were talking to *me*." I cleared my throat, which had suddenly gone dry. "Would Nate really have gotten out of hand? Because I'm pretty sure I could have handled him all by myself."

"Number one, Nate talked to you first," he said, taking a quick sip of coffee from his mug. "I mean, it makes sense— who would spot a beautiful girl across the room and not want to talk to her?"

I'd heard that same kind of line dozens of times from guys, but somehow coming from him it felt more real. More direct. More sincere.

I felt a slow burn smoldering in my stomach, so I decided to deflect how affected I was by his words. "Is there a number *two*?"

"Huh?" He moved his gaze away from my lips and back up to my eyes.

Something stirred inside my chest—most likely his chromosomal superiority revving me up. "You said that was number *one*."

"Oh . . . yeah," he said, tucking a smirk in the side of his cheek. "And number *two*, I figured you were the kind of girl who ate guys up and spit them out for sport. But even still, I thought it was best to say something. Nate can be a dick sometimes."

Was that his way of admitting that he was intimidated by me?

In an ideal world, I wouldn't be such a player, because I wanted him. All to myself. Right this very moment.

I leaned against the window ledge. "What gave you that impression of me?"

"The way you carry yourself." He shrugged. "Confident. Self-assured."

"Is that a bad thing?"

"No way." His fingers fumbled through his hair. "It's sexy as hell."

Right now our pheromones were breathing the same air. Nuzzling up against each other. Swapping saliva.

"I figured, I . . . I mean, *Nate*, would be no match for you, anyway," he practically mumbled. "You know, *some* guys like to take things a bit slower."

Was this guy for real? Suddenly I felt like a bona fide man-eater. A Slutasaurus rex.

"Huh, guess I didn't take *Nate* as the relationship type of guy," I said. A deep shade of plum tinged his cheeks. We were speaking in code here, but we both knew the real deal. "And just by association, as Nate's *friend*, I figured *you* must be the same way."

"Not true. I'm a commitment kind of guy." His voice was low and smooth. Like he was very sure of himself on that one point. "If the right girl comes along."

Suddenly the walls of his apartment closed in on me. I'd never be that kind of woman for him, so I needed to move the hell along right *now*. Mr. Tattoo Artist was proving to be a very intriguing and mysterious guy. There was a story under there somewhere. Maybe he'd been badly burned and no longer wanted to sleep around. Or maybe dedication to one person was part of his religion or something.

No matter—I couldn't stick around long enough to find out.

Bennett was holding my gaze solid as steel, but I finally managed to break away.

"Well," I said.

"Well."

That one word said nothing and everything all at once.

I placed his coffee mug in the sink and headed toward the door. "Thanks again, for everything. Your bed is really comfortable."

"Anytime."

I snorted. "Is that an open invitation, Mr. Reynolds?"

The trace of a corrupt smile stretched across his lips, telling me that maybe he'd actually consider it despite everything he'd just told me. That maybe I'd be the Kryptonite to his very values and ideals.

And that's when I knew I needed to make my exit. *Fast.*

Yet, he'd decided to keep on talking. "Sometimes it's nice sleeping next to someone. I forget what that's like."

I stopped and spun around. "Has it been a while? For someone who looks like you?"

He looked down, his eyelashes combing his cheeks. "Yeah."

"Been hurt that bad by someone?"

His head snapped up, and he arched an accusing eyebrow. "Have you?"

"Touché, Mr. Reynolds." I could tell neither one of us was going to budge. "Have a good one."

Bennett's words stuck with me throughout the day.

I kept spacing out, and Mrs. Jackson called me on it. "You must be thinking about that man again," she said, her hand hovering over the remote control. She loved watching her soap operas during the day. All smut and disappointment and makeup sex.

I grinned. "You are insufferable, woman."

Her husband had just left for the day, and I filled her vase with fresh water for the white daisies he'd brought. Sometimes he stayed to watch TV with her, gently holding her hand. You could feel the affection rolling off of them when they were together, and I imagined their sex life had been blazing hot when they were young and agile.

"You know I'm right. C'mon, talk to me about it." Mrs. Jackson tapped the side of her bed. Sometimes we'd have heart-to-hearts while I was feeding her. She'd tell me about her life and I'd tell her about mine. Most of it, anyway. She grew sad whenever I mentioned my mother. Told me my mother's priorities were misplaced. And I could tell she was concerned about my brother. Said he should live with me after graduation.

"I'm not going anywhere; I've got all day," she said.

"And I have rounds to do." I adjusted the Velcro on the blood pressure cuff. "Besides, your son and grandchildren should be here soon."

"Excuses, excuses. You better take a chance on that boy," she said, patting my hand. "He must be something special. You never come in here looking like that."

"Looking like what?" That was the hazard of seeing someone every single day. They got to know your moods almost *too* well.

"Like there's fire in your eyes," she said, wistfully.

I shook my head, not wanting to admit to anything out loud.

33

"Let me guess," she said. "He's a confusing young man. He makes you feel things. Giddy and frustrated and wound up all at the same time. Am I right?"

"I don't know. Maybe." I wanted to tell her that I had no intention of having anything more to do with Bennett. That he was looking for something else. Someone else. That the most we'd be was friends. That I couldn't even think of him as a one-night stand anymore. That somehow he'd gotten under my skin and I needed to let him go, clear my mind of him, and move on.

But I knew saying any of that would disappoint her. She was a true romantic and had a husband who proved true love existed. At least for them.

"Honey child, that's roots taking shape."

"Roots?" I slanted my head sideways. Mrs. Jackson was always quoting something.

"'Two seeds destined to grow in concert, planted together in the field of love.'" She took in a lungful of air and continued. "'The sky cast wet buckets of dreams and desires, the roots took shape, and the leaves tangled as one.'"

"'Roots took shape . . .'" I repeated to myself. "Wow. That rocked. What was that?"

"It's from a poem called 'The Roots of Love.'"

"Your photographic memory amazes me."

"When you find love, you'll start quoting poetry, too."

I turned away so she couldn't see me roll my eyes.

# CHAPTER FIVE

"So what's up, girlie?" Ella asked, sitting across from me at the campus coffee shop. "Still freaked about the break-in?"

"A little," I admitted. "My gorgeous new neighbor helped me out, though."

"I bet he did." She grinned, leaning back in her chair, like she was settling in for a good story.

"No, nothing like that," I said, watching the students out the window strolling by on their way to class. "Unfortunately."

She arched an eyebrow. "Oh come on, you didn't jump his bones?"

"I swear," I said. It did sound unbelievable rolling off of my tongue. "We just slept in the same bed. He rubbed my back and I fell asleep. It was sweet."

"No way, dickhead," she said, sipping her cappuccino.

"Way, dill weed," I retorted.

"And how do you feel about that?" She leaned forward. Her blue eyes, which were two shades bolder than mine, sparkled in the sunlight. My eyes were more gray blue, like murky ocean water.

"I don't feel anything," I lied. "He was being a friend."

She twisted her lip. It was the thing she did instead of calling bullshit—when she didn't believe a word I was saying. We sat in silence while I got lost in my own thoughts.

Ella swirled the liquid concoction in front of her with her spoon. "Is he someone you *could* be friends with?"

"Probably." I said it like I meant it. Yet, I still wasn't certain. I mean, sure, I could be around him. But without wanting something more from him?

"That's actually a good thing," Ella said.

"Why?" I took a bite of my strawberry cheese Danish.

"So you can finally see that not all men will do what that prick did to you," she said, twirling her brown locks around her finger. "You don't have to fight off all men. Or use them. Or control them. And you know I'm not referring to some lunatic trying to break through your window."

My mouth hung open. Normally Ella was bashing me for my antics with guys while still acting like she reveled in the details. Like she was living vicariously through my vagina or something.

"You're a strong, gorgeous, independent woman who just happens to carry around so much emotional baggage that it weighs her down." She patted my hand across the table. "But sometimes it's okay to let someone in."

I wiggled my eyebrows. "Oh, I've let plenty of guys *in*."

That got a snort out of her.

"As a *friend*, you slut. Someone who can warm your heart, not your bed."

"You sound like a fucking Hallmark card," I said. "And a lot like Mrs. Jackson."

"How's she doing?" Ella's eyes brightened. She'd met her once when she'd come to my job to take me to lunch. Mrs. Jackson was being wheeled around the grounds by her husband and she had insisted on meeting Ella. They'd ended up talking for an hour and I'd missed my lunch. "God, I love that lady. I'd take her as my surrogate grandmother any day."

"She's probably the only representation of a parental figure I have," I said. "Except I'm the one taking care of *her.*"

"I don't know about that. I'd say it's mutual." Ella's eyes softened. "Hey, have you talked to your bro lately?"

"Of course. I need to keep daily tabs on him." I sighed. "He's still dating Andrea. He's taking her to prom. I just hope she doesn't break his heart."

"He's a good egg—somehow has his head screwed on straight, despite that mother of yours." Ella would never be a fan of my mother. She knew our situation only too well, and I was grateful for her friendship.

She'd saved me from jumping off the nearest bridge a few times in high school. Her parents were understanding and let me sleep over, too many nights to count, after my mother and I had had one of our screaming matches.

But our friendship definitely went both ways. I knew Ella's optimistic front sometimes hid a lot of pain. Her family had its own share of heartbreak when Ella's brother passed away in high school. Ella admitted my sleepovers helped her get through some rough nights, too.

"So back to the hottie-neighbor-friend," she said. "Describe him, five words or less, and *go.*" It was a game we'd played since high school called Five Fingers, but I wasn't in the mood.

Besides, the only words I could think of at the moment to describe Bennett were *hot*, *hot*, *hot*, *hot*, and *hot*.

"C'mon, tell me *something*," she said.

"He works at Raw Ink." I said it like I was proud or something. "He's also an art major at TSU."

"No way—think he can do my tattoo?" Ella had wanted a tattoo for as long as I'd known her. Even after graduation when I went to get mine, she'd wanted one, but then chickened out. "You'll come with, right?"

"Sure," I said, even though I wasn't totally sure. Why did I ever hook up with Bennett's boss that night? If I showed up at his place of employment, Oliver might think I was still interested. And then if Oliver and Bennett got to talking about me—yikes. Although I wasn't even sure why I cared what Bennett thought of how I spent my nights. "Maybe you could go to the shop, view his work. Tell him your ideas and see what he comes up with."

After kickboxing, I studied my butt off for my critical care class. I needed to keep a B average so I didn't have to repeat the course again. Next semester my nursing rotation would be in the university hospital's intensive care unit, and I was excited to learn something new. The nursing home had prepped me well for end-stage care and crisis intervention. And maybe there'd be a job waiting for me at the hospital upon graduation.

I knew I'd be decent at nursing because I could keep my emotions at bay while helping people who were too vulnerable to care for themselves. It was important to me, plus the pay was good, because nurses were in such short demand.

Deep down, I'd wanted to make my grandma proud. She'd been a nurse's aide—had never taken the steps to get her degree. She'd encouraged me to go to college, even at an early age. Said I'd be the first in our family to graduate, since Mom had never finished high school.

Mom and Grandma were always bickering. "Your daddy would roll over in his grave if he saw you traipsing around town with all of those men," Grandma had said on more than one occasion. She'd begged Mom to set an example for Adam and me of a strong and proud single mother. "Only *then* will a man respect you."

Guess I'd internalized that lesson more than Mom had.

Despite Grandma and Mom being as different as night and day, when Grandma got sick, Mom was as wrecked as I'd ever seen her. She had planned on moving Grandma into our home while she went through chemo, but the cancer took her pretty quickly.

Now I flipped through a gossip magazine, all the while considering whether or not I could sleep in my own bed again. I had brought my pillow and blanket out to the couch and made sure I had the sharpest knife from the kitchen in view on my counter.

Despite the landlord placing motion-sensor lighting near the main door and a locksmith drilling more secure clasps onto my windows, the shadows moving across those blinds in my bedroom made my stomach lurch.

Last night, a man with the intent of robbing or raping

chose my window to climb through. And had Bennett not shown up, my day would have looked starkly different. I'd be a robbed or raped or dead woman because I had frozen in my bed, unable to move.

I pulled out my phone and considered texting Rob and asking him to sleep over. Rob had never slept all the way through the night in my bed because I had never allowed him to, but maybe after sex he'd agree to stay on the couch.

I'd tell him I was a little spooked, and he'd understand because he was a guy and probably liked having a female depend on him. He'd be shocked because never once had I relied on him for anything except my own orgasm.

But it might turn him on a little—or send him packing. It was not part of our arrangement, that was for sure.

My fingers hovered over the keys and finally I gave in.

Me: Hey, Rob, have anything going on tonight?

Rob: Nothing. Want to hook up? I can be over in thirty.

My fingers froze, considering whether I truly wanted to cross over into that realm with him. He wasn't my protector or even my friend. Just my fuck buddy.

A knock on my door startled me, and my phone slipped from my fingers, dropping to the couch.

When I looked through the peephole and saw it was Bennett, my heart strained against my rib cage. He was wearing the same clothes I had seen him in that morning, but his shirt was more wrinkled and his hair more messy.

I opened the door before realizing how I was dressed again. Same sleep shorts as last night, but a pink tank top this time. And still no bra.

Bennett's eyes gave me a once-over before landing squarely on my breasts, and I swear my nipples rose to greet him. He swallowed roughly before saying, "Um, hi. I just got home and I thought . . ."

He just stood there staring at me, like he was debating with himself.

"What?" I found I was panting at the sight of him. Hoping, praying the words I wanted to hear would come out of his mouth.

"Um, want some company again tonight?" He rubbed the back of his neck, looked down at his feet, and it was so damn sexy. "I just figured . . . if it were my mom, she'd want me to check on her for a couple more days."

My eyes closed in relief as I released the breath I was holding. I could even overlook the fact that he'd just compared me to his mom. Talk about mixed signals. But I wasn't faring much better in that department.

"Are you still nervous about sleeping here?" His voice was earnest, like he hoped I'd say yes.

I could tell him *no* to prove how strong I was, but my resolve was crumbling fast. My fingers were trembling on the doorknob because I wanted his company so damn badly.

"N-not sure."

"Want to watch a movie upstairs and sleep over again?"

My heart flapped and wavered. This boy was going to be the death of me.

He reached out his hand for me. "No questions asked?"

I nodded. "Just let me put on some clothes and I'll be right up."

He looked down at my bare legs and swallowed. "Good idea."

I closed the door and gulped down my hesitation. *No questions asked,* he'd said. I threw on sweatshorts and a T-shirt over my tank. I looked in the mirror and fixed my raccoon eyes a bit. Then I threw on some lip gloss for good measure.

When Bennett pulled open his door I noticed he'd cleared off his couch and had taken some things out of boxes. His flat-screen TV and Xbox were on a walnut-and-glass stand, and an open box of DVDs lay directly beneath.

"Your pick," he said, motioning toward the television and the movies piled high. "I'll even agree to finding a chick flick on TV—anything to make you feel comfortable tonight."

I would be anything but comfortable. All of my senses were heightened around him. His lips looked yummy enough to eat. His hair was begging for my fingers to glide through it. But I needed to remember that this was probably a friendship thing. Maybe we *could* be buddies.

"I'm not a chick flick kind of gal."

He smirked. "Why doesn't that surprise me?"

His box of DVDs was an eclectic mix of blockbusters and independent films, a few comedies, and even a couple of romances.

I pulled out the *Lord of the Rings* boxed set. "Now *this* I can do."

"Seriously?" His eyes lit up at my revelation.

"Absolutely," I said.

"Which is your favorite?" His question came out as sort of a test, like he didn't believe I could be into Tolkien and fantasy.

"*The Two Towers.*"

His brown eyes sparkled like they contained flecks of gold. "Mine, too."

"Let's *do* it then," I said.

Bennett's eyes became dark and hooded, causing my breathing to escalate.

We settled in on the couch with some distance between us. My phone vibrated with a text message and it occurred to me that I had left Rob hanging downstairs. *Shit.*

Rob: I guess this means no about tonight?

I quickly typed back.

Me: Sorry, friend stopped over, catch up with you later.

Bennett looked at me curiously. "Boyfriend?"

"No. I told you I don't do boyfriends."

His eyes were a bit guarded. "Someone who *hopes* to be your boyfriend?"

I figured I'd go for honesty. "Nah, we're more like friends with benefits."

The look of shock on his face was evident before it crossed over to something else that looked a little like jealousy. Or maybe it was just curiosity.

"C'mon, you can't tell me you haven't had your share of those kinds of nights."

He cleared his throat while I waited for him to say something. Anything. But he didn't.

"You're a hot guy, Bennett." I tossed up my hands. "I'm sure plenty of girls throw themselves at you."

His face quirked into a lopsided grin. "You think I'm hot?"

"You're avoiding the question."

"The answer to your question is no, I haven't."

I had to pick my jaw up off the ground. I had expected him to say something like *Sure, but that was in the past. Now I want a commitment*, or . . . something.

"Don't get me wrong," he said in a low voice. "I've made out with my share of girls. I'm only human. And sure, girls have come on to me . . ."

I cringed inwardly. Is that how he saw me? I'd never thrown myself at anyone—I'd never had to. Guys came on to *me*. Except for that one time at that party, when I saw Bennett for the first time.

I needed to change the subject, pronto.

Noticing he had unpacked some pictures and placed a couple on his desk in the corner of the room, I stood up and made my way over. "Are these your mom and sisters?"

His mom was a pretty lady with blond hair cut to her shoulders. And she was next to a pair of twins and a very striking teen girl who was bound to have guys falling all over *her* as well.

"Yeah," he said. "The twins are twelve and my sister Taylor just turned seventeen."

"Wow, you've lived around a lot of estrogen your whole life." I looked back at him. "Where's the testosterone?"

"Nonexistent." Anger flashed hot as an iron and Bennett's

features turned into a scowl. "Let's just say I've been the only decent male role model in their lives."

That might explain a lot. I noticed they all looked different from one another. Did their father leave or die, or did they come from different men, like my brother and me? I'd save those questions for another day.

"So, do they live around here?"

"About twenty minutes south, in West View. I see them every week for Sunday dinner. I lived at home until about a year ago, when my mother met her current husband." I saw his jaw tick. "Then it was time for me to go."

"Oh, I know that feeling too well," I said, not offering any more information. I checked out of my house when I was sixteen and slept at Ella's most of the time. And then checked out emotionally after that. "Did you have a beef with your new stepdad?"

"Not really. It's just that I helped Mom pay the bills and raise my sisters for as long as I could, but now he can be responsible for all of that. As long as he sticks around." There was quite a story there, I could tell, but I didn't want to push the topic.

Maybe he was one of these super responsible kids who could never let loose.

"Sounds like our moms could have been BFFs in another life."

He turned his head sideways, studying me, wondering about me. "Where does your family live?"

"About an hour from here. I don't visit very often, but I talk to my brother, Adam, almost every single day. He's a senior in high school, and I try to keep tabs on him. He's a good kid, though."

"What about your mother?"

I grew silent. He had shared stuff with me, so I really wasn't being fair.

"You don't have to tell me any more if you don't want to."

I shrugged. "What can I say—she's my mother. The biggest pain in my ass." And the biggest betrayer in my life. "So I keep my distance."

"Your dad?"

"Let's not even go there." There was nowhere to go, anyway. I wasn't sure if even Mom knew who he was. Or even his name. Either way, she'd never talked about him.

"Another time, then," he said. I noticed that he had shifted closer to me and our shoulders were almost touching. "Want a beer while we watch the movie?"

"Sounds perfect."

He opened two beers and joined me on the couch. The opening credits rolled and he scooted over close enough that our knees almost touched. I sipped and watched the screen, not even registering what was happening in the movie. Thankfully, I'd seen it half a dozen times already, in case he wanted to make small talk.

I was cognizant of Bennett's every move. Like a current humming through the air. Every swallow of his beer, every time his arm came down with the bottle and brushed alongside mine. When he reached over to turn up the volume on the remote, his thigh rubbed against my shorts and I nearly flinched.

I was like some lovesick tween desperate to have my crush finally notice me.

As the movie played on, I finished my beer and became increasingly drowsy. During the big battle scene, my head slumped toward his shoulder in the twilight of sleep. Bennett's arm slinked behind my neck as he nudged closer. When his fingers made small circular motions up and down my arm, my heart pumped an inordinate amount of blood through my veins.

I wasn't sure if he realized the impact his touch had on me.

I became intensely aroused, but pretended that I was still nearing slumber. If Bennett's fingers inched anywhere southward, he'd be fondling my chest. My breast practically stretched toward his hand—begging for his undivided attention.

I couldn't help wondering if my nearness was affecting him as well.

I'd caught him checking me out earlier, and he obviously wanted to spend time with me. I didn't get the sense that his invitation was out of obligation or pity, though I might have been mistaken. He'd mentioned a girl he was seeing in one of our earlier talks, yet he still asked me to sleep over tonight.

I sighed and snuggled into his chest, carefully placing my fingers against his thigh. His leg muscle tensed and the hand on my shoulder paused. His breaths were brisk and warm against my hair.

So he wasn't immune to me after all.

I didn't know what the hell I thought I was doing. He specifically told me he was a commitment kind of guy, and here I was messing with him, trying to prove some kind of point.

What was wrong with me? Did I need so badly to see what he was made of?

But I was entertaining other thoughts as well. Like maybe Bennett would eventually be open to the kind of arrangement Rob and I had. Except that I was terrified I could lose myself in a guy like Bennett—he'd be like a drug I couldn't get enough of. And that was hazardous to a girl intent on being in control. Being her own person—which didn't gel with having any kind of relationship.

Bennett didn't breathe a word as my fingers raked softly against his thigh. He sucked in a breath and brushed his hand up and down my back and against the nape of my neck. The fire between my legs only intensified. I resisted the urge to squirm and moan into his chest.

Once the end credits began rolling, Bennett straightened himself. But I was still against his shoulder in a feigned state of sleep. When he removed his fingers from my hair, I lamented the loss.

"Avery," he whispered. "Ready for bed?"

"Mmmm . . ."

He shifted away for a moment before I felt my body being lifted by strong arms. He smelled like coconuts and white sandy beaches. My eyes remained closed but I nuzzled into his neck, my lips resting against his smooth skin. He stifled a groan.

His lips brushed against the top of my head as he carried me to his bed, and a wave of euphoria pulsed through me. He laid me down facing the wall, the same position I'd slept in last night. I heard his labored breaths as he stepped out of his jeans and removed his shirt. Then he slid in beside me.

He hesitated for the longest time before finally scooting forward. His hand came around and braced my stomach, so warm and strong and protective that I couldn't hold in my gasp.

"Is this okay?" he whispered. I could only nod, my limbs felt so weak.

His breathing intensified and I felt his bulge growing against my back. But Bennett said nothing more and made no other moves. I got the feeling he was trying to hold himself back, and there was no way I was going to throw myself at him.

It was the single most sensual moment of my life.

We lay there for some tense and aroused minutes before I finally heard his breaths soften into sleep. Eventually, I drifted off as well.

# CHAPTER SIX

slept in Bennett's bed for the next three nights, in much the same way. I'd head up to his place and we'd dine on takeout, watch a movie, or listen to music. I helped him unpack most of his boxes and he directed me where to place his things.

I got a bird's-eye view of his art. I'd known he was an art major, but seeing his work revealed another side to him. It was earthy and eclectic and stunning, just like him. It was mostly charcoal drawings of city life or scenic landscapes that he somehow transformed into ethereal, picturesque, and peculiar versions of themselves. Like *Starry Night* meets *The Scream*.

Then we'd snuggle into bed together, his chest against my back and me aware of how completely aroused he was. If I had an appendage growing on the outside of my body, he'd have known how entirely stirred up I was as well. It was completely nerve-racking and overwhelming yet provocative and comforting all at once.

I had never done any such thing with a guy. And I didn't know who was more stubborn, me or him. Neither one of us was willing to make the next move. For him, it may have been because he didn't want to become one of my friends with benefits. And for me, it was because there was some small, desperate part of me that didn't want him to think I was so easy, or easily led—into commitment, that is.

I asked him about the girl he was seeing, but he never answered me, so I assumed he was having the same problem—no desire to be with anyone else for the moment.

Rob even drunk-dialed me and threatened to show up on my doorstep because he needed it so badly, he said. Obviously I did, too, like I'd never needed it before in my whole damned life, but it felt weird to let Rob come over, especially if Bennett accidentally ran into him. I had no earthly idea where either of us stood or how blurred the lines had become.

So I decided I needed to be the bigger person—the person who had an ounce of control and sense left—and put an end to my sleepovers with Bennett. I needed to sleep in my own damn bed.

So I didn't go up to his apartment and he didn't come down to get me and somehow that made me feel even worse. My chest had an ache I couldn't shake until I fell into a restless night of sleep. I figured he got the message I was sending. That I was no longer interested in whatever little game we were playing.

In the morning I was proud of myself for making it through the night without the help of a man. I needed to get my life back. I was strong and unattached, and I liked it that way.

Mrs. Jackson noticed a difference the following morning in the activity room. "You look resigned today. Maybe with a hint of sadness underneath."

"Nope, you don't have me pegged today," I said, laying

down my pair of aces. I'd promised her a quick game of rummy. "I am confident and self-assured."

"I am woman, hear me roar?" she said, snickering. Her fingers trembled as she balanced her stack of cards. It was a skill that had become difficult for her, given the numbness in her hands since the stroke. "Trying to play the independent game with him, huh?"

She was frustrating as hell and always saw right through me and I loved her for it.

I waved to Mrs. Jackson's daughter, Star, as she strode through the door for a visit. "Oh good. Now you can complain about how Star and her husband work too much and need more date nights." I winked as I exited the table.

That night I tried to have a quickie with Rob—at his place, instead of mine. I had so much pent-up sexual frustration I didn't know what to do. Rob had two roommates, and they were pains in the ass. Always high as kites in front of the PlayStation. The place was a disaster, and I refused to ever use the one bathroom they all shared. No way did I want to see nasty pubic hairs clinging to the wall or yellow trails of pee on the floor. Men had disgusting habits; that was for sure. One of the many reasons I was better off without one in my life.

After Rob brought me up to his room, he immediately lifted my shirt and began pawing at me. No erotic foreplay there. Not that I'd ever needed it before.

His hands were rough, his kisses sloppy, and for the first time I asked myself how I'd ever been with him so many times. It suddenly felt different, and there was definitely no damn fire in my belly.

It might be the first time I'd have to fake it, but I didn't want to disappoint Rob. We used each other for just this purpose, and if he needed to get off, then I'd oblige. But damn, I needed it, too. My vibrator had been a poor substitute for flesh and bones. Or boner, in this case.

An hour later, I was on my way home and less satisfied than I'd been in a good long while.

The second night I slept alone in my bed, I told myself things were finally getting back to normal. I ignored the tightness lodged in my throat that I was missing something—missing someone—and convinced myself that Bennett was fine with it as well, because he never tried to contact me, either.

I was going to a party with Ella and Rachel that evening and was excited about being out with my friends again. But as I got dressed I couldn't help wondering if Bennett would show up. It was the same frat house throwing the party as a couple weeks ago, and Bennett had mentioned that the one jock was a customer of his. Said he had inked two tattoos on his biceps in the past year.

And so I found myself dressing for Bennett as much as for me. *Pathetic.* I wore my favorite skinny jeans with a flowing top that I left unbuttoned to the center of my chest. I wore a white cami underneath that had a built-in bra. It made my small breasts look firm and round.

When we first arrived I begrudgingly admitted to myself that I was disappointed that Bennett wasn't there. His friend Nate was, but I refused eye contact with him. It didn't stop me from drinking shots of tequila with Rachel and Ella and having a good time.

The music was pumping, the bodies were wall to wall, and

the girls and I danced a few songs. I felt myself letting loose and not thinking so hard. We let a couple of guys dance with us, but when one started getting frisky, I turned him down. Definitely not because of Bennett. I just wanted to ease back into the game slowly.

We sipped the margaritas that Rachel mixed especially for tonight, and they felt good going down. She leaned toward me and shouted above the music. "A yummy guy keeps looking over here. If you don't want him, I'll take him."

I looked up and saw Bennett leaning against the wall, a beer in his hand. He practically knocked the wind out of me he was so stunning. He lifted his hand in a wave and I smiled back.

"That's him, isn't it?" Ella shouted into my ear. "Your neighbor?"

"Yep." I bit my lip while my heart performed impossible tricks in a jump rope tournament.

"He is smoking hot," she said, sipping her margarita through a straw.

"Yeah," I said. "Too bad he doesn't want to get it on with me."

"Maybe he does but he's waiting," she said, looking over my shoulder and checking him out again.

I rolled my eyes. She was closer to the truth than she knew. Bennett had slept in the same bed with me and never touched me once. "For what?"

"For you to want him in the same way, asshead."

I hadn't told her all the details of our nights; just that we had hung out some more. And that it was totally innocent.

"Think about it," she said, all smug.

Oh, I was thinking about it. Every single day.

And I knew what Ella was getting at.

I *did* want him.

I wanted to get him out of my *damn* system already.

Rachel headed toward Bennett like she was on a mission, and I felt my stomach bunch up. She kept her dark hair short, and her face was unbelievably striking—full lips and dramatic green eyes. Guys fell all over themselves to talk to her.

She used her you-are-so-getting-some-tonight smile on Bennett. He was polite and said hello, but kept his eyes trained on me the entire time. Rachel looked back, shrugged, and mouthed *All yours* before she was pulled onto some huge linebacker's lap.

Ella tugged at my hand. "C'mon, I can't find Joel, and I need to dance to this one."

"Okay," I said, standing up and taking one last glance at Bennett. He had his back turned and was talking to Nate. Nate said something and they high-fived and chugged back their beers.

We pushed our way to the middle of the writhing bodies and I started swaying my hips in time to the music. I raised my arms in the air and got lost in the slow and sexy song.

A minute later, I felt warm breath stroke my neck and a strong hand brace my stomach. I knew it was him without turning around. Those same long fingers had been splayed against my body all week long. I closed my eyes and savored his skin touching mine.

"I like when you wear your hair down." He twined his fingers through the ends of my curls and it sent a shiver ricocheting through my body.

"You haven't come up," he breathed against my ear.

"I figured it was time to be a big girl and sleep in my own bed," I said.

"Understood." He held on to my waist and swayed along with me. His fingers trailed beneath the hem of my shirt and a couple of inches upward. I fought to keep my breaths under control.

"I know this is going to sound crazy," he whispered. "But I kind of missed you."

He pulled me flush against him and I sucked in a breath. I felt the hard wall of his chest, the strong and steady thud of his heart at my back. I laced my fingers around his neck and leaned into him.

His fingers blazed a trail along my rib cage and stopped just above my navel. I rocked my hips back and forth in time with the music and he let out a slow groan.

"Jesus, Avery," he said. Suddenly he pushed away from me. "I need some air."

He stormed off the dance floor, leaving me speechless and way too aroused.

Ella raised an eyebrow at me.

Why the hell was he resisting so badly?

"That boy's got it bad for you," she said. "So what the hell just happened?"

"I'm not sure," I said, my mood having shifted to ugly. "You okay if I just take off?"

"It's unlike you to get bent out of shape over a guy," she said. "I think you're feeling more than you're letting on."

I just shrugged and stomped off. That was the problem

with friends who'd known you forever. Too perceptive. Especially Miss Psychology Major.

When I got home, I only stopped long enough to pull off my jeans and top before I fell into bed, tipsy and more than a little frustrated.

I had enough drinks in me to drift off to sleep.

# CHAPTER SEVEN

A sharp knock on my door woke me out of my restless sleep. My heart jammed in my throat. Body taut as a rope, my eyes immediately stole to my bedroom window, hoping it wasn't another neighbor alerting me of a potential break-in. I had managed to get to sleep the last couple of nights without completely stressing over it, especially after taking an extra kickboxing class that morning.

I did, however, move the biggest knife from my kitchen drawer to beneath my mattress. And now my fingers were reaching for it.

My blinds remained dark, however, the only pinnacle of light from the streetlamp on the corner. I was safe.

So who the hell was knocking?

I heard his voice before I padded my way to the door. "Avery?"

Bennett stood there, a bit unsteady on his feet.

I folded my arms. "Are you drunk?"

"Maybe a little," he said, his hand wandering to the back of his neck. "More nervous than anything."

I had the power to make this beautiful man nervous?

"What the hell are you nervous about?" I asked, hands on hips.

"That you're pissed at me." He leaned forward. "That you won't let me in so we can talk."

"I'm not mad. Frustrated, maybe." I opened the door wider to allow him to pass. I wasn't sure what I was doing, but I knew I wanted to see him, talk to him, spend time with him.

"Were you hoping to test the coziness of *my* bed tonight?"

He stretched his gaze across my body, and a shiver bolted through me. "More than anything."

"Well, good." I turned and walked away. "Because I'm exhausted, and I need to go back to sleep."

I marched to my room, and felt him follow closely behind. I slid back into the comfort of my sheets while he inspected the photography on my walls and the trinket boxes on my dresser, like he was memorizing everything.

My heart throbbed in my chest as I watched him unbuckle his belt and then unzip his pants. His gaze remained locked on mine the entire time, like this striptease was for me, and me alone. So damn sexy.

He took off his jeans, flicking the material down one muscular leg at a time to reveal his blue boxer briefs. Then he reached for the hem of his shirt and pulled it over his head. The light from my bedside lamp highlighted his ripped biceps and his lean abdomen. I caught a glimpse of the tattoo on his rib cage. Swirls of black letters curled along his smooth skin, and I hoped for the chance to examine it more closely one day.

"So you *do* sleep on that side," he said matter-of-factly as he slipped into my bed. "Not just at my place."

We lay facing each other. Studying each other. Drinking each other in.

"Bennett," I said, taking a deep breath. "What happened to that girl you were seeing?"

"Dunno. Haven't talked in a while," he said. "Guess I've had other things on my mind."

He reached out and skimmed his fingertips over my shoulder and then up to my jawline, sending a bolt of electricity through me. Anticipation coiled into a tight ball in my stomach. I couldn't take it anymore. I wanted him. I needed him.

I wasn't sure if I'd ever been more desperate to kiss someone.

Chill bumps broke out on my skin and raced up and down my arms and back.

"Avery?" Bennett stroked my lips with his fingers, and the heat from his touch shot straight through my stomach and whispered a trail along my thighs.

I panted out a breath. "Yeah?"

"I don't know what this is or what the hell we're doing," he said. "But if I don't kiss you right now, I might explode."

His fingers curled over the nape of my neck and into my hair, tugging me nearer.

"God, Bennett." My voice was breathy and my head rolled back against his fingers.

He whispered soft kisses against my neck, along my jaw, and below my ear. Then he nipped at my bottom lip, and I fought for air. He slid his thumbs over my cheeks and stared deeply into my eyes, right before his lips brushed over mine, so gently that I shivered.

Did this man have to take everything in measured steps? I was dying a slow, erotic death.

He positioned his body over mine. "I love your eyes. They remind me of a rainstorm."

My hands rested on his chest and I moved them up to his hair. It was silky-smooth, and I closed my fists around the velvety strands.

Then the soft pillows of his lips hummed in concert against mine.

When his tongue slipped between my lips, I whimpered. He explored my mouth slow and careful, and all the nerve endings in my body began to pulse against him.

He reached into my hair, tightening his hold and deepening the kiss.

His tongue lapped against mine like his life depended on it. Something that sounded like a growl emerged from the back of his throat and sent another heat wave ripping through me.

Bennett was kissing the shit out of me and I couldn't breathe but I didn't care because if this is what kissing him felt like, I could get my fill of oxygen later.

He pulled my lower lip into his mouth, and then my top lip, taking his time sucking each one as my fingers dug deeper into his neck.

His hands never traveled south even though I would have welcomed them. All of his focus was on my lips. And then on my neck. And then on my ear. His hot breath making my toes curl.

This man knew how to kiss.

He shifted again and the entire length of him covered me. I felt every place on his body that touched mine—his chest, his stomach, his pelvis. Bennett claimed a patch of skin at the base of my throat and drew it into his mouth hungrily. The ache between my legs intensified and I tilted my hips against his.

His tongue slid back inside my mouth, wet, deep, and forceful. Like he was starving and I was his last meal. I fought to keep my breaths steady. They were as reckless as my thundering heart rate.

An eternity passed before Bennett took a breath, but I immediately grieved the loss of his tongue. My lips were swollen and my face stung from his stubble, but I'd welcome him back in a heartbeat. No questions asked.

He looked into my eyes for a long, silent moment before kissing the hell out of me again. His mouth captured mine in a desperate, frenzied, heated rush. I was jumping off a cliff, sinking, drowning, and couldn't have cared less about being saved as long as he kept kissing me.

I was aroused, flying sky-high, and could barely take anymore. I wanted this man, if he'd have me.

He pulled me on top of him, and I could feel his hard-on bumping against the thin material of my underwear. He was hot and throbbing and I was panting and desperate from need.

I traced my hand down his stomach to the top of his shorts, and he shuddered out a breath.

He latched on to my hand to stop me. "Avery, I don't know what you're doing to me."

"The same thing you're doing to me," I said between heavy breaths. "Bennett, I want you."

His whole body stiffened. And then he moved from under me. "I . . . I can't."

"What do you mean, you can't?" My voice had raised an octave. "Why the hell did you come over, Bennett?"

"Because I can't stop thinking about you." He placed his head in his hands. "You're the sexiest woman I've ever met."

This man was the personification of sexy, so Bennett think-ing the same about me was mind-bending. A shiver of gratitude raced through me, only to vanish, like that vivid moment when a snowflake lands on your fingertip, pure and whole, the second before it dissolves.

"What's the problem, then?"

"Avery." He reached for his shirt on the floor. "I'm . . . waiting."

"Obviously," I said. "Waiting for what?"

"For the right girl," he said, sitting up.

So he *did* think I was some kind of whore. A *sexy* whore, at that.

I balled my fists and considered using them on him. "Oh I get it, I'm nice to sleep next to and grope on the dance floor . . ."

I didn't know what I was getting so uptight about. He had clearly explained to me that he wanted a commitment. And I had made it clear I wasn't girlfriend material—so why did it upset me that *he* didn't think so, either?

"No! You don't understand, Avery," he said. "I want you. Damn it, I want you like I've never wanted anyone before."

"But . . . ?"

"But . . ." The look in Bennett's eyes was resigned, dutiful even. "I'm a *virgin*, Avery."

I slumped forward as if I'd been sucker-punched in the gut. "What do you mean?"

"I'm pretty sure you don't need a definition," he said, rushing his fingers through his hair.

I stared at him for what seemed like hours, thoughts tick-ing through my brain. A slide show of our time together. The party, the sleepovers, the dance floor.

"Go ahead, get it out," he said, arms crossed over his chest. "I've heard it all."

I shook my head, not sure what he wanted.

His voice went up a register to sound distinctly female. "Maybe I'll be the one to *break* you, Bennett . . ."

Hadn't *I* tried to break him? My pulse pitched at that realization.

"Or how about this one—I'd rather be with someone who knows what they're *doing*."

That last girly imitation made me sit all the way up. "Seriously?"

"Seriously," he said, looking crushed and angry all at once.

"Okay, I get it," I said. "This is like breaking headline news for some women, including me."

"Obviously." He pulled his shirt over his head and then brought it down over his smooth chest.

"I guess I just want to understand." I fisted the sheet in my hand. "Can you explain it to me?"

He narrowed his eyes. "Do I really have to?"

"No, you don't. I'm sorry." I averted my eyes, feeling like an idiot. "You have the right to your own privacy. That was stupid."

"No, Avery, I'm the stupid one," he huffed. "I don't know what I'm doing here. I want to know you, I crave being around you. But you've made it clear you don't do relationships."

"And you've made it clear that you do. So I'm to blame as well." I wanted to tell him I hungered after him, too, that I felt the exact same way—but the very thought of sharing that was terrifying and would have blurred the lines even further.

"Look, I've been taking care of my mom and sisters for as

long as I can remember. My mom was a teenager when she had me, and we had to live with my aunt for a while," he said, explaining himself after all. And I didn't want him to stop talking, so I kept my mouth shut. "My mother's been in so many crappy relationships. Men treated her like garbage."

"Same with my mom," I whispered, more to myself than to him.

"And what a great role model she turned out to be, because my sister got pregnant at sixteen, too." He was up and pacing at this point. "I swore to myself I would never have casual sex and knock a girl up. I've always worked odd jobs to help Mom pay the bills. No way in hell was I going to support my own kid, too."

"But don't you think that's extreme?" I asked. He rolled his eyes, like he'd heard that one before, too. Probably from the hordes of girls that wanted him so badly. But still, I tried making my point. "There's plenty of good birth control out there, and lots of people are having sex and not getting pregnant."

"Like you?" he said before a look of regret shot through his eyes. "Damn it. I'm sorry, that was uncalled for. Guess I'm feeling defensive."

"I deserved that," I said. "And for the record, I don't always have sex. But I'm not ashamed of wanting it sometimes, either."

"I hate that you saying that makes me jealous." He stared at me, distress in his eyes. "Shit, this is so messed up."

A guy jealous over me was a feeling I wasn't accustomed to.

"But it's more than all of that, Avery," he said. "I saw how casual guys were with my mother, how they threw around the word *love* to get what they wanted, when I knew it was all a bunch of bullshit."

I nodded, knowing full well what he meant. I'd seen it plenty in my house, too.

"I want something *real*," he whispered. "And I'm willing to wait for it."

My throat closed up at his words.

"Are you . . . waiting for marriage?"

"No." He looked me dead in the eye. "I'm just waiting for *love*."

Those words rocked me hard. He sounded so honest and sincere and brave.

"Have you never been in love before?" I asked.

I had, once only. Gavin and I were sixteen and about to make love for the first time. And then Tim ruined it for me. For us. Like a big, dark shadow that turned our love into fear, and eventually hatred.

If I could have a redo of my first time, I'd take it in a heartbeat. I wouldn't be so scared, so distrustful. Maybe then Gavin wouldn't have been so shitty to me after all was said and done.

"I thought I was in love once, but then I realized how very wrong I was," he said. "So I don't plan on making that mistake again."

Here was a guy who actually valued women. And he had to meet someone like *me*.

"Believe it or not, Bennett," I said. "I respect you so much more now."

"Is that all you feel for me—respect?" he asked, inching toward me. "Because the way you were kissing me . . ."

He wanted something from me that I couldn't give him. Not now. Not ever.

Man, this was tough. I wanted him, *bad*. But there was no way in hell I could have him. Not when our goals were so vastly different. So why did the idea of walking away slice somewhere deep inside my core?

He was just another guy. A hot and deep and irresistible guy. Who happened to be a *virgin*. And happened to live in my building, where I'd be forced to run into him all the time. Fuck my life.

"I feel . . . *horny*," I said. He shook his head and his jaw ticked. "I'm sorry you have to be attracted to someone like me. I can't be that girl for you, Bennett."

His eyes drilled a hole through me, trying to reach inside and grasp on to something. "You can't, or you won't?"

I shut my eyes tight against the truth. "Both."

# CHAPTER EIGHT

(( H e's a virgin?" Ella screeched. I ducked my head from probing eyes.

Rachel, Ella, and I were back at the campus coffee shop in a cushioned corner booth in between classes.

Rachel was a business major, and after Bennett's declaration that one day in the laundry room that my field of study should have been something more cutthroat, I couldn't help thinking it was the perfect major for her.

Ella was a psychology major, and she liked to use her mumbo jumbo terms on me, saying that I was repressing my feelings about Tim and projecting them onto men everywhere.

"Holy crap!" Rachel said. "You realize how messed up it sounds that he just happens to be attracted to a bitch-ass like you?"

I rolled my eyes. "Geez, thanks a lot, dickhead." I may have acted nonchalant, but I wanted to pound her one. Was it really that far-fetched of an idea?

"She didn't mean it that way," Ella said, giving Rachel big

eyes. "You're a lot of things, Avery. A lot of wonderful things—for a bitch-ass."

"But you are definitely emotionally unavailable," Rachel said, smoothing her hair behind her ears.

My eyebrows drew together. "Pot, meet kettle."

"I'm not denying that," Rachel said, laughing. She was busy making eyes at a prospect across the café. She was in constant player mode. I paled in comparison to her antics. She had something to prove, and I had something to . . . avoid.

Ella grabbed my hands. "Do you have feelings for this guy?"

"I . . . I don't know," I said. Then I saw the look on Rachel's face. The one that said that our solidarity would be ruined if I said yes. "Of course not. Other than lust."

"Okay, pretend Rachel's not here and your slut-o-meters are not in mutual heat," Ella said, shooting daggers at our other friend. "You are *so* feeling something. You just don't want to admit it."

"Does it really matter?" I huffed. "I'm a train wreck. You've said so yourself."

"As a joke, yes. You're *so* not." Ella squeezed my hand. "You just think you are, asshead."

"She kind of *is*." Rachel snickered with those disgustingly perfect pouty lips.

Rachel's story was different than mine. She'd been in a five-year relationship with her first love. They got engaged and she joined him at an out-of-state college. Then she realized that she just wasn't ready for the 'burbs and marriage. She broke it off with him and moved back home to attend the local university.

We met Rachel at a party last year. The same drunk guy

was trying to hook up with both of us—together, I might add—and instead of Rachel's claws coming out, as might be the case with other girls, we laughed it up and decided to play a little prank.

Rachel was decidedly more evil than I was. She got the guy naked and horny as hell in one of the frat bedrooms. Then she hid his clothes instead of coming to find me, which was what she told him she'd be doing. He was ready for a ménage à trois and what he got was a limp dick and a bunch of jocks razzing him.

Rachel admitted to blazing through all the men she hadn't been able to have for the last five years. Ella thought she was still in love with her ex-boyfriend, but she'd never admit it. I assumed she just needed a break to grow up a little and figure things out. She wasn't into talking about feelings, so we kept things light—when it came to discussing *her* life, at least. But she was funny as hell and great for comic relief.

"Besides, how totally cool would it be to bed a virgin?" Rachel's eyes gleamed with something I recognized—the hunt. "Teach him what to do. He'd be like an eager puppy, wanting to please the hell out of you."

"In case you've forgotten, I've already been with a virgin," I said. "Gavin, my boyfriend in high school?"

"Yeah, but that was different. You both were virgins. Neither one of you knew what the hell you were doing."

"How did I end up friends with the two of you?" Ella rolled her eyes. "You're both full of shit, no matter how many boys you mess around with."

Ella was always telling us how we were both just running away from our own hearts. More of her psychology bullshit.

"I'll tell you one thing," I said, taking a huge breath. "That boy knows how to kiss—he's no virgin in the tongue department."

"That's a damn good sign," Rachel said, high-fiving me. "Wear that boy's defenses down."

As I imagined Bennett's tongue tangling with mine, a heat wave broke out over my skin. I also entertained thoughts of what might have happened had we not had to stop the other night.

I was bummed that I wouldn't be feeling those lips, those strong arms, or that sinful body of his again. It *was* more than that, but I'd never come clean to Rachel. To anybody, really. But I also enjoyed Bennett, the person—his sense of humor, his taste in music and movies, that look in his eyes when he described his art.

But that still didn't change the fact that we wanted different things, despite wanting each other.

Bennett and I hadn't seen each other in a few days, and I missed him. But I was moving on with my life. And I was sure he was, too. Maybe he'd call that girl he had been seeing and give it another chance. I thrust those jealous thoughts out of my head.

Besides, I was getting together with Rob tonight. I knew it might be reckless considering what had happened last time— how unfulfilling it'd been—but now that I'd had some distance from Bennett and his amazing lips, maybe I could see Rob in a new light. Which would really be the *old* light. I did used to think he was cute and sexy. Plus he'd never given me any reason to dislike him. He wasn't into relationships, either, so really, the arrangement was perfect.

As soon as my apartment door shut behind Rob, he was ready for action. He dug the foil wrapper out of his pocket and was already slipping off his shoes. His lips instantly found mine, and my legs easily slid around his waist. He carried me to my bed, and even though I didn't feel scorching-hot for him, I prayed he could meet my needs tonight.

Sex with Rob was always quick—no words and no foreplay. But I couldn't help wishing for the build-up, the smoldering burn that I'd had with Bennett the other night.

"Rob, wait," I said, scooting away as soon as my back hit the bed. "Give me a minute."

I shut my eyes and winced. I wasn't feeling it for Rob tonight. And I didn't think I could pretend again. "I changed my mind. I just can't tonight."

"What?" He stared at me with his fingers frozen on his zipper. "Why'd I come all the way over here, then?"

"I'm sorry—I thought I was in the mood." I stood up and walked out of my room as he followed behind. "I just have too much on my mind . . . with classes and work and stuff."

I bit my lip, silently cursing myself for not going through with it. It was so unfair to Rob. But as I looked him over I knew I'd never get off tonight. Not when I wanted someone else.

"Whatever, Avery," he said, gripping the door handle. "Next time, don't text me unless you're sure. So I don't waste my time."

"Whatever *yourself*," I said, gritting my teeth. My frustration spilled over. "Don't forget the couple of times you were too wasted to follow through and left *me* high and dry."

He waved his hand dismissively as he trudged through the door. I knew he felt as frustrated as I did. But I couldn't help him out tonight.

Damn it, what in the hell was wrong with me?

I lay in bed and closed my eyes, picturing the other night with Bennett. His tongue in my mouth, his warm body on top of mine, his hard-on against my very wet underwear, and I became instantly aroused. My fingers worked their magic and I had the most powerful orgasm I'd had since meeting that beautiful boy upstairs.

Two days later, I was in the university library checking out nursing pharmacology books when I saw a familiar red baseball cap across the room. My heart strained at the very sight of him. He had on a worn pair of jeans and a white concert T-shirt with a gray hoodie.

As soon as I checked out, I jerked my head down and strode toward the exit to outpace my racing heart.

Before I could make it through the sliding doors I heard his voice. "Avery, wait."

I slowed down and turned, afraid to make eye contact lest his voodoo magic work on me again.

"How are you?" he asked.

"Good," I said, telling myself to breathe. I focused on the Van Gogh book tucked beneath his arm.

"I . . . I just . . ." he sputtered. "Listen, isn't there any way we could get past the awkward and just become friends?"

I bit my bottom lip and shrugged. Finally, I got up the nerve to glance at him. I noticed how his long eyelashes brushed across his cheeks when he blinked and how his five o'clock shadow made him look decidedly more handsome. The guy still knocked my socks off.

"I really like hanging out with you," he said in a gruff voice.

"Um . . ." I said, finally getting my breathing under control. "Me, too."

His shoulders seemed to unwind as he stood up straighter. He'd been as uptight and uncertain as I was. Maybe this could work. Maybe if we put in the effort we could just be friends.

"Where are you off to now?"

"Just walking home," I said.

"Can I . . . walk with you?"

"Sure."

We stepped out into the chilly fall temperature. I adjusted my sweater and kept pace with him. The wind had picked up and I heard the rustle of leaves in the trees.

Bennett leaned down to pick up a red maple leaf that had fluttered to the ground in front of us. He twirled the stem in his fingers. "We used to collect leaves and make collages in grade school."

"Or iron them between wax paper." I grinned. "I love fall. The crisp air, the colorful leaves, football season."

"Football?" Bennett raised his brow. "I guess that shouldn't surprise me, but it does."

I shrugged. "I'm in the fantasy football league at work. Last year, I kicked an orderly's butt. Won myself a couple hundred in cold hard cash."

He laughed and shook his head. "You are one tough cookie, you know that?"

"I guess." I got the impression he was talking about more than just football.

"So, what are you up to this weekend?" I asked, trying to

75

keep the conversation light. Hopefully he wasn't going to tell me he had a date. Although I supposed I had to get used to that idea if we were going to be friends.

I mentally kicked myself for staring at his lips again.

"Actually, on Saturday I'm driving up to Lakeland for an art exhibit," he said, picking up another leaf. "I'll be back Sunday night."

"An exhibit that you're a part of?" I asked, thrilled for him.

"Yeah." He stepped around a pile of brown leaves on the sidewalk. "I've done shows before, but this one is huge. They get a large turnout every year, and my pieces will be for sale."

"That is so awesome." We turned the corner to our street. "People are going to snatch up your stuff, I just know it."

"That would be cool," he said. "But I'm just psyched to be part of it."

Our strides matched as we trudged toward our building. I felt lighter somehow, being with him.

"So how about you?" he asked. "Weekend plans?"

"I'm actually off for the first Saturday in forever. Originally, the girls and I were supposed to drive up to that new casino about an hour away, but then Ella remembered that Joel invited her to some family reunion thing this weekend." I sighed. "I've got studying to do, anyway."

The girls from work had invited me to some in-home jewelry party Saturday night, where you got pressured to buy stuff. But the pieces were always pricey and I just wasn't feeling it.

A kind of melancholy settled over me, knowing Bennett would be gone this weekend. Even when we weren't talking these past few days, I still tried to catch glimpses of him going in and out of the elevator. Now that we were back to friend status, I secretly hoped he'd want to hang out—get takeout, watch a movie. Sitting far away from each other on the couch, of course.

"Bummer. But at least you still have the day off," Bennett said, pulling open the door. "Hope you have a good weekend."

"You, too," I said. "And good luck. I expect a full report about how much art you sold on Monday."

He waved on his way to the elevator. I slid my key into the lock, feeling that pull toward him again. Maybe it was best he'd be away this weekend.

Just as I was stepping inside my door, I heard Bennett call my name.

I spun around. "Yeah?" I heard the elevator doors grinding shut behind him.

"Um . . ." He shut his eyes as if to gather himself. When he opened them again, they were a dazzling caramel brown. "Want to come . . . to my show this weekend?"

My stomach squeezed into a ball. "You mean, drive up to see the exhibit?"

"Yeah. I mean, drive up with *me*."

He looked down at his shoes and simultaneously rubbed his neck, waiting for my answer. After I picked my jaw up off the floor, I considered what he was asking. But I wasn't doing a good enough job of putting any of the pieces together. All my brain could muster was: him, me, out of town, two days.

"I . . . um . . . It's just for one night, and my hotel room has two double beds. Or you can get your own room," he spat out. "I just . . . It would nice to have a friend along. I mean, unless you think it would bore you to tears."

Damn. I so wanted to say yes. Was it the smart thing to do? Probably not. But I wasn't known for my amazing intellect when it came to anything involving Bennett. Besides, if we were going to be friends, we should be able to hang together— even out of town. And who was I to dispute his attempt at making this friendship work?

"Yeah, that would be fun. Thanks for asking."

His smile lit up the whole damn hallway, and I held onto my doorjamb for support. Man, he was gorgeous.

"Cool. We'll leave at eight o'clock on Saturday morning."

# CHAPTER NINE

Bennett met me in the parking lot at eight sharp Saturday morning. He held out a large cup of coffee, and I could've hugged him for that. But I restrained myself. "You rock. Thanks."

"I went to fill up the tank, so I got the coffees while I was at it," Bennett said, holding open the passenger door to his used silver Jeep.

Lakeland was a couple of hours' drive north.

It felt good to be with him, despite having tossed and turned about my decision the previous night. I couldn't help wanting to know more about him, especially if we were going to be friends.

He let me control the radio station, and I bit my tongue about how he rode other cars' bumpers on the freeway. On the last leg of our drive, after belting out U2 at the top of our lungs and playing punch buggy a little too aggressively, things got quiet. Bennett was still nursing his shoulder, saying I had a mean right hook.

"Want to play another game?" I asked, focusing on the orange barrels lining the road. I hoped we didn't run into any construction. My legs were already cramped, and I couldn't wait to stand up and stretch.

"Sure." He adjusted the rearview mirror. "What is it?"

"It's called Five Fingers. Ella and I used to play it with our high school friends."

"Should I be scared?" he asked, inching his arm away from me.

"Nope," I assured him. "One person asks a question and the other person has to answer in five words or less."

His eyes brimmed with mischief. "What if you *can't*?"

"Well, normally you have to drink something. But we won't be playing it that way."

"Okay, I'm game," he said. "We can always sip our coffees."

"Not if you don't want to stop at every rest area so I can use the bathroom."

"True. There's something about chicks and bathrooms." He grinned. "And I should know; I grew up in a house full of girls."

"Secret discussions take place when girls congregate in restrooms—like how to rule the world."

"Ah, to be a fly on the wall."

"Okay, me first." I was eager to start our game, especially since it meant getting to know him better. "Your most embarrassing moment?"

"Um, let's see . . . ." He smoothed his fingers over his jaw.

"You just used up three words."

"Shoot—no, wait." His eyes grew wider. "I didn't realize I couldn't deliberate out loud. Can I get a second chance?"

I smirked. He was cute when he was flustered. "Sure."

He took his time thinking of his answer and finally said, "Zipper stuck . . . in hair." He punctuated each word with one of his fingers.

"Good job," I said. "And . . . really?"

"Ugh, use your imagination," he said.

"I guess I'll have to if you're not going to share."

"Nope," he said, smugly.

His answer could have gone a couple different ways, making Bennett way more mysterious now. *His* hair stuck in a zipper, or someone else's?

"Okay, me next." He grinned like a little kid. "Um . . . your favorite childhood book?"

I held up my fingers to count. This one was easy for me. "*To Kill a Mockingbird.*"

"Impressive. One of my favorites, too."

"My turn. What were you like in high school?"

He scratched his chin in deep thought. "Well-rounded, responsible, studious . . ."

"I knew it," I blurted out.

He held up his last finger to finish his answer. "Sneaky."

My mouth hung open. No way would I have guessed he'd had a sly side. "You're becoming a bigger mystery, Mr. Reynolds."

"Am I? I mean, most teenagers have their devious and resourceful ways, right?"

"True." I thought of how many times I had snuck out of my house to be with Gavin. But Bennett had said he worked jobs to support his family. That had to be tough. Hopefully that meant he had a little fun on the side, too. "Did you play any sports, or were you always into art?"

"I believe it's my turn, Ms. Michaels."

"Oops. Right you are."

"What do you like about your job at the nursing home?"

I'd asked myself this question a few times lately. Especially after a hard day of work. But the pay was good and I needed to have a plan B if Adam ever needed to live with me.

Nursing homes were filled with throwaways. People whose families had essentially given up on them. Not all families, but more than a few. You could always spot those residents a mile away. Zero visitors, vacant eyes, low energy.

I knew what it felt like to not have someone on your side—someone who didn't fight for you. Support you. Believe in you.

To curl in a ball and feel hopeless. Frustrated. Despondent.

I tuned back in to Bennett's question about my job. He was waiting on my answer.

"Helping . . . learning . . . experience . . . Mrs. Jackson."

"Mrs. Jackson?" he asked, cocking an eyebrow at me.

"My turn," I said, hoping to get away from the topic. Her name had slipped out before I could stop myself.

I was too flustered to remember my other question, so I came up with a different one. "What's the strangest tattoo you've ever inked?"

He thought about it forever, like there was a catalogue in his brain of all his past customers. I could tell he was struggling for a good enough answer.

"If that's too hard to answer, then at least the strangest one this month."

His answer came immediately. "Tree stump, kids' book, dude."

My heart pumped out one large thump. "From *The Giving Tree*?"

His eyes widened as he nodded.

"The most depressing kids' book ever," I mumbled, never admitting that I cried like a baby first time I'd read it. I'd pulled it from Ella's bookshelf back in high school. It had left an indelible impression on my brain. She told me it was her favorite book, that her mother had dedicated it to her, and then I broke down in front of her.

I knew inherently back then that no one had ever—*would* ever—sacrifice themselves for me like that tree character had in the book—most of all, my own mother.

But I'd do it for Adam, in a heartbeat. He was my brother, my responsibility, my heart. Even though he was pretty good at taking care of himself. Just like I had to.

Bennett reached out his hand. He could tell I'd drifted off on him. His warm fingers squeezed mine briefly before pulling away, bringing me back to the present.

"My turn," he said. "Mrs. Jackson?"

"Wise, hopeless romantic, grandma figure."

"A resident?"

I nodded. His mouth pulled into a sad little smile. Like he realized she was pretty important, but he didn't want to press the issue. I turned away from him to look at the passing landscape.

"My turn. What do you hope to be when you grow up?" I asked.

"Artist who actually makes money," he said, and then we both laughed.

His voice became low and gravelly. "What made you notice me at that party?"

I gulped down my surprise. Were we really going there?

I kept my gaze turned to the window and said the most honest thing I could think of. "Sexy . . . magical smile . . . soulful eyes."

*Gorgeous. Amazing. Special.*

His breath hitched but he remained silent. I noticed how his hands gripped the steering wheel. It was the same way that I now grasped at the door handle.

I adjusted myself in my seat, but refused to meet his eyes.

"What made you want to kiss me?" I whispered. I wasn't even sure if he heard me, until he finally spoke.

"Explosive chemistry . . . powerful conversations . . . beautiful."

I tipped my head forward, unable to breathe. I pretended to fish for my cell phone in my handbag on the floor.

I felt his warm fingers on my back and heard him swallow roughly. "We're here, Avery."

I looked up as he turned into the Holiday Inn hotel. He pulled into a parking space, and we still didn't make eye contact.

"Let me grab our bags," he said, and then rushed out of the car. I took several deep breaths, trying to get a grip on myself.

*They were only words, Avery.*

I met him in front of the car, and our eyes locked. His searing gaze reached straight through my chest and grabbed hold of my tattered heart. It stroked and soothed the bruised places like a salve before finally releasing its penetrating hold.

Bennett strode toward the hotel lobby. My legs started working again, and I stumbled toward the front desk as he gave his name and waited on our room key.

"You here for the art fair?" the hotel manager asked.

"Yep," Bennett answered.

I cleared my throat. "Are there any other rooms available?"
Bennett stiffened beside me while the manager punched
keys on her computer. "We're pretty booked because of the
fair and another conference this weekend. The only availabil-
ity is a smoking room on the third floor."

I cringed. I hated anything having to do with smoke. I
knew those rooms stunk to high heaven. "No, I'm good. Thank
you."

She handed Bennett the room cards, and as we walked to
the elevators he gave me the extra one without even a glance.
When the doors to the elevator shut, he said, "*Damn* it. I'm
sorry if you feel uncomfortable. Maybe this wasn't such a good
idea after all."

His pained voice made my stomach clench.

"No, Bennett, I agreed to come because I wanted to," I
said. "I just had a moment of doubt at the desk, like maybe
being near you and those beds . . ."

"Not if we don't let it," he said. "I promise I'll sleep on the
very edge of the other bed."

We got off the elevator, found our door, and slipped inside.
It was a plain but clean room. Two queen beds sat side by side,
separated by a nightstand. A bathroom was across the room,
along with a closet, a mini refrigerator, and a sink.

"I call this one," I said, pointing to the bed closest to the
window.

"Sounds good to me." He lifted the corners of his cheeks.
I smiled back. "Now, let's go sell your stuff."

. . .

We drove to the art exhibit, which was in a huge space in one of the local shopping malls. I helped Bennett bring in his pieces from the back of his Jeep and find the table where he was to set up his display.

The event coordinator assigned him one of the last tables in the far corner of the largest section and he got to work placing his art on easels as well as on the long table provided him. His pictures were of varying sizes, and though all of them were black-and-white charcoal drawings, a couple had hints of added color.

Like the one he set on the easel that resembled the eye of a tornado—black and gray and angry. But when you directed your gaze to the center of the storm, you saw that Bennett had inserted splashes of green and orange. The effect was awe-inspiring.

There were dozens of other exhibitors setting up, and I found myself moving down the line passing table after table of artists and their wares. There were sculptures, photographs, and abstract paintings. And almost every artist held that same intensity in their eyes that Bennett had. Like gratification restrained by sheer nervousness. Maybe pleased with their craft, yet still reserved. Not quite ready to show off their art, to perhaps give it away, for the world to see.

Bennett had encouraged me to bring my books to study from during the setup, but I was too jazzed up to pull them out of my bag. There was too much creative energy in this room and spilling over its sides.

When I headed back in the direction of Bennett's table, he was talking to a short redhead with pretty blue eyes—another artist? She placed her hand on his arm, a personal gesture that made my chest constrict.

"Avery, this is my friend Rebecca."

Rebecca turned and smiled, all the while appraising me closely, from my jeans to my sweater to my hair.

"Are you also exhibiting here?" I asked to be polite.

"Yeah, my sculptures are at table fourteen." She pointed in the direction of her art.

"I saw those," I said, looking back to the table I had recently passed. "Your stuff is really good."

Bennett cleared his throat. "Rebecca and I know each other from the Bane Center for the Arts, in our hometown."

"Yep, and I haven't seen you in months," she said, pouting out her bottom lip. It gave me the impression he had known those lips more intimately. "Next time you're home, give me a call so we can grab coffee."

He nodded, and she walked away, throwing a smile over her shoulder. I wanted to ask him about her, but it was none of my business.

Although maybe it *was* my business—because we were friends too, right? Besides, I was more than curious about who and how much Bennett had dated. Or maybe he just had hordes of female friends—like me—all of us waiting, hoping, to jump his bones someday.

Ugh, my imagination was getting the best of me.

"So what did you think of the other artists?" he asked, placing an empty box beneath the table.

"Some amazing stuff," I said. "But I'm partial to this *one* artist's work."

"Oh, really?" A deep red splattered across his cheeks. "Why is that?"

I looked down at his display and noticed a piece I hadn't seen before. It was so stunning I couldn't help being drawn to it, tracing my fingers along the outer edges, trying to understand it. "Take this breathtaking one, for example."

Two charcoal figures stood on opposite ends, as far away as the canvas would allow. They were drawn in swirls of stormy grays, browns, and blacks. But in the space between them, the entire center of the drawing, were abstract colorful objects floating in midair, like a misshapen hourglass, melted books, and ghostly trees.

As if the objects represented all of the stuff between them, cluttering their path, keeping them apart. Swirls of reds and yellows and purples offset the dull colors of the androgynous figures, as if their lives were colorless in comparison to the bits and pieces in the center.

The two characters couldn't see each other clearly—there was so much in the way. But one of the figures leaned to the side trying to see around all of that *stuff*, trying to get a good look at the other one. And the look on this figure's face was unabashed want and need and desire.

It occurred to me that the drawing could have been a metaphor for Bennett and me. An absurd one, at best, because I was pretty sure it wasn't at all and that Bennett had created it long before he had met me.

But for some reason this drawing spoke to me. To something deeply rooted inside of me. I was so moved by its intensity, I felt the stinging of tears behind my eyes.

Bennett was directly behind me now, so close I could feel

the heat radiating from his body. His mouth moved close to my ear, and my stomach quivered at the feel of his breath on my neck.

"Tell me what that drawing makes you feel in five words or less," he murmured against my hair.

And as the first tear rolled down my cheek, the words came to me. "Pain, melancholy, beauty, longing . . ."

The sound had whooshed out of the room, like he and I were the only two people standing in the entire place, discussing the brilliance of his drawing. And unlike those two figures he had drawn, we had gotten past all of that *stuff* and were standing in the space between, close enough to touch.

I turned to him, and he wiped the tear from my cheek with his thumb. "And?"

"Hope," I whispered.

He said nothing more. Only searched deeply in my eyes for something—but I wasn't sure what. Maybe my tattered and bruised heart.

"Is that one your favorite?" he asked.

And then the moment was lost, because there was an announcement and the doors were swung open and the public was let inside. Bennett steered me to one of the chairs behind his table before the pandemonium hit. People mobbed the artwork, asked questions, shouted prices, and moved in herds to the next table and the next. And so the morning passed in that way, with very few lulls.

When I returned from getting us a couple of sandwiches for lunch, I noticed Bennett had sold another two drawings to a man who was hunched over the table writing a check. Bennett moved the pictures under the table so he could wrap them in brown butcher paper and have the man pick them up on his way out to his car.

One of the drawings he was storing away was the one I had developed an affinity for. I felt a stab of regret, because all morning long I had considered buying it for myself. But now that it had sold, I was happy for him. Besides, I could barely afford much beyond rent, food, and gas.

As the afternoon wound down, I looked up from the nursing textbook I had finally pulled out only to see Rebecca staring at me from across the way. I turned to Bennett, who was busy playing a game on his phone, and realized she was probably staring at him instead. Or maybe it *was* me. Maybe she was curious about my relationship to him. As curious as I'd been about hers.

I could understand why. He was one hot boy.

"Your pretty redhead friend is looking this way," I said as nonchalantly as possible.

Bennett heaved a long sigh. "Remember when I told you there was a time I thought I was in love?"

My eyes widened. "It was Rebecca?"

He nodded and put down his phone.

Now I looked at her in a whole new light. Her face was striking and she had a smoking body—tight butt, bigger boobs than mine. "What happened?"

"She was my girlfriend in high school," he said, taking a sip of the soda I had brought him for lunch. "My first love, or so I thought. But she cheated on me—more than once, apparently."

"Hussy," I said to get a laugh out of him, and it worked. "Should I assume she got to experience the sneaky side of

Bennett and maybe even got her hair caught in a certain some-one's zipper?"

"*Maybe,*" Bennett said, with mischief glistening in his eyes.

I gulped down the green-eyed monster. That was a long time ago. "Does it still hurt?"

"Nah, water under the bridge and all that."

"Well, she's looking at you like she has some regrets."

"Doesn't matter; there's no going back," he said, shaking his head. "Don't feel a thing for her anymore."

I couldn't help wondering if, in a few months' time, he would say the same thing about *me*.

# CHAPTER TEN

Exhausted and starving, we headed back to the hotel. We decided on dinner and drinks at the hotel bar. We shared wings and mozzarella sticks, along with a couple of beers each.

"Gosh, bar food. It's yummy, but so bad for you. How do you stay in such good shape?"

"I like to work out," he said. "And to answer your earlier question, only one sport in high school—wrestling."

He took a giant swig of his beer. "How about you? How do you keep that little rocking body in shape?"

"Kickboxing." I dipped my head so he wouldn't see how rosy my cheeks were. "But I've always had a boyish figure. I was a late bloomer in the curves department."

"I'd definitely never call you *boyish*, Avery," he said, before throwing his napkin down. "I'm beat—want to head up?"

When we stepped off the elevator, it was hard to miss the couple getting it on in the hallway. His hair shaved short, the guy wore military fatigues and whispered, "I love you," over and over while tenderly kissing the neck of his leggy brunette.

Bennett threw me a sideways grin and opened our door with lightning speed.

"How long do you think they've been separated?" I whispered.

"Probably for a long-ass time," Bennett said. "That would be hard."

"Oh, it's *hard*," I snickered, and Bennett burst out laughing.

When I stepped out of the bathroom, I noticed the way Bennett's eyes scanned over my body, despite the fact that I kept my bra on this time and wore long flannel bottoms. Bennett had gone for modest, too, in the pajamas department. He wore black, knee-length gym shorts and a blue YMCA T-shirt.

I gave him a quick hug good night, inhaled his coconut scent, and thanked him for bringing me. He held on to me for longer than expected, and I realized how nice it felt to be in his arms again.

He nuzzled his face in my hair, causing a tingling sensation at the base of my neck, then pulled back.

"Did you just sniff me?" I asked.

His cheeks lifted into a crooked grin that blazed a trail down to my toes.

Despite my best attempts, my attraction to him was only increasing this weekend.

Now we stood silent on opposite ends of the room, gazes locked on each other. I was about to say good night when I noticed Bennett close his eyes and swallow forcibly.

I thought about making a crack about our double beds, but he was so concentrated and intense. I couldn't stop staring at the raw emotions on his face, at his clenched fists—it was completely unnerving.

Every fragment, every substance, every element occupying the space between us, began to pulse and vibrate. There was so much electricity in the air I could almost hear it sizzle.

I wasn't sure if it was the alcohol I had consumed, or if it was that gorgeous specimen of a boy standing across from me, but I became increasingly aroused.

I arched my back and squirmed, my body betraying me, as I imagined Bennett pulling me to his bed, ripping off my clothes, and telling me that he wanted to fuck me senseless.

As the tension between us grew denser, I noticed something steadily swelling across the room. Bennett attempted to adjust himself, but it was plain as day.

Finally, Bennett turned away, inhaled a deep breath, and then charged toward the bathroom. "I'm going to shower," he mumbled in my direction.

He was as turned on as I was and trying to get as far away from me as possible.

"Bennett, it's okay," I said. I felt pinpricks all over my body. It was all I could do not to reach out to him.

"Give me a minute." He closed the bathroom door, and I heard him lean his full weight against it.

"Wait, Bennett." I had this desperate desire, this powerful need to be near him, to do something about all of this pent-up frustration. If not for me, then for him.

I heard the shower turn on right before he yanked open the door. He stepped back in the room to grab something from his bag, which was on the floor by his bed. "I'll be fine in a few minutes."

CHRISTINA LEE

The spigot was turned on full blast and steam was already escaping beyond the glass shower door. When he straightened himself, toothbrush holder in hand, I noticed his breathing was labored.

I scanned down his body to his full-blown erection and his shaking hands.

I felt this overwhelming hunger to touch him as he brushed past me, his stride purposeful.

"Bennett," I whispered. "I want to help."

He stopped suddenly and sucked in a breath. "Fuck, Avery."

I took a step toward him. "Please."

One step closer and he didn't move away. I stood in front of him and saw his dark and hooded eyes, overwhelming desire coursing through them.

I inched my fingers to his waistband and he groaned, the container in his hand clattering to the floor. When the tip of his erection poked out of his shorts and met air, his breathing only intensified. Edging my hands beneath his shirt, I pulled it over his head.

When he twisted to deposit his shirt on the floor I spotted a second tattoo, low on his back. I remembered what he said about them being well-placed.

I smoothed my fingers down his chest as goose bumps broke out over his flesh. I eased his shorts down and let his erection spring free. *Damn.* He was taut, smooth, and all kinds of exquisite.

I trailed my hands down his belly to his hips, teasing the area around his erection with my fingers. He grabbed my face and kissed me with such passion and conviction I was begging for air. His mouth was on fire as his tongue tangled deeply with mine.

"Bennett, you're beautiful," I whispered against his lips.

Then I tugged his fingers away from my face and down to his sides. I watched as he balled his fists, but he kept his hands there.

I looked into his eyes. "Can I touch you?"

His response came out in a muffled pant.

I traced my thumb over his silky tip and watched how his chest heaved and his eyes glazed over. When my fingers grasped the length of him the breath caught in the back of his throat. He felt firm and smooth in my steady hands.

Bennett knotted his fingers in my hair and then skimmed them along my neckline. I relished every touch, every breath, every time he whispered my name.

I pulled his shorts all the way down his legs, and he stepped out of them. "Get in the shower."

Without hesitation he moved backward, crossing over the threshold of the door, and then under the stream of water. I watched as it cascaded off his shoulders and beaded down his chest. I reached for the hotel soap, unwrapping it and running it under the water stream, despite my arms getting wet. I lathered up and then washed the front of him—his neck, his chest, his stomach. When my fingers traced down below to his dark and curly hair, he squeezed his eyes shut and moaned. My fingers were sufficiently soapy, and when I worked my hand up and down the length of him, he braced the shower wall. "Jesus, Avery."

As I moved my fingers fast, and then slow, and then fast again, his hands gripped my shoulders and then trailed down to my breasts. He ran his thumbs over my nipples, which became instantly hard through two layers of clothing. As my breathing intensified, so did my caresses. My hands stroked up and down his warm and soapy shaft.

"Oh God. I'm close," he panted.

"Come for me," I whispered against his lips.

That was the breaking point as he groaned out his release and tucked his head against my shoulder.

The milky white substance washed off his stomach with a swipe of my hands, and I stepped back, dazed, and more than aroused. His eyes locked on mine, and if they hadn't loosened their hold soon after, I might have come right then and there.

I turned away from him as he finished his shower. I brushed my teeth and changed into a dry shirt, and then lay down in my bed, facing away from his. He took five minutes more in the bathroom and I nearly fell asleep, except my mind was far too busy processing everything.

When he stepped into the room, I felt his eyes on me, but I didn't stir. I hoped he thought I was asleep because I didn't want to have a discussion about what just happened. I didn't regret it for one moment, but I didn't want him to read too much into my actions or think it meant more than it did. I wasn't even sure what it meant at this point. All I knew was that some part of me—some raw and carnal part—longed to reach out to him. Touch him. *Please* him.

My mattress caved in from the pressure of his knee, and I squeezed my legs together. I was still cooling down from the intense experience of seeing him naked and making him come.

It made me feel powerful in ways I couldn't explain.

"Avery," he whispered in my ear. "Why did you do that?"

"I wanted to," I mumbled. My eyes fluttered open and I stared out the dark window. "I *needed* to. God, Bennett, you're amazing. Just leave it at that."

I heard a sharp intake of breath, and then felt his warm fingers on my shoulder. "What if I wanted to do things to you, too?"

I shook my head, even though my underwear felt instantly moist. "No, Bennett. It's okay."

*God. Just the sound of his voice.* "Besides, you'd be breaking your own . . . code. Just . . . go to bed."

He was silent for so long I wasn't sure if he hadn't drifted off to sleep. Finally, he sighed and said, "Good night." He reached down and placed a hot kiss in the crook of my neck. My shoulders stiffened and I tried unsuccessfully to hold in a moan.

"Damn it, Avery." Then his tongue was stroking my ear and I almost came unglued. I curved my head toward him, my breaths shooting out in hard gasps. I heard a groan in the back of his throat right before he sealed his mouth over mine.

His tongue performed a slow dance inside my mouth—relaxed, lazy, and all kinds of sexy. The exact opposite of my pulse, which was steadily climbing to the stars.

His hand edged under the hem of my shirt to my stomach and I flinched. His fingers slid to my bra, pushing it up to let my breasts loose. He nudged me flat on my back and lifted up my shirt, exposing me. His eyes raked up and down my body before he swung his knee over my stomach to straddle me. Lifting my arms above my head, he held them captive while he kissed me, soft and gentle, trailing his tongue along my lips.

I squirmed beneath him, feeling his hard-on grow against my belly. He tugged off my shirt and unhooked my bra, pulling the lacy material from my arms and then dropping it on the bed. He caressed the length of me with his eyes while my chest heaved.

"Perfection," he whispered against my lips.

He lay down on his side while his fingers stroked my breasts and stomach, trailing his nails up and down the center of my chest, driving me insane. My breasts felt swollen and my need turned to desperation. When he traced his thumb around my nipples, my fingers fisted the blankets so tight I thought they might gouge holes.

As his hand fingered the edge of my pajama pants I nearly jumped out of my skin. He rose to his knees and gently pulled the pants down my legs and tossed them aside. I had on a pair of pink cotton underwear, and when his gaze moved up my legs and landed on my crotch I was nearly finished right then and there. I knew I was almost a goner. I wanted him so damn much and had for so damn long, all he had to do was keep looking at me like that to make me come.

"You are stunning," he murmured. I squeezed my eyes closed and fisted the covers again. As his hand moved up my thighs, my legs began to tremble.

"I want to touch you," he said as his fingers reached the lacy edge of my bikini bottoms.

I sucked in a breath as he shifted my underwear to one side. "Damn, you're so wet," he groaned.

He trailed hot and wet kisses up my neck to my mouth. He nibbled on my bottom lip as his finger slid through my wet folds. I gasped loudly and he pulled my tongue into his mouth, sucking it until I reared against him. When he slipped one finger and then two inside me, I whimpered. I knew I wouldn't last much longer.

My hands reached for his hair, and I yanked him toward me. My tongue darted inside his mouth, lapping greedily against his while his fingers explored me. When his thumb inched up and found my sweet spot, I moaned into his mouth. His thumb pressed and circled and rubbed.

Then his thumb stilled, applying constant delirious pressure—until my entire world came undone.

Bennett held me while I trembled and pulsed and finally came floating back down to earth. He nudged me on my side and pulled my back against his chest, until I fell into a deep and delicious sleep.

# CHAPTER ELEVEN

When I woke to the sound of Bennett's phone alarm, I was alone in my bed. Bennett was already dressed and had apparently left the room to get two coffees, one of which he now handed me.

"You're a lifesaver." I sat up, keeping the sheet in place against my nakedness.

Bennett glanced at the top of my covered breasts and then away. "Figured you'd need your caffeine."

"You figured right." I smiled and then took a long sip.

He grinned back, and it didn't feel forced. This wasn't as awkward as I thought it might be, after last night.

"So we just have until noon today. Then we pack up what's left and hit the road."

"Sounds good. Maybe I'll even get more studying in today."

Bennett was acting a little too calm and collected. Like either he was cool with what had happened between us or he wasn't planning on bringing it up.

Fine with me. I didn't want to bring it up either.

I guess part of me figured he'd want to discuss the whole relationship-status thing again, but maybe he knew it wouldn't get us anywhere. Or maybe he realized I wasn't going to be that girl. Even if he'd entertained that idea at some point.

So why did I feel so unsettled, so unfinished? My stomach was in knots, and every time he looked at me with those beautiful and soulful eyes, those knots changed to flutters.

Flutters so fierce I felt them down to my toes.

I was afraid to admit that maybe he didn't think I was good enough for him. That I wasn't girlfriend material, after all. And I guess, really, I wasn't.

*So get over yourself, Avery.*

I raised my coffee cup to him. "Here's to not having anything to pack up after the exhibit today." Bennett had done well yesterday, selling half a dozen of his drawings. He clinked his cup against mine, grinned, and started packing up the things around his bed.

I stood up and adjusted the sheet to fit around me. "I'm going to shower. I can be ready in twenty." I felt his eyes on my body, and I pushed back that flicker of desire I felt low in my belly.

Last night was all kinds of earth-shattering goodness. I mean, he got me off with just his fingers. That's how worked up he made me. And watching him come—the way his eyes became unfocused, his brow furrowed, his jaw clenched. Hot damn. That image alone would be enough to last me—and my vibrator—a long while.

The crowd was thinner at the exhibit that day, and Bennett and I fell into a comfortable silence. I pulled out my nursing textbook and began reading chapter twenty-two sitting in the chair beside him. We still had redhead staring at us across the way, but since Bennett didn't seem to notice or even care, neither did I.

Something had shifted in the air between us, despite never discussing the previous night. We had shared something so intimate it gave me chill bumps just thinking about it. I was able to make him feel things—really powerful things—and somehow that changed everything.

Even though I wasn't trying to be closer to him, not in that way. Just in a friend kind of way. And I'd keep telling myself that lie until I believed it. Because I was so not ready for someone as amazing as Bennett Reynolds. And I never would be. I was fucked up, and it wouldn't take him long to figure that out and hit the road running.

It didn't matter, though; there was no chance of last night occurring ever again. We'd had the perfect kind of storm brewing. The hotel room, the passionate couple in the hall, the intense talk on the ride up. It was something that had just happened given our circumstances, and I'd be on high alert to avoid a repeat occurrence.

Except, the truth of the matter was, I felt closer to Bennett as a result. Because I came on this trip and learned new and incredible things about him, and was grateful for that. He'd be an amazing friend for me to have. For anyone to have, really.

Bennett's phone buzzed, and he fished it out of his pocket. "Hi, Mom."

I heard her tinny voice and some of what she said, even though I tried not to listen. She was asking if he was coming for Sunday dinner.

"I told you I had an art exhibit this weekend. So I need to skip it this time."

He listened as his mom's voice changed to a frustrated tone.

"No, Mom, I—" He huffed and listened some more. "My friend Avery is with me, and I need to get her home."

He turned his back to me, intent on more privacy, and I pretended to be immersed in my book. "The girls will see me next week. No . . . Okay, maybe. I'll ask her."

He gritted his teeth. "I'll let you know in a couple of hours. Good-bye, Mom."

I closed my book. "You look as exasperated as I feel when I talk to my mom."

"Yeah, well, she knows how to push all the right buttons." He sighed. "Guilt trips have always worked in her favor."

"Tell me about it," I mumbled. "You were supposed to do something with them today? Sorry, wasn't trying to listen."

"Our weekly dinner. You wouldn't by chance . . ." He rushed his fingers through his hair. "Never mind."

"Ask me," I said, my pulse picking up speed.

He took a deep breath. "Would you mind stopping at my mom's house with me on our drive back? I won't torture you with a family dinner, but if I stop in I can at least see my sisters and . . . check on things."

I could tell he was struggling with that last part—maybe how I did with my own brother. Making sure he was okay. He was surviving. He still felt loved.

"Of course I'll go, Bennett. No problem."

The surprise in his eyes was evident. "Cool, thank you."

We were packed up and on the road by twelve thirty. Bennett had sold one of his smaller drawings and he seemed satisfied. I helped him wrap the rest of his artwork in butcher paper and bubble wrap and store the pieces in the back of his Jeep.

106

"Mind if we go to a drive-through? I'm starving."

"Me, too," I said, and got comfy in my seat by removing my shoes and propping my feet up on the dash.

He pulled into a McDonald's and we got two burgers, sodas, and fries to share.

"After that greasy food last night and now this, I'm going to have to eat salads for the rest of the week," I said.

"See, that's the beauty of working out," he said, biting into his burger. "I can eat what I want as long as I work it off at the gym."

"Yeah, and I'm pretty sure your genes have nothing at all to do with it," I said, rolling my eyes. I kept my gaze away from his muscular biceps in that blue T-shirt.

We got back on the road and downed the rest of our burgers. I ended up feeding Bennett my fries, only because he grabbed my hand after it came out of the bottom of the bag. When his tongue touched my fingertips I held my breath.

"More, please," he said, gobbling up the fries.

"What am I, your servant today?" Heat was pulsing low in my belly. "Grab your own damn fries."

"Hey, I'm the chauffeur, so it's only fair," he said, yanking the fast-food bag onto his lap and digging in.

Around a mouthful of fries, he said, "Want to play Five Fingers again to pass the time?"

I wasn't sure if that was such a good idea, but he seemed like he was in a good mood, so I went with it. "Sure."

"Okay," he said, wiping his fingers on the napkin I handed him. I resisted the urge to pull them in my mouth one by one and suck the salt off. "Me first."

I nodded and then braced my hands on my knees.

"Tell me about that tattoo behind your ear."

My back went rigid. I got the tattoo in that location so that few people would ever notice it. It meant something to me. It represented a time in my life that I'd needed to be strong. The time I made a conscious decision to never be fragile again.

But somehow, around Bennett, I felt all kinds of weak. And that scared me.

*Here goes nothing.* "Eighteen . . . Gaelic symbol . . . means *survive.*"

Bennett's eyebrows rose to his hairline as he considered my answer. I held my breath as he thought about it for long moments. Then his fingers reached for my hair. I felt my skin pebble beneath his touch.

Keeping one hand on the wheel, he brushed the strands over my shoulder, exposing my ear, so he could get a glimpse of the tattoo again. I was waiting for him to say something—anything—like that it sucked, it was ugly, or it was poorly designed.

But he didn't breathe one word.

"You probably could have done a better job," I mumbled.

"Nah," he said. "Would be cool to ink something else on you, though."

Sparks flickered inside me as I imagined how sexy that would be. Lying on his table, letting his fingers work their magic.

"That reminds me," I said, glad for the distraction. "My friend Ella needs an appointment with you. She's wanted a tattoo forever, but always chickens out."

"Happens to a lot of people," he said. "Cool, guess I'll be seeing her soon."

"Okay, back to our game," I said, and he glanced over at me. "Turnabout is fair play. Your tattoos?"

His cheeks turned up into this ridiculously sexy smile, as if he was recounting our night together. Seeing his tattoos on his stark naked body. *Damn.* I crossed my legs and squeezed my thighs together.

He cleared his throat two times. "An hourglass and a poem."

Drat, he got out of that too easily. I knew the hourglass was on his lower back, and it seemed to resemble the one in the drawing I liked so much. And the scripted letters—the poem— were on his rib cage. But I needed more information.

"Can I see the poem?"

His eyes expanded. "What—now?"

I shrugged. "We've got the time."

He swallowed thickly and his eyes became hooded. Shit, maybe this wasn't such a good idea. But I'd been curious about the tattoo on his rib cage for weeks.

Bennett's eyes met mine, and he nodded. I unbuckled my seat belt and slid closer to him. He white-knuckled the steering wheel like he'd crash if he didn't pay more attention to the road.

Thankfully, the tattoo was on the side closest to me. With shaky fingers, I lifted his T-shirt, and he sucked in a breath. The poem was written in a heavy black script and it curved inward, in the shape of a mini tornado. It reminded me of his drawing from the exhibit.

I moved my face closer to his skin and noticed how his chest rose and fell in quick succession. How my breath caused goose bumps to break out over his smooth flesh.

CHRISTINA LEE

I found the beginning of the poem, which was marked by a small star and read it aloud. "Unfurl your muscles. Slip off your skin. Drop your guts in a heap on the floor."

I felt my airway constrict. Damn, this was profound. I continued. "Nuzzle inside the hollow of my bones. Let our breaths mingle as one. Turn liquid for me. Only for me. Bury your essence inside of my soul."

I sat up and let the fabric of his shirt fall back in place. I was lightheaded, my tongue thick in my mouth. I stared straight ahead at the cars in front of us on the freeway, trying to digest what I had just read of that beautiful and multilayered poem.

"Bennett, that's just . . . wow," I said, trying to meet his eyes. But he kept them trained on the road. "What does it mean to you?"

"I believe it's my turn, Ms. Michaels."

"No! Time out, Bennett," I said, gritting my teeth. "I *really* want to know. Please, tell me."

He stared at me for a lengthy moment, then back at the road again, before answering.

"It's written by a modern-day poet," he said, almost reluctantly. "And it's a reminder to me—of two very different kinds of love."

I held my breath, praying for him to keep going. This man, this gorgeous man, continued to astound me at every turn. I pleaded with my eyes for him to continue.

"There's the kind of love that's unhealthy, all-consuming. You give up entirely who you are for that other person. Like my mother has done her whole damn life."

He took a deep and meaningful breath.

"And the other kind of love is freeing. It allows you to be

110

your best self. You're seamless when you're with the person you love unfathomably—but *never* invisible."

As I sat there listening to him, something profound happened in the very center of me. Stuff began rearranging and clicking into place. My heart burst through my chest and landed at Bennett's feet—asking, pleading, begging him to smooth out her creases, soothe all her wounded parts, mend her shattered center.

I couldn't even talk any sense into her.

"Why aren't you saying anything?" he whispered. He gave me a nervous sidelong glance.

"Because I have no words," I said, still in awe of him. "What you just said . . . it . . . it left me . . . breathless."

We didn't speak for long minutes afterward, both of us lost in our own thoughts. I waited for my heart to get her butt home, back inside my chest, so I could breathe freely again.

Bennett was the first to speak. "Why the word *survive*?"

Bennett had shared some deep beliefs with me. It was only fair that I opened myself up, too. At least a little. I'll admit he was way braver than me.

"Because I survived my mother. Growing up with her and all her . . . men. Her shit. Her selfishness." Her *betrayal*, I left out. I huffed out a breath. "And I hope against hope that I can help my baby brother survive that woman, too."

He grabbed my hand and tugged it toward him, squeezed it. "Thank you, Avery, for sharing that."

Like he knew how tough it was to open myself up to him. Damn, he got me sometimes.

# CHAPTER TWELVE

"My family lives just off this exit," Bennett said, pointing east. "You ready for this?"

"I'm ready," I said, fisting my seat belt strap.

Meeting Bennett's family? What the hell was I thinking?

He pulled into the first development off the exit and then down the second side street. The house was a ranch with peeling paint and half-dead flowers in the garden. But it had a sweet white picket fence that surrounded the property, and the lawn looked freshly cut.

We waited at the door as he knocked. A lady who was unmistakably his mother swung open the door. "Why didn't you use your key, honey?"

She looked different from that picture I had seen in his apartment. Her hair was a mess, her blouse wrinkled, and a cigarette hung from her lips, like she needed a long drag to help soothe her nerves.

Hell if she didn't remind me of my own mother.

"Mom, this is Avery," Bennett said as we stepped inside.

"Nice to meet you," I said, my palms sweaty and slick. I wondered what this family would think of me and my friendship with Bennett. I was glad I at least put on mascara and ran a brush through my wavy hair this morning. Not that I should want to look presentable for them. Or pretty.

"Benny!" the twins sang in unison, and came bounding down the stairs. They were identical and had long brown hair, and I wondered how anyone told them apart.

"Benny?" I mouthed to him. He narrowed his eyes at me.

"Lex, Soph," he said picking each girl up and twirling her around. "Where's Taylor?"

"Taylor," his mother bellowed around her cigarette. "Get your ass down here!"

"Coming." Taylor appeared at the top of the stairs with a baby in her arms. He was maybe a year old, and I remembered Bennett saying something about her getting pregnant last year. I just never considered her raising the baby. I don't know why.

When she landed on the bottom step, she said, "Hey."

She was stunning. She could have been Bennett's twin, with her dark curly locks and perfect complexion. Her eyes were blue, like his mother's. The twins had hazel eyes.

"Everybody, this is my friend Avery," Bennett announced. Right on cue the baby started wailing. Bennett took his nephew from Taylor's arms and circled the room. "Toby, what's wrong, buddy?"

Toby stopped crying and stared at Bennett. Bennett made some crazy face and Toby cracked up.

"Again," Toby said. Bennett made the same face over and

over, until Toby was laughing so hard no sound came out of his mouth. It was completely endearing.

"Can I get you something to drink?" Mrs. Reynolds asked. She ran her cigarette butt under the faucet before pitching it in the garbage can under the sink.

Well, at least she knew about fire safety. But all of that secondhand smoke around these kids. Who was I kidding? I was probably a walking billboard for what a parent's second-hand smoke did to you.

"Got anything with caffeine?" I asked.

Taylor opened the refrigerator and turned to me. "Diet Coke?"

"Perfect." I looked around the kitchen. It was a wreck. Baby toys were everywhere, the counters were cluttered, and the dishes were piled a mile high. Bennett came around the corner carrying Toby.

"Haven't the twins been doing their chores?" Bennett asked, looking at the kitchen sink. "Mom, you've got to en-force that stuff."

She fished another cigarette out of her pack. "They haven't been listening to me."

"Alexis and Sophie, start on the dishes," Bennett said in an authoritative voice. "Now!"

I'd never heard him sound like that, and it took me by surprise. The twins dragged themselves to the sink, both sets of eyes glaring at him.

"Do they listen to Henry?" Bennett mumbled to Taylor.

"Yeah." She sighed. "When he's here."

"He's been working a lot of hours," his mother interjected. "Don't start, Bennett. You know he's a good man."

"Just making sure, Momma." Bennett narrowed his eyes at Taylor in a silent form of conversation and she just shrugged. For the first time, I noticed the bags under her eyes, and I wondered if it was because of staying up late with the baby and then getting herself to school every morning.

I thought about how tough being a teen mom would be, and Bennett's vow about not raising his own child so young suddenly rang true. I was starting to get it. *Really* get it.

"How do you and Bennett know each other?" Mrs. Reynolds asked.

"We live in the same building and attend the same university," I said. I noticed Taylor had taken the baby back from her brother and was now feeding him a bottle.

"She's an LPN—which is a kind of nurse," Bennett said, placing his hand on the small of my back. "She's working on her RN degree."

His warm fingers made me flinch, but I also liked his hand there; it felt safe and protective, and I wasn't sure I wanted him to remove it.

His gesture didn't go unnoticed by his mother or sister, either.

"I'm interested in health care," Taylor said, her voice soft, almost humble. "I'm taking an elective at my high school."

"I'd be happy to talk to you about it, anytime," I said. "Just say the word."

"Cool," she said, adjusting the bottle for Toby. "Thanks."

"How are you doing on homework, guys?" Bennett asked the twins. "You keeping up?"

"Taylor's been helping us," Alexis said, wiping a dish with a soapy sponge.

Damn, I felt sorry for Taylor. Sounded like she had a huge

load. And I couldn't help wondering if Toby's father was involved in their lives. Somehow I doubted it.

Bennett gripped Taylor's arm. I saw concern in his eyes. The same concern I had for my own brother. "You doing okay, Tay?"

"Hanging in there, Ben," she said. "Actually, Henry's helping me with calculus and rides and stuff." Henry. The stepfather. Sounded like he might be involved with these kids.

I shivered, remembering Tim taking an interest in my schoolwork, and hoped Henry's intentions were sincere.

I noticed these siblings spoke as if their mother weren't even in the room. And she didn't seem to mind at all. In fact, she had planted herself at the kitchen table with another cigarette and a soda. At least I hoped that was what was in her glass. It reminded me so much of home that I wanted to slap her silly and tell her to get ahold of her family and her responsibilities.

Now I understood why Bennett felt so damn accountable for this family.

"We've gotta head back soon, Mom," Bennett said.

"I'll let Henry know you'll be here next week," she said. "He'll be disappointed you didn't stay. He planned on grilling steaks and chicken for dinner."

I wondered again about this Henry guy and whether he was a decent man. I felt protective of Taylor, like I wanted to invite her to live with me or Bennett. That was just how it felt to have so much responsibility put on you as a kid. When you finally broke away, the anxiety still lingered.

"Tay, you wanted to show me something upstairs?" Bennett asked, and a look passed between them that told me they needed to talk about something. "Do you mind?" Bennett asked me. "I'll be right back down."

"No problem," I said, looking at some of the kids' artwork on the refrigerator. The twins were still washing dishes and arguing about some video game.

I watched Bennett and Taylor make their way upstairs, and then turned to his mother. I wasn't even sure what to say to her. Like with my own mother, I was pretty sure we had nothing in common.

"He's smitten with you," Mrs. Reynolds said out of the blue, puffing out a ring of smoke. "Hope you're not a heartbreaker."

"We're . . . we're just friends."

"Sure you are." She took a sip of her drink. "I see how he looks at you."

"I'm not really sure what to say to that."

"He doesn't bring any girls around here," she said, and then sighed. "He's a good boy."

"I agree," I said, and sat in the chair across from her. "The best."

"Well, he's needed around here . . . a lot," she said, her voice wavering. "So he doesn't have time to get all caught up in some girl."

What she was really saying was that she continued to lean on her son, instead of relying on herself, and that just boiled my blood.

"I hear you loud and clear," I said, meeting her hard gaze.

She puffed her cigarette and turned away. Like she'd said her piece and was done with me.

"He's an adult now," I said, more for Bennett's sake than for hers. And maybe a little for mine, too. "He's bound to make his own life, live his own dreams."

I looked up and saw Bennett paused on the top step of the staircase. His brows were drawn together.

"You starting stuff, Momma?" The question was one he'd probably said to her a thousand times, and I realized it wasn't my place to be here saying anything at all. They had a long history together, and even though I thought I understood it, I knew there was plenty more I didn't.

"Everything's cool." I stood up. "It was nice meeting your family, Bennett. I'll wait in the car."

When Bennett came outside, his face was drawn, his jaw set tight. As he backed out of the driveway, he said, "I'm sorry I brought you here."

"I'm not." I placed my hand on his arm and felt him twitch. "Thankfully, Bennett, neither one of us is defined by our families." I stared out the side window and felt him relax beside me.

We didn't speak again until we got on the freeway. "What did she say to you?"

"She was just being a protective mother," I said. It was a lie mixed with the truth. A partial truth.

"Then you've got the wrong mother," he hissed. "The only person she's protective of is herself."

"Maybe," I said. "Or maybe it's not so black-and-white all the time. I mean, you turned out pretty okay."

"Yeah, I guess so."

"And remember, I've got one of those moms back home. So I'm pretty used to selfish."

His fingers patted my knee. It was a light and quick tap but I felt it shoot up my arms and lodge in my chest.

"So, what do you think of your new stepdad?" I held my breath as I waited for his answer. I was hoping Taylor was safe.

But somehow I doubted Bennett would leave her vulnerable if she wasn't.

"I think he's the most decent guy she's been with," he said. "The truth is, he's the twins' dad—he came back after all this time."

"Seriously?"

"He didn't know about them. He and my mom had a one-night stand, and she never told him she got pregnant," he explained, and again, I understood his logic about not sleeping around. It came to me in waves. All of those things added up to Bennett's self-assigned values and beliefs. "Then they had a chance meeting all these years later."

"Now that's crazy pants," I said. "But I understand crazy." His grin lit me up from the inside.

"I think Henry will do right by the girls. It's Taylor I'm worried about."

"She's got to be under a shitload of stress," I said. "But she also seems smart and responsible."

"She is. But taking care of a kid and still finishing high school? It's a hard life." He sighed. "I offered to take her off my mom's hands. Told her Taylor could come live with me. But Henry wasn't having it. He told me to finish college and let him be the man of the house for a change."

My chest felt lighter hearing that man's words. "Did you feel relief—hearing that?"

He shrugged. "What do you mean?"

"That someone acknowledged all that you'd done. It would have felt better coming from your own mother—but still," I said. "And now you can concentrate on taking care of yourself."

He rushed his fingers through his hair. "I know it's fucked

up, but it's all I've ever known. Besides, it's nice being needed sometimes."

"Yep, that's fucked up all right." I pushed his shoulder playfully.

"Hey!" He gave me a sidelong glance, mischief twinkling in his eyes. "I'm a work in progress."

"Aren't we all," I mumbled.

"I just pray my mom doesn't blow it. She's got a good man right under her nose—she's never had that before," he said. "So I hope she doesn't try to screw it up and throw it all away."

His words wedged in my throat like a cold, harsh truth, and I had trouble gulping them down.

# CHAPTER THIRTEEN

Raw Ink was located in a little strip mall on Vine Street. Ella had made the appointment a few days ago and begged me to go. I knew she wouldn't take no for an answer. She honked twice when she picked me up and yelled, "Get in the car, bitch!"

Since our weekend trip, Bennett and I had settled into a new kind of normal. We didn't spend any more planned time together, but if we happened to run into each other in the building, we'd get takeout and watch a movie, or Sunday afternoon football. He'd suggest players to start for my fantasy football league and I'd argue with his horrible logic and choices.

All of it was purely platonic. At least from the outside.

Still, I was dying to know what that weekend meant to him. It had definitely connected us in a deeper way—despite the crazy sexual tension between us. We were more honest with each other about our families and friends and jobs—just not about what was going on between us.

I should have been thankful for that. Nothing had changed

on my end. Except for wanting to jump his bones every two minutes. And it was messing with my head. But I knew he'd never let sex happen between us. And I still respected him for that.

But the craving to be connected to him in an intimate way had become visceral—I felt it dead center in my chest, traveling south to between my legs—almost animalistic, pining over something you knew you'd never have.

The receptionist at the front desk of Raw Ink fit the part, with her purple spiked hair and a feminine sleeve of tattoos up the length of her arm. She checked off Ella's appointment on her calendar and told us to have a seat.

She walked down the hall to the third door on the left and dipped her head inside. "Bennett, your sketch consult is here."

I heard his throaty voice next. It slid down my spine like warm fingers. "Tell her I'll be out in few; just finishing up with a client."

We sat down on the black leather couch and waited. The walls were decorated with graffiti art and alt rock piped through the stereo, loud and menacing. I still had trouble picturing Bennett working here, even though he was a few doors down.

Yet, he was probably in his element here. I could picture his drawings lining these walls.

A couple minutes later, Bennett walked out with his female client. He had on tight jeans, black Doc Martens boots, and a black, long-sleeved, fitted T-shirt. The girl was fiddling with the bandage on the inside of her wrist, and clear slick ointment glistened along the edges.

"All set," Bennett said. "Keep it clean and don't mess with

it too much. Follow the instructions on the handout. Holly will check you out."

"Thanks so much," she squealed, her eyes roving over him. It occurred to me that Bennett probably got lots of numbers slipped to him after well-placed tats. My cheeks inflamed thinking about his hands hovering above me and then slipping over my skin as he tattooed my stomach or my lower back.

One thing was for certain: Not only did Bennett know how to use those magical lips—he knew how to use his fingers as well.

That boy had skills. So he had to have had some practice. Or he was just a natural.

Bennett scanned the waiting room before his eyes locked on mine. Then they reluctantly glided over to my friend. "You ready, Ella?"

"Yep." She hopped up. "Okay if Avery comes back, too?"

"No problem," he said, giving me a sidelong grin. He knew how nervous Ella was about this appointment. My eyes roamed around the room, nervous I'd see Bennett's boss, Oliver, here. But maybe he'd act cool about seeing me. I was only a one-night stand. One that he'd tried to turn into a date the next night. But I'd turned him down, and we hadn't been in contact since.

We followed Bennett through the tight hallway lined with framed pictures of tattoos on actual clients. A colorful butterfly on someone's lower back caught my eye. The smell of antiseptic filled the air, but another odor infiltrated my senses as Bennett moved confidently through the space: coconuts.

"Right in here." He motioned to a large glass table with four chairs. I noticed a small black desk along the far wall where Bennett's laptop and iPod were plugged in. The music piping through this room was different—more soothing, less angry. Probably helped his clients relax.

"Let's get down to business, Ella." Bennett sounded much more formal than I'd ever heard him. "What did you have in mind?"

Ella bit her lip. "I'm pretty sure I know what I want, but I'd like to see some of your work first—do you have any samples?"

"Of course." He reached down to the ground for a thick white binder and placed it in front of her. "Here's my portfolio."

"Don't even roll your eyes at me, dickhead," Ella hissed. "I'm just making sure."

I shook my head and snickered. "Dude, I haven't said a word."

Ella opened the book and started paging through. I tried looking with her, but Bennett's gaze pressed into me like a weight, and I couldn't look away, or take a decent breath for that matter. He seemed different here in his element—more confident, sure of himself—and I'll admit it unnerved me.

I wore my hair in a low ponytail and I could tell he was trying to get a good view of the tattoo behind my ear. I absently glided the stray pieces of my hair behind my ears. I looked down at the book every time Ella pointed something out, but Bennett's eyes were like a magnet. I had trouble glancing anywhere else.

The way Bennett gazed at me was so different from other guys—it wasn't vulgar or offensive, just plain hot. *Blistering.* And it only made me want him more.

"These are amazing, Bennett," Ella said after another five minutes.

"Thanks." Bennett's cheeks grooved into a shy grin. "So, did it help you decide?"

She flipped to the page bookmarked by her thumb. It showed a small dragonfly, an image I knew she had been considering, and had hoped to find in Bennett's work. She pointed to it. "This one. Except, can I get different colors shaded in?"

"Of course. You need to make it what you want," he said. His voice was smooth and confident, different than he'd been when he'd first kissed me and that night at the hotel when I'd gone to him in the shower. I liked this confident side of Bennett. He'd been this way with his family, too. "So, why a dragonfly? What does it mean to you?"

"Um . . ." Ella stumbled over his question, possibly unsure of answering him. Maybe she thought her reasoning was lame, but I knew it wasn't. It was meaningful and powerful.

Bennett cleared his throat. "When a client's about to get something permanently inked on their skin, they should ask themselves an important question."

"What's that?" Ella asked.

"'Am I getting this because I like dragonflies this year, or is this symbolic—does it have a deeper meaning?'" Bennett said, digging out a drawing pad and pencils. "Because tastes change. And I'm telling you this because you seem nervous about it."

Ella's shoulders relaxed and she took a deep breath.

"It does mean something to you, Ella," I said, nudging her along. Ella's brother died when we were in high school, and understandably, she was devastated. We all were. Ella said when they were kids, they loved weekends at their grandmother's cottage, where they'd swim and fish and try to capture dragonflies that raced across the lake—along with every other bug under the sun. On the day of Christopher's funeral, Ella swore up and down that a dragonfly flew by her at the cemetery.

"Hey, it's really none of my business. You don't have to explain anything to me," Bennett said, low and gentle. "I was just trying to help—to give you more confidence."

"It . . . it reminds me of my brother—he died a couple of years ago."

Bennett's eyes softened.

"Goddamn, I'm sorry, Ella," he said, his voice strained. "The dragonfly is a nice idea if it's a tribute to your brother. Do you feel better about your decision?"

"Yes, I do," she said. "And thank you."

Bennett nodded as he drew on his sketch pad. His hand moved fast and steady as a dragonfly began taking shape. After seeing his other drawings, I knew this one was small potatoes for him. He could probably do it in his sleep.

"Where did you want the tattoo to go?"

"I was thinking above my ankle," Ella said, wringing her hands. "What do you think, Avery?"

"Sounds perfect," I said, suddenly glad I'd decided to come with her. Not that she would've given me the choice. "And you can cover it up if you need to."

"What colors do you want me to shade in?" Bennett asked, his fingers roaming over the colored pencils next to him.

"Blues and greens," she said, her eyebrows arching upward in excitement.

He chose two colors, and then swirls of cobalt blue and sea green came alive on the page. "Something like this?"

Ella squealed. "I love it."

"If you want to wait out there, or grab some coffee and come back, I can draw this up on transfer paper," he said. "We can have it done and over with today."

"Today?" Ella suddenly looked nervous again.

"Perfect." I stood up and pulled Ella with me. "Enough deliberating. Bite the damn bullet already."

Bennett smiled. "Give me some time and I'll come get you."

"We'll go across the street and make her eat something," I said. "Text me when you're ready."

Bennett reached for his phone when it occurred to both of us that we didn't have each other's cell numbers. I guess it was unnecessary when we lived in the same building. I punched my number into his keypad and handed it back to him. "See you soon."

Ella and I walked to the bagel shop across the street, where we ordered coffees and sandwiches. Ella only nibbled on a few crumbs, she was so nervous.

"It's small, and it'll be over with before you know it," I said, trying to reassure her. "It's going to look so cool. And you'll be happy you finally got it."

My cell buzzed with a message. My stomach clenched with the anticipation of Bennett texting me. I looked at my phone and saw it was Rachel.

Rachel: Did she do it?

Me: She's about to.

Rachel: Tell the bitch I said good luck.

Me: Will do.

"Rachel says good luck," I said. I left off the *bitch* part. It was such a common term of endearment connecting the three of us, Ella probably added it in her own head automatically.

"If Rachel were here, I bet she'd have no qualms about getting that huge tattoo on her back that she's always talked about," Ella said, snorting. "God, I envy you guys some times."

"Envy us for what?" I asked, biting my bagel.

"For just letting loose and going with the flow."

"Um, obviously you haven't gotten my latest memo," I said around a mouthful. "I haven't been able to let loose and go with anything lately. Not even with Rob."

"You had an amazing, orgasmic weekend with Bennett, and now he's ruined other guys for you," Ella said. "Don't even try denying it. See what Hot Boy's done?"

"Oh, I *see* it every night when I'm lying in bed alone. Or should I say, *feel* it."

"It's not so bad having the same boy in your bed every night. You should try it some time," she said, and I scrunched up my nose. "In fact, I'll have me some Joel tonight. Can't wait to surprise him with my new tattoo."

"You'll for sure get some tonight."

My phone buzzed on the table and I felt that familiar pull in my belly.

Bennett: I'm ready for you.

Damn if my heart didn't leap at those words. And certain other parts of me, too.

Me: Are you now?

Bennett: I am. Are you?

Me: Been ready. ☺ See you in five minutes.

"What's the goofy grin for?"
"I don't have a goofy grin. C'mon, Bennett's waiting."
"I doubt he's waiting for *me*."
"Whatever."
"You may not want to admit this, dickhead, but you're already in deep," Ella said, following me to the door. "You haven't picked up any other guys since you met Bennett."
"Then I guess it's time to change that." My words sounded about as hollow as my determination.
"Whatever you say, bitch," she said, swinging around me to push through the exit. "You're coming to the clambake at the frat house this weekend, right?"
"Absolutely."
We stepped inside Raw Ink, and receptionist Holly motioned for us to head to the back.
Bennett wore black plastic gloves and was fiddling with his tools as if he were about to perform a sexy experiment. The longing in his eyes upon seeing me told me all I needed to know about whether he still thought about our weekend together.
"Lie back in this seat and get comfortable," Bennett said. Ella folded herself into a black leather chair that reminded me of something from a dentist's office. Then he pulled the lever to make a footrest pop up. "There you go."
After he set up his work area, he picked up the transfer paper. He rubbed a light layer of ointment on her ankle, placed

the transfer paper on her skin, and pressed down. I realized again just how intimate this type of procedure could be.

When I got my tattoo, the girl was totally professional. And I expected nothing less from Bennett. So why were my palms sweaty just watching how his fingers delicately braced my best friend's leg?

"What do you think?" Bennett asked her once the transfer was complete. This drawing was even better than the sample he'd sketched for us at the table. He had taken more time to make it shine, obviously.

Ella beamed. "I think it's awesome."

"Cool," Bennett said, and then looked at me. "How about you, Ms. Michaels? Do you approve?"

His eyes became hooded, and I crossed my legs in response. "Looks good, Mr. Reynolds."

"Enough with the formality, you two," Ella said. "Unless this is some sort of Regency-era sexual fantasy being played out."

I flipped her off and Ella rolled her eyes. "Now get over here, bitch, I need you."

Bennett looked down at his tools, his neck splotching red. "You can pull up a chair, Avery."

Ella practically wrenched my arm from its socket as Bennett raised the tattoo gun. "One word of caution. If you need a break or feel light-headed, give me a warning so I can remove the needle before you bolt out of your chair."

The look on Ella's face was now one of sheer terror.

"Oh, Ella. It'll feel like teeny prick marks, and then you'll get used to it," I said. "Squeeze my hand if you need to."

As Bennett positioned the needle, Ella grabbed onto my hand like she was having fucking contractions or something.

"There we go. It'll be over before you know it." Bennett spoke to her in a soothing voice. I bit down on my tongue because my hand was being clutched so tightly my knuckles were turning white.

Ella squirmed initially but held it together after that. She squeezed her eyes shut and tilted her head upward just waiting for all of it to be over.

I enjoyed watching Bennett work—he licked his lips and slanted his head in deep concentration. His hands were accurate yet tender. He also hummed a tune so low that I couldn't decipher if it was a made-up song or not. The low vibration from his voice mixing with his soft breaths created a path of goose bumps down the center of my body and a soft tickle between my legs.

"You okay?" Bennett rubbed excess ink from a section of Ella's skin with a wet paper towel.

"Hanging in there," she squeaked out. "It feels less painful than it did at the beginning."

"Good. I finished the outline, so now you can take a breather while I change needles to do the shading. This time will feel different—a little better."

Ella puffed out a breath and opened her eyes. She let go of my hand and I shook it out. "Shit, you dickhead. Remind me not to be in the room if you ever go into labor."

Bennett's back was turned, and I heard him chuckle while he prepped his next set of tools.

When he twisted back around, his gaze bonded to mine like it was the glue holding me together. "So, have you decided what you're going to let me ink on you next?"

"Haven't given it much thought," I said, trying to tear my eyes away from his hold.

"No? Hmmm, I've got some ideas."

"Listen, you two can grope each other after I'm done," Ella said. "But right now I need you to finish my tattoo."

"Knock it off, asshat." I gave her knee a firm shake.

"There will be no groping," Bennett said, and came toward her with the needle again.

I watched him work again but tried to tone my breathing down. Our attraction was becoming way too obvious.

"All finished," he announced several minutes later. "That wasn't so bad, was it?"

Ella's eyes glowed with admiration. "It was worth the pain. I love it so much."

"It looks great, Ella." I mouthed a thank-you to Bennett, and he winked.

"Let me give you our aftercare instruction sheet. Don't take the directions lightly," he said, placing ointment and a Band-Aid over the tattoo. "Follow them to the letter. You don't want to mess around with getting an infection."

Ella stood on shaky legs, and I helped her get her footing.

I slipped into the hall behind Bennett, but had stopped to admire a framed tattoo when I felt a pair of arms slide around my hips.

Then Oliver's low voice. "Hey there, sexy girl—are you back for more?"

I cringed. Bennett whipped around, shock registering over his features.

I pushed Oliver's hands from my waist. "Hey, Oliver. Just here for moral support. My friend got a tattoo from Bennett."

"Yeah?" Oliver looked at Ella as she stood before Holly at the front desk. "She hot, too?"

"She's got a boyfriend," I said, and took a step away. Bennett's jaw was set so tightly, I found it hard to look anywhere but the floor.

Normally, I gave it back good to grabby guys and could tell them where to shove it, but something about Bennett hearing this private conversation made my ears blaze and my stomach ball into a hard fist.

"I know for a fact that you don't do boyfriends, sexy girl," Oliver drawled in my ear. "So we can go at it again tonight, if you're free."

"Stop, Oliver." Now smoke was pouring out of my ears. "I'm just here for my friend. Nothing else."

"Hey, O, you don't give all our female clients this hard of a time, do you?" Bennett had a tight smile on his face. I could tell he was trying to joke with his boss, but there was a serious underlying tone to his question.

"Of course not, Ben," Oliver said, straightening up and taking a step back.

"C'mon, Avery," Bennett said through gritted teeth. "Let's get your friend checked out."

Bennett avoided eye contact with me after that.

Like he was disappointed by the very idea of me having had a one-night stand with his boss.

Or maybe even disgusted.

And I was ticked. Fuck him. He didn't have the right to make me feel that way.

When Ella waved as she went out the door and Bennett turned back toward the hallway, I had the feeling this might be our final good-bye.

# CHAPTER FOURTEEN

My phone rang early Saturday morning. Too early. When I saw it was my brother, I immediately went into panic mode. The kid always slept late. "Adam, what's wrong?"

"It's Mom." He sounded breathless. "She didn't come home last night, which didn't surprise me—you know, her usual Friday night at the bar. I just figured she went to someone's place and got laid."

Hearing my brother talk like that about my mother was normal, but it still bothered the shit out of me. Did other kids have these kinds of fucked-up conversations about their own parents?

"And?" It had to be something serious for Adam to call me this early.

"Anyway, she came home this morning and tried to hide in her room," he said. "Avery, she's one hot mess. She's got a swollen lip and a black eye."

"What the hell?" I sat up in bed. "Did she say what happened?"

Adam sighed. "I'm pretty sure I already know."

"What, Adam?" I reached for my jeans on the floor and pulled them on. "Goddamn it, tell me."

"I didn't want to mention it to you before, but she's been seeing Tim again."

The blood drained from my face. "What?"

"She asked me not to tell you, and I figured it would go nowhere fast," he said. "He hasn't been over more than two or three times. But last night I heard her on the phone, so I knew she was meeting him."

"That son of a bitch," I said, and smashed my fist into my mattress. "I'm hopping in the shower and driving down right now."

"Mom will be pissed, but I didn't know what else to do," he huffed out. He sounded relieved. "I need you, sis."

"You did the right thing."

The hour drive home just made me more furious. Maybe now Mom would finally believe what a sick fuck Tim was and that he was prone to violence. I couldn't stop my hands from gripping the damn steering wheel so hard that my fingers were beginning to swell from the pressure.

I almost wished I would have killed Tim when I had the chance. But I might be sitting in jail right now if I had. There were no witnesses, and my mom sure as hell didn't believe me. Tim had been a cop at the time, and the force was a tight-knit group. The only reason Tim finally left my mom is because my ex-boyfriend Gavin's father was the mayor and my threat against him worked.

But I knew Mom still blamed me to this day for running him off.

When I turned down Maple Drive, I felt that familiar tension in my stomach. I hadn't been here in months, but just driving through my old neighborhood still had the power to make me feel like an outsider, like I no longer belonged. Hell, I was proud of that fact. But somehow, passing by the city hall and high school stadium reduced me to lost-teenager status again.

I pulled up the busted concrete driveway and parked next to Adam's brown beater, still going strong after two years. The trees had turned a golden orange and some leaves had already fallen to the lawn.

Adam and I had loved jumping in leaf piles out front while Mom yelled at us to help rake. Most of my good memories involved Adam. Mom was always with one guy or another—some who tried to parent us, others who ignored us completely. I couldn't even remember half of their names.

But I remembered Tim. He and Mom drank heavily on the weekends, so there was no telling what I'd walk into. Sometimes they were half-dressed and passed out on the couch. Other times, friends were over and they were high as kites from the bong they'd been passing around.

Tim had tried to insert himself into our lives at every turn. He'd won me over for a minute there—I'd actually thought he was sincere. He'd show up to my softball games and piano recitals, dragging my mother with him. But I realized now he had only been grooming me, prepping me for what he'd tried to do to me later. What he'd tried to take from me.

I'd tried shielding Adam from all of Mom's men, but by the time he reached high school, he knew the deal. He wasn't naive or dumb. And the biggest surprise of all was that he wasn't *jaded*. He was upbeat, social, and hopeful. So when I left for college I was hopeful, too, that he'd finish high school and blaze his own path in life.

Adam came charging out of the house toward me. He was tall, lean, and handsome, but still had a baby face. I hopped out of the car and pulled him into a hug.

"You need a haircut, baby bro." I ruffled his golden locks. "But I bet the girls like it."

His cheek lifted in a dimple. "Only one girl could request a haircut, and it's not you or Mom—you know that."

I pulled Adam's shoulder against me and we walked side by side to the front door. He was over six feet, so he had to scrunch down to keep in step. "How'd you get so whipped by a girl, huh?"

It hit me how much Adam reminded me of Bennett. And that made me feel strangely satisfied and optimistic. Adam was sweet and vulnerable and in love with his girlfriend, Andrea. He wasn't a virgin like Bennett, but I knew he was being smart about using protection.

The old aluminum door swung open, creaking on its hinges, and the noise from the TV came at me like a blast, smacking me upside the head. Mom always had the TV turned up too loud. "Where is she?"

"Kitchen."

She sat in a chair with a damn cigarette dangling from her busted-up mouth. When I got a good look, my hand shot to my face. A purple bruise formed beneath her left eye, and her top lip was cracked and split.

"I don't know why Adam called you." Her voice was

gravelly and harsh. "Not like you've shown your face around here in months."

I ignored her pity party. I talked to her plenty on the phone, and to my brother even more. I left this place for me. To save myself. And I would have taken Adam with me if she'd have let me.

"What did he do, Ma?" I asked, hands on my hips. "Punch you in the face a couple of times?"

"You don't know anything about it, Avery," she said, pointing an accusing finger at me. "Don't come marching in here acting like you own this place. You left *us*, remember?"

"Mom, I'm in college, *remember*?"

"You left long before college." She looked so vulnerable then. Like she was just hanging on to her sanity by a thread. I'd wondered if her lifestyle would ever catch up to her. Accepting any man into her home, into her bed, hoping they'd "love" her back and stick around long enough to help pay some of the bills.

That's where she and I parted ways. I accepted only men I *wanted* into my bed, and then kicked them to the curb immediately afterward. And no way in hell did I ever beg them to care about me, help me financially, or do any special favors for money.

"I tried to tell you why I was leaving back then, Mom," I said. "But you didn't believe me."

She refused to meet my gaze, just taking long drags on that cigarette and blowing smoke into the air. I wouldn't be surprised if her coffee was spiked with something strong, too.

"You need to ice that shiner." I pulled a bag of frozen peas from the freezer, knelt down beside her, and held it to her eye.

When she finally looked at me, I saw that her resolve was softening.

"Do you believe me now?" I whispered, forcing the matted blond hair away from her face with my fingers.

Tears sprang to her eyes and rolled down her cheeks in fat trails. She'd probably never say it out loud, but I took that as her admission.

"He'll just make it hell for you," I said, adjusting my knees on the tile. "You'll have to get a restraining order against him."

"A restraining order?" Her bottom lip hung open and then started to quiver.

I nodded. "You still love him?"

She shook her head. "Thought maybe I did. But he's changed."

I bit my tongue to keep from telling her that he was just putting on a show for her all those years ago. When in reality he was proving his true colors in my bedroom, in the middle of the night.

"You afraid of him?"

She squeezed her eyes shut. Again, her only admission.

"Get in the car," I said, standing up. "Adam, too. We're going down to the station."

She wouldn't move. Just stared at me with those puppy dog eyes. One of them with a black and purple ringer.

"Don't you dare try to argue with me," I said through gritted teeth. "You have an underage child in your home. You need to protect him until he graduates from school."

I went down low, right next to her ear. "At least do right by *him*, if you couldn't do right by *me*."

She inhaled a lungful of air that left her gasping. She stood on shaky legs and moved toward the door, grabbing her purse on the way out. Adam gave me a sidelong glance, but didn't ask what the hell was going on. A hundred bucks said he'd already figured it out.

On the way into town, I dialed the one person who'd be stunned to hear from me. But I still had his number saved in my phone.

He answered on the first ring.

"Gavin, it's Avery."

There was a long pause. So I filled in the silence. "I know it's been a long time, but I need your help. Your father's, too."

I dropped my mom and brother at home after we filed the temporary restraining order at the police station. I had an afternoon shift at the nursing home and needed to get my butt back on the road.

Mom would need to attend a court hearing to make the restraining order stick, and Gavin promised to have his father look into it as soon as I told him who the charge was against.

Even though we ended our relationship badly, he knew I went through hell with that man.

Mom assured me that Tim had gotten back on the road already—that he had a wife forty minutes away in Russell Township. *Scumbag.* But Mom would have taken him back anyway.

Regardless, I made Mom call one of her old flames to stay the night—nothing like a damsel in distress to make the men come running; look how Bennett took care of me after my almost-break-in.

The thought of me sleeping in Bennett's bed again lit the usual fire in my belly, but I pushed the thought away.

I begged Adam to stay at my place this weekend. Even offered to have his girlfriend come, too. But he refused. Said he wanted to stick around home, just in case. He promised to come up next week instead and to call me first thing in the morning or sooner, should he need me.

The moment I walked into Mrs. Jackson's room that afternoon, she knew I'd had a tough day. "You look like hell, princess."

"Are princesses *allowed* to look like hell?" I asked, adjusting her position in bed. She hated lying flat on her back. She needed to have a view of the grounds beyond her window. "Even princesses have bad days," she said, touching my shoulder. "Tell me what happened, sweetie."

I told her about my mother, leaving out details about exactly who Tim was and what he'd done to me years ago. I didn't need her blood pressure rising any higher today. She'd been having a rough time of it lately. Her feet were swollen and her temperature had spiked earlier in the week.

"You're a good daughter," she said, patting my hand. "And big sister."

I smiled, prepping the thermometer.

"And if I was your grandmother," she huffed, "I'd knock some sense into that mother of yours." I thought back to my real grandma and how she was just as strong-willed as this lady in front of me. A smile tugged the corners of my lips. They'd certainly *both* have given my mother a run for her money.

"I believe you would," I said. "If you were my grandmother, my life would be immeasurably happier. Adam's, too."

"Consider me an honorary grandmother then," she said. "I insist. I already love you like a granddaughter."

"That means more than you know." I felt the stinging of tears behind my eyes. "Now tell me where that husband of yours is. I haven't gotten my flower fix today."

"You'll get your own flowers someday," she said, a twinkle in her eyes. And I knew what was coming next. "So, how's Pretty Boy doing? You haven't talked about him in a while."

"His name is Bennett. But he *is* pretty," I said. "And nothing is going on with him. We're just friends." Although I wasn't sure if even that was true anymore. Not after what had happened with Oliver at the tattoo parlor.

"Mmmm-hmmm . . ." she drawled. "I don't believe you for one minute. Not with that fire blazing in your eyes."

After recording her temperature, I tucked her in and waved good night. "See you on Monday."

I got a text from Rob on my way home. I almost didn't check it because I was too tired and definitely not in the mood. At least not for *him*.

Rob: You home?

Me: Not yet.

Rob: Think I left my Ray Bans at your place—can I pick them up?

Me: Why do you need them so bad? They're only shades.

Rob: Mom bought 'em for me, they're pricey as hell, and I'm seeing her for brunch 2morrow.

Me: I'll be home in ten minutes.

I had changed into my flannel pajamas and had already poured myself a glass of wine when I heard my buzzer. I grabbed Rob's sunglasses off my kitchen counter and went to meet him at the door.

Maybe he'd get the hint that I wasn't into anything more tonight, in case that was on his mind. "Looks like somebody's ready for bed," he said, looking down at my fuzzy slippers.

I was so covered up, I probably knocked the thought of a quickie straight from his head.

"Yeah, I'm beat."

We stood in my doorway chatting about Rob's plans with his buddies for the night when Bennett stepped off the elevator. I straightened as tension radiated up my spine and across my shoulders. He wore a gray hoodie, baggy jeans, and a pair of worn-in blue Converse sneakers. Wow, he made casual look good.

Bennett adjusted his red ball cap lower on his head when he spotted me. His shoulders hunched up and he looked behind him, like he hoped the building had a rear-door exit so he could made his escape.

"Hey," he said, and dipped his head as he passed. He didn't even look at Rob and probably assumed he was just another one of my friends with benefits.

But maybe Rob wasn't. Not anymore.

Bennett Reynolds was messing with my head.

I didn't want him to get away so easily. I wanted to talk to him, to make sure we were still cool. Even though I was pretty sure we weren't. "Where are you headed tonight, Bennett?"

Bennett paused at the door and seemed to be weighing the decision of whether or not to turn around. My stomach pitched and rolled.

"Up to the corner bar," he said. His eyes were dark and stormy. "To meet a friend."

The way he said the word *friend* made my insides curdle. Was he just giving it back to me, or was he actually meeting a girl?

"That's cool," I said, not meaning a word of it. "Um, this is my friend Rob."

Bennett gave a simple nod and turned again to leave. And suddenly I wanted to usher Rob the hell out the door as quickly as possible.

"All right, Rob, I'm gonna hit the hay." I said it loud enough for Bennett to hear. The door slid closed behind him, and I watched him walk down the sidewalk to the street. He never missed a beat and never once looked back at us.

Rob looked between me and the door, his expression dark. It was an emotion I'd rarely seen before—he'd always been pretty laid-back and happy-go-lucky. Which made him the perfect fuck buddy. No questions asked.

"So, um . . . thanks for the shades." Rob twirled the sunglasses in his fingers with a jerky, odd motion, like there was something else he wanted to say. For the first time I had the impression that maybe he was wishing for more tonight. That maybe he *had* hoped I'd invite him in. He sighed. "Tired, huh? Catch you later, then."

I stayed up a bit later to watch a home-decorating show in bed. But my concentration waned. Every time I heard the sound of a key turning in the front entrance door, I imagined it was Bennett coming home, possibly with a girl.

I pictured Bennett lying beside me, his strong arms embracing me, his warm mouth against my lips. I wanted to inhale his coconut scent, map every inch of his skin with my tongue, and hear my name tumble from his lips again when I made him come undone.

I hoped that Bennett might stop over after the bar because he was alone and wanted my company. But he never did.

# CHAPTER FIFTEEN

The clambake was tonight, and it had been drizzling all day. But fall days are unpredictable, and Ella said they'd have large tents set up to shield the partygoers from the elements. Joel apparently had been working on shucking corn all day with his frat buddies. They'd also been hitting the keg early, and Joel was napping before the big party.

I figured this was the night I needed to get my shit together—take back control of my life. Bennett had too much of a hold on my thoughts and fantasies, and I needed a reality check.

I'd gotten to a point in my life where I was content. I worked hard, attended classes, and had good friends. When I was horny I called Rob or picked up guys at parties or bars and made out with them, let them feel me up, or let them get me off. It made me feel desirable and a little less solitary for that short period of time.

Plus, I played by my own rules. *I* was in control. Simple as that. I didn't need anything more complicated.

Besides, it was now blatantly obvious that Bennett was done with me as well. Maybe the girl he had gone to meet at the bar the other night was the one he'd begun dating before he met me.

Ella and Rachel honked to pick me up just as I was texting Adam. He told me all had been quiet on the home front, Mom was going out with her girlfriends tonight, and he and Andrea were staying in to watch a movie.

I made sure to dress warm. Skinny jeans, red sneakers, and a thick black sweater. When I slid into the backseat, Rachel squealed. "Let's get laid tonight, bitches."

We high-fived each other and were on our way.

The rain subsided, so the two-block trek from the car was pleasant. The temperature was warmer than expected, so when my sneakers got wet from all the puddles, I didn't mind so much. I could have walked to the party from my apartment, but Ella had insisted on picking me up because of the rain.

The white tents were gleaming against the night sky and the smell of clam broth was in the air. It reminded me of autumn, crisp leaves, and cozy nights. Rachel grabbed us some beers from one of the coolers lining the fence while Joel pulled Ella into a mini make-out session.

Rachel and I chugged our first beers while we checked out the crowd. The usual suspects were there—frat guys and sorority girls, jocks, friends of friends, and everyone in between. It was one of the frat's biggest parties of the year. I knew Bennett might be here, and I wondered if he'd bring a date. I planned on staying far away from him and finding my own guy tonight.

The beer felt good going down, and when Rachel moved

in on a group of jocks smoking in the garage, I headed off to grab another. Jocks were Rachel's specialty. I figured it was because she was missing her ex-boyfriend, who was a star basketball player.

I knew for certain she'd hooked up with at least two of those guys in the garage before. I told her I'd join her after my next drink, but I knew none of them would appeal to me.

And I was afraid no one would ever compare to Bennett.

I popped open my beer and stopped to warm my toes at the huge bonfire in the backyard. The smell of weed was in the air, and I noticed some blond chick passing a roach to one of the guys sitting in the lawn chairs by the fire.

Bennett was standing directly behind her, next to Nate and a tall, pretty brunette. I shut my eyes to steady my breathing. I felt like I'd never be rid of him. Like he'd haunt me until I either graduated or moved, or both. I wondered if this girl was the one he'd met up with the other night or if he'd decided the same thing as me—to move on to someone else tonight.

The song "Fix You" by Coldplay was pumping through the speakers and I couldn't help snickering at the absurdity of this moment. Me, across from Bennett, the guy I wanted to sleep with—and who was I kidding, just *be with*—but I couldn't because I needed some heavy-duty *fixing*. And I wasn't ready or willing to be fixed by anybody.

Nate spotted me and waved me over. I shook my head, hoping to get away with a simple nod instead. But he wasn't going for it. He walked over and pulled me around the fire to stand closer to Bennett and the brunette, whose fingers were now sliding up his sleeve.

"Hey, Ben, look who I found," Nate announced, slinging his arm around me.

Bennett did a double take, gave a curt, expressionless nod, and then turned his attention back to the girl. My stomach clenched so tightly that I felt like I might puke. For some reason his indifference hurt worse than his anger.

What the hell was wrong with me? I came here to have a good time with my friends and find someone else to make out with. To be in control of my own emotions; not the other way around.

I thought of something to say to Nate that wasn't as dumb as asking him what his major was. "So, are you still moving into my building at the end of this month?"

"Change of plans," he said sheepishly. "Now it's the end of the semester. Couldn't get out of my other lease as easily as I thought I could."

"Got it," I said, trying like hell to keep my eyes on him instead of sliding them over to Bennett and the girl. In my peripheral view, she was doing some hair flipping and hip jutting. And apparently she cracked him up, too, because then he howled with laughter over something she said.

Nate leaned closer to me. "He's not with her, by the way."

I shrugged, trying to keep my shaking hands at my sides. "It's okay if he is. In case you haven't heard, we're just friends."

"Well, in case *you* haven't heard, my boy's got it bad for you," he said, shooting a look at Bennett over my shoulder. "And he's, like, the best guy that I know. So you should give him a chance."

My heart was thrashing in my chest from his words. "It's a bit more complicated than that, Nate."

"I hear you. No strings attached and all that," he said, obviously having heard a few choice details from Bennett. "But if I found a girl that I had that much chemistry with, I wouldn't want to let her go so easily, either. Just saying."

We did have undeniable chemistry, that was for sure. I could feel the undercurrent in the air this very instant, yanking at my core. It was thick and suffocating.

Not knowing what else to say, I took a step back. "Gonna find my friends."

I felt Bennett's gaze bearing down on me, so I looked his way. Heat, uncertainty, and anger seemed to roll off of him. The brunette was trying to get his attention, but he wasn't having it.

I could barely catch my breath. I backed away until I was under the canopy of the giant maple tree at the rear of the property. I tilted my head to look up at the top branches and colorful leaves. My cheek was pelted with a fat raindrop, and it cooled my heated face. The tree sheltered me as the drops came faster and heavier. Everyone else sprinted to the protection of the tents.

But I chose to disappear behind the trunk of the tree instead. I caught my breath and had a good talk with myself about burying my feelings for Bennett once and for all. Focusing on school, and Adam, and my career. It was quiet and dark, like I was in my own little secluded world. Until the rain came down in hard sheets and drenched me. I pushed away from the tree to make a run for the tent.

All at once I saw a blur of red as I was forced against the tree trunk, the bark digging into my sweater. Bennett's soaked hair swung against my forehead, his hands gripped my face, and his mouth sealed over mine, fusing our wet lips and tongues together.

I scraped my fingertips up his chest to his hairline and felt him tremble against me. My heart thudded against my rib cage as Bennett's mouth devoured me—like he was pouring all of his frustration into me.

We were sopping wet, our clothes clinging to us, and the rain wasn't letting up anytime soon.

I swept my tongue across his lips and the hottest fucking growl erupted from his mouth. He flattened his body against mine, crushing me with the weight of his passion.

"Is this how you like it?" he mumbled, but my mind couldn't register what he was asking. It had turned into a foggy haze and I couldn't even remember the letters of the alphabet at that point.

Bennett was entirely lips and fingers and raw passion and I felt his arousal pulsing against my stomach. His hands were rough and they rushed down my body to palm my ass. He lifted me off the ground, and my legs gripped his waist.

"Tell me you want this." He slid down to the grass with me straddling him, and all I could do was moan into his lips. It was as if all the pleasure receptors in my brain had expanded and then shot rapidly into my core, setting me on fire.

He licked the water from my neck and then moved up to my mouth. His lips fastened around my tongue and he sucked it hungrily while I whimpered against him.

His hands moved to my breasts and he thumbed my nipples in a frantic and angry rhythm. "Is this how the other guys do it?"

I jerked back from him and went completely still as a memory washed over me.

*Is this how you let your boyfriend touch you? He's too young to know what he's doing. Let me make you feel good.*

Bennett kissed me hard again and I wrenched myself out of his grasp.

"You let every other guy have you. You give away pieces of yourself like they're candy." I went rigid, trying to make sense of this different side of Bennett. He looked lost and miserable and desperate. "Maybe this is the only way. Maybe if I pretend to be like *them.*"

And then another memory made my throat seal shut as I struggled for a decent breath.

*What is with you, Avery? We've been planning our first time for weeks. I'm so fucking hard, I need a release. Let's just do this.*

I smacked Bennett hard across the face and then pushed myself off the ground. Bennett was stunned into silence. He shot up, his hands shaking, and tried to reach for me, but I backed away.

"They don't make me feel *anything.* Not one. Damn. Thing." I shoved against his chest and his face crumpled.

"But *you* . . . you already own a piece of me. Don't you *get* it?" I yelled, stumbling back.

"Wait, Avery. I'm so sorry." His voice sounded rough and tortured. "Please don't walk away."

I stood frozen under the tree, the rain pelting my body, my eyelashes gluing together.

"I don't know what else to do," he said. "I can't stop thinking about you. I want you so damn much."

I turned to him. "What you want from me is too goddamn scary. I can't . . . I can't . . ." My shoulders shook as sobs wracked my body.

"What happened to you, Avery?" His arms gripped me from behind and his lips closed in on my ear. "Please. *Please* tell me."

"Just"—I pushed out of his grasp—"leave me the fuck alone!"

I took off running. Away from Bennett. Away from my memories. Away from my fucked-up feelings.

As soon as I got home I jumped in the shower and stood under the scalding hot water to wash it all away.

Ella left me a dozen text messages until I finally replied that I was fine and going to bed.

Bennett banged on my door and pleaded with me to talk to him.

I ignored him until he finally gave up and went away.

# CHAPTER SIXTEEN

The following morning I slipped into my scrubs to get ready for my shift. I turned my phone back on and saw there were dozens more text messages from Ella. My finger hovered above the delete button before I decided to just weed through them all.

Ella: If you're not going to pick up the phone and talk to me, I'll just text bomb you all night.

Ella: Damn it, Avery! What happened tonight between you and Bennett was bound to happen with any guy you got close to.

Ella: You have to tell him what happened to you. Please tell him already!

Ella: He would stick around and work through it. That boy has deep feelings for you.

Ella: And I think you might feel the same way. In fact, I KNOW you feel the same way.

Ella: And I know you don't want that, it scares you shitless, you feel out of control, but please, bitch, for the sake of all the fake players everywhere, take a chance on somebody.

Ella: You should have seen him last night. He tried to go after you, but Nate stopped him. He looked miserable. Felt sick about what he said to you.

Ella: Don't worry, I told him nothing. Only that you'll talk when you're ready.

Ella: That boy is a damn good egg. Just like Adam.


I let out my breath slowly and stared at myself in the mirror. At my puffy and swollen eyes. The light rash on my jawline from Bennett's rough stubble last night.

He'd been sensual and passionate and fiery. I felt safer with Bennett than I'd felt with anyone else, ever.

I knew he'd never hurt me on purpose, but his harsh words rocked my world. I felt off-kilter, unglued, out of control. The same feelings I'd successfully stamped down for years.

And did Bennett seriously think I gave myself away so easily? Was that what I was doing?

He was so damn frustrated with me. Just like I was frustrated with myself.

Adam. Bennett. Mr. Jackson. Maybe there were decent guys out there.

But I didn't let myself see it. I didn't want to see it. I didn't want to feel it.

I grabbed my purse and keys to head to work. I heard a

thump as I swung open my apartment door. A large package that had been leaning against the doorjamb had fallen over. It was wrapped in shiny silver paper with a note attached.

I went back inside, rested the package on my coffee table, and opened the letter.

> *A,*
>
> *I'm sorry. Please believe that I never meant to hurt you. I'm so ashamed of myself.*
>
> *But I heard you loud and clear. You're not ready for this. For me. For us.*
>
> *So I'll leave you alone—I'll walk away.*
>
> *But if you decide you want to talk, you know where to find me.*
>
> *I'd planned on giving this gift to you someday. I figure now is as good a time as any.*
>
> 

*Take good care,*

*B.*
> 
>
> *P.S. Here's what I think of you in five words or less: Fierce, determined, scorchingHOT (yes, that's one word), incredible, beautiful.*

Fat tears rolled down my cheeks as I ripped open the pretty wrapping. I inhaled a lungful of air when I saw his gift. It was my favorite drawing from the art show.

He'd never sold it. He'd saved it for me.

My fingers were trembling so badly that I had to set it down before it fell from my grasp and broke.

But the drawing looked different today.

Now it seemed like the one figure was trying hard to reach across all the junk—in the spaces between—to the other side. But the other figure was so well hidden he could barely find her. And she didn't plan on coming out anytime soon.

I read Bennett's letter three more times, dried my eyes, fixed my makeup, and left for work. The rain had cleared and the air felt warm. The walk would do me good.

My phone buzzed while I was crossing Albert Street, and I saw it was my mom. I so wasn't ready to talk to her—to anybody, really—but because of recent events, I needed to.

"Hey, Mom. On my way to work. Everything okay?"

She was silent, but I heard her breathing. Prepping herself for something she needed to say. I gripped the phone tighter. "Just spill it, Mom."

Her voice was a hoarse whisper. "What did Tim do to you?"

I stopped in my tracks, nearly tripping over my own two feet and causing a collision at the crosswalk. My voice was low and rough. "You know what he did. I told you everything, hoping my own mother would believe me."

I heard her take a long drag on her cigarette. I could picture her sitting at the kitchen table chain-smoking. "Is that why he left us?"

What the fuck. Is that what this was about?

She had some sick need to know he didn't leave her because of something *she'd* done? She was always so weak when it came to Tim.

"He left because of what I threatened him with."

She let out a long breath she obviously had been holding.

"Is that why his arm was bandaged up the night he walked out the door?"

I'd been proud of that moment. Proud of myself. I had seen the fear in his eyes. Had the sharp utensil slipped just an inch the other way, I would have gouged his heart. "Yes."

We were silent for a long minute, just listening to each other's breaths. Would this woman ever tell me she was sorry? Or that she was proud of me? Or . . . something that showed me she was a *mother*?

"That's why he beat me up."

"What?" My heart raced a thousand miles a minute. "Damn it, Mom. Tell me what the hell happened the other night."

"We got in an argument . . ." I heard the tears coming. "About you."

"What about me?" I saw the nursing home in the distance so I slowed my steps. No way could I head into work without knowing what went down.

"He'd been asking questions about you every time I saw him lately—when you had moved out. If you were ever coming back. What you looked like now." She was sniffling and coughing and all worked up. "I got the impression he was either afraid of you or had some kind of sick desire to see you again."

She caught her breath for a moment while I let all of that sink in. My stomach churned just thinking about the low timbre of Tim's voice.

"So I pressed him about it that night. I needed to know."

*Shit.* This is where her story was about to get ugly. "What did you say?"

"I asked him if what you accused him of was true."

I had trouble swallowing. "And?"

"He denied it up and down, of course," she said. Now her words were rigid and hate-filled. "But this time, I wasn't buying it."

*Was this finally Mom's lightbulb moment?*

I knew my mother would never apologize for betraying me. She didn't have it in her. And I'd gotten to a place in my life that I didn't need it. Not anymore. Besides, this was as close to an apology as I would get.

"Were you alone somewhere with him?"

I could picture this going down. Tim getting more manipulative, more irate. Switching from his soft and soothing words to his harsh and threatening tone.

"We were in the parking lot outside the bar." One, two, three puffs of her cigarette. "So I warned him that people would see us inside his car and call the cops."

"God, it could have been so much worse, Mom."

"I told him if he stayed away I wouldn't go to the police," she said. "I don't think he'll come around again. He doesn't have buddies on the police force like he once did."

"What else, Mom? I know there's something you're holding back."

"So . . . I don't think this restraining order is necessary." And there it was. She was still protecting him. "It'll only draw more attention to the situation, mess up his other family."

"You assume his other family isn't already messed up." A cynical laugh escaped my lips. "How many times will Tim get away with stuff, huh? He got away with it years ago and now you're letting him off again."

"I'm not saying I won't go through with it," she said. Yes, she absolutely was saying that. "I just . . . I'll think about it."

"Geez, Mom, do you realize how fucked-up your relationships with men are?"

There was a long, drawn-out silence before she said, "Is that why yours are, too?"

checked in at the front desk ten minutes late. Thankfully my supervisor was in a staff meeting down the hall.

"I'm so sorry, Lillian," I said to the nurse I was replacing on the floor.

"Uh-huh. Thought someone forgot to tell me you called in sick or something."

"Won't happen again," I said. "Shift change report?"

Lillian grabbed her purse from the drawer beneath the desk and then handed me the notes. "Mr. Brody in room 105 is waiting on an EKG, and Mrs. Jackson in 108 needs another vitals check in an hour."

My stomach clenched. "What are her symptoms?"

"Some blurred vision, slurred speech, and weakness in her limbs. Doc wonders if she had another small stroke last night. Scheduled her for a CAT scan."

I loaded the med trays, trying not to get choked up about Mrs. Jackson. The logical side of me said that I worked in a nursing home and patients didn't stay here forever. They either recovered or died.

Which led to my emotional side. I wanted to pull away from her, stop talking to her so damn much, so that it would be less painful when she left. But that would only hurt her.

Just like I was hurting Bennett. I immediately shook that thought away.

When I entered her room, she was resting on her side. Her normally dark complexion looked a bit paler. I ran my fingertips over her forehead to wake her up. "Med time."

Her breaths were short, and she squinted at me through slits. "H . . . Hey, sunshine." I noticed how the words broke from her lips in a lazy, sluggish pattern.

She blinked the sleep away, and I positioned her pillows to help her sit up. She studied me with concerned eyes. "Nah, I take that back. I'd say someone got rained on instead."

She couldn't be closer to the truth if she tried.

"It did rain a lot last night," I said, trying to keep my voice light.

"You could say that again," she said, and then narrowed her eyes. "But I wasn't speaking literally."

"I know," I said, my voice strained and quiet.

She grabbed for my hand. "S–something happen with that gorgeous man who's chasing after you?"

I didn't want Mrs. Jackson to know that I was in fact worried about *her* today, so this time I relented on her Bennett questions.

"Maybe."

"He's getting too close, isn't he?" She raised her eyebrows. "And you . . . you're pulling away."

This lady needed an award for mind reading.

"Why do you always think it's me causing trouble?" I asked, my hand on my hip. "Maybe *he* did something wrong."

"If he did something wrong, it was only out of fear," she said, downing her pills and water. "And fear is the flip side of love."

"Huh?" I massaged her weak and trembling fingers.

"Honey, I know there are things you haven't shared with me." She squeezed my hand with the little strength she had. "Painful things."

Wow, this lady was good. *Damn* good. I didn't deny it or try to make light of what she was saying.

"Your whole life can't be defined by that one single moment. Or even a series of awful moments." She held my gaze, and it was difficult not to want to look away. "You are strong and courageous. But it doesn't mean you can't lean on others sometimes."

My eyes felt glassy and full. I blinked to keep the tears at bay. I was overwhelmed with emotions today. About Bennett. My mom. Mrs. Jackson.

"Especially very handsome *others*." She winked. "Take a chance on him, girl."

Man, people were dishing out advice left and right today. Maybe the universe was conspiring against me.

"Let me get the circulation going in those feet," I said, to change the subject. I pulled back the covers to reveal her swollen legs. Water retention made the skin bloat and stretch, giving it a shiny and fake look, almost like plastic.

As soon as I began rubbing her ankles, her forehead relaxed, her back slumped in relief, and she became more animated.

"I want to hear about your grandmother today," she said, her voice still a bit rough. "You've only mentioned her a couple of times."

How had she known I'd been thinking a lot about her lately?

I couldn't help wondering whether, if Grandma had been

alive when mom dated Tim, *she* would have believed me, and held me those nights I lay shivering and crying.

I knew, without a doubt, the immediate answer to my question. Of course she would.

Mom had a blind spot when it came to handsome and charming men, and Grandma always called her on it. Asked her where she'd ever gone wrong for Mom to want to rely on a man so completely.

I'd asked myself the same question a thousand times. Wondered if there was something in Mom's past that I didn't know about. Would *never* know about. Something that made her cling so recklessly to any string of false security.

Was it the death of her father at an early age? Or seeing how Grandma had worked two jobs to support them? Did Mom hope that by getting pregnant with me, she'd snag the guy who knocked her up? It didn't work the first time—or the second time, either, for that matter.

I heard Mrs. Jackson let out a whimper at a certain sensitive spot around her ankle, and that snapped me out of my thoughts.

"My grandma was a lot like you. Feisty, compassionate, and wise." I massaged her calf muscles and up to the back of her knee. "A pain in the ass, too."

That got a grin out of her. "No wonder you like me so well."

I returned the smile as I started on her other leg.

Mrs. Jackson closed her eyes and let out a sigh. "What happened to her?"

"She died of cancer when I was twelve." I remembered the day we got the call, how it brought me to my knees. I'd never prayed before in my life, but that day, I prayed and begged and pleaded that the news wasn't real. That she'd come waltzing through that door and scoop me into her lap once again.

"Well, isn't that a damn shame." Mrs. Jackson was looking at me now, her eyes soft around the edges. "I'll bet she taught you a lot. Had a hand in making you the woman you are today."

"Absolutely. I learned to be independent and go after what I wanted."

And if I was being honest, my own mother had pushed me to become the person I was, too—by forcing me to stand up for myself. Lord knows *she* never did.

Mrs. Jackson's cheeks lifted. "If she was still around, I bet she'd agree with me."

"About what?"

"About giving pretty boys a chance."

I shook my head and laughed. "See, I told you—a pain in the ass."

# CHAPTER SEVENTEEN

A few nights later, I stood at Bennett's door, my hand poised to knock.

I'd hung his drawing in my bedroom and studied it every night before bed. It reminded me of Bennett. His laugh, his eyes, his warmth.

The fact of the matter was that I missed him. And I owed him an explanation, at the very least.

I wasn't ready for anything, but at least it was a start. I'd never opened up to any guy before, but something told me he was worth it. That he'd understand.

He lived by a preconceived code to protect himself. And so did I. And he needed to know why.

I knocked three times and waited. I heard movement inside, and then a voice. A female voice. "Someone's at your door, Benny."

*Benny?* I'd only ever heard his family call him that.

Did someone else know him as intimately?

The door opened just as I considered making my escape.

It was Rebecca. The ex-girlfriend that I'd met at the art show. My heart froze instantly. I couldn't blink, move my lips, or walk away. I could only stare at her blue eyes and shiny red hair. Her pretty face and impressive figure.

"Hi," she said. "You're Avery, right?"

And then I became unstuck, for self-preservation's sake. "Hi, Rebecca. I was just going to talk to Bennett about something. But he has company, so I'll come back later."

"He's in the shower," she said with a hint of satisfaction in her voice. "We're going out for a bite to eat. But I'll tell him you stopped by."

I practically sprinted to the elevator, my stomach throbbing. He had definitely moved on. Maybe seeing Rebecca again made him curious about rekindling something with her.

I lay on the couch, the TV turned to a random channel, a tub of ice cream melting in front of me. I told myself I couldn't get upset over this. I was the one who'd pushed him away. Just because I was ready to open up to him didn't mean that would fix or even define our nonexistent relationship.

We were in limbo. He was in limbo.

So I could understand him wanting to forget, to move on.

I thought I heard them walk by my door, joking and laughing, so I blasted the volume on the television. Not two minutes later, my phone buzzed on the coffee table.

Bennett: Rebecca said you came by. It's not what you think, Avery.

Me: I'm not thinking anything.

Bennett: Don't pretend. Not with me.

Me: Okay. How about this: I have no right to think anything.

Bennett: True. But I still wanted you to know.

Me: Why?

Bennett: You know why. How come you stopped by?

Me: It was nothing.

Bennett: When it comes to you, Avery, it will never be nothing. It will always be something. BIG somethings that I'll always want to know about.

A shiver raced through me. Even the tone of his damn text message got to me.

Me: ☺ Get back to your friend. I'll catch you later.

After eating a good chunk of that ice cream and watching a lame comedy, I decided to go to bed. Apparently my sappy button was fully charged tonight.

I realized I was practically standing guard over Bennett's purity; his damn virtue. And I needed to cut that shit out. Just because I couldn't have him—at least not according to his conditions—didn't mean that nobody else could, either. So why did the very thought of him being with Rebecca—with any girl really—make it so fucking hard to breathe?

When I heard the knock at my door, I closed my eyes and made a silent wish that it was Bennett and not Bennett all at the same time.

As soon as I pulled the door open, he said, "She's thinking about transferring her credits and coming to school here."

"So she can be closer to you?" I moved aside to let him in. His dark-wash jeans and messy hair didn't go unnoticed. Had Rebecca's fingers been in that hair?

"Who knows? Not sure I care," he said, and the heaviness in my chest lifted. "Anyway, I told her I'd show her around campus today. So, I did."

"And where is she now?" I sat back down on my couch.

"On her way home." He sat next to me. Close enough that our knees touched. "It's only a thirty-minute drive. She could commute here for classes."

I stared at the TV infomercial. "And stay at your place whenever she needs to crash."

He elbowed me gently. "Avery Michaels, do I detect a certain tone in your voice?"

I arched an eyebrow. "What tone?" I was so full of shit, and he knew it.

He turned to face me. "Five words or less: How did you feel when Rebecca opened my door?"

I fumbled with the remote. "I felt nothing."

"Really?" A crooked grin draped his lips. He wasn't letting this go anytime soon. "Let me see if I can help you out. Maybe the same way I felt when I heard how Oliver talked to you at the shop, or when you were standing at the door in your pajamas, with *Rob*."

Heat splashed across my cheeks.

"And how's that?" I mumbled.

He inched closer and fused his eyes to mine. "Surprised . . . curious . . . PISSED . . . jealous, jealous, jealous."

"You're bending the rules. That's six words."

He arched an eyebrow. "I thought I'd let you borrow one."

I felt an electric current coursing through me. "Why?"

He smirked. "If you can't say it out loud, then I'd be helping you out."

My fingers fisted the blanket.

All at once he grew serious, his eyes large and sincere.

"Why *did* you stop over tonight?" His voice was soft, like a caress.

"I . . . I owe you an explanation for the other night."

"No, you don't," he said. "I scared you, and I'm still sick about it."

"You *did* scare me," I said, and his head dropped. "But not in the way you think."

He looked up at me. "How, then?"

"The way you were talking to me." I took a deep breath. "It brought up some memories I had locked away."

"Shit." He rushed his fingers through his hair. "I'm so sorry."

"No, Bennett. It's not like I thought you'd hurt me," I said, and then cleared my throat. "Actually, I've never felt safer with anyone else."

His breath hitched in the back of his throat. He raised his fingers to touch me, but then dropped his hand. "You *are* safe with me, Avery."

"It's an idea I need to get used to."

He nodded and then sat back, waiting on me. He became so still. As if he'd dissolved into the furniture, afraid to even stir the air. Afraid I'd changed my mind about talking to him.

"When I was sixteen, my mom had a boyfriend named

Tim, who was a cop." When I looked at Bennett, his eyes were wide and intense. "I always got the feeling he was checking me out or looking at me in a different kind of way. The way he should be looking at my mom."

Bennett put his fist to his lips, but remained silent.

"He took an interest in me—in my schoolwork, my activities—he tried to build my trust. When I started dating Gavin, my first love, Tim acted strange. Almost jealous."

Bennett reached for my hand and I offered it willingly, even though I was ashamed of what I would tell him next. Revealing this to him was like stripping the nerves from my body one strand at a time. Painful, nearly impossible, and scary as hell.

What if he didn't believe me, either?

I shook those thoughts away. He was not my mother. And he certainly wasn't Tim.

There were few people in this world I trusted—and Bennett was quickly making the short list. He had somehow embedded himself beneath my skin, made me feel secure and protected, and here I was telling him one of my deepest, darkest secrets.

The flip side of telling him was that it felt necessary. Because saying it out loud made it more real. And would help clear the shadowy corners of my soul. At least, I hoped it would.

My breaths came out in sputtering gasps. Was I brave enough to do this?

"Hey, Avery, it's okay. You don't have to tell me anything." He tucked a stray piece of hair behind my ear. His scent wrapped around me like a warm blanket.

"Yeah, actually, I do. If not for you, then for me."

He nodded in understanding as his fingers grazed my cheek.

"Tim and Mom drank a lot together and I wondered sometimes if he was trying to get her drunk enough to pass out." I sucked in a deep breath. "Tim started coming into my room in the middle of the night. It began innocently enough. He'd feign being drunk and crash next to me, or he'd just rub my back or stroke my hair. I never had a real dad, so in some twisted way, it felt kind of nice. Like maybe something a real dad would do."

Bennett was holding on to my hand for dear life, anticipating what I'd say next. But his face remained neutral.

"But then things changed. He started talking dirty to me. I was a . . . a virgin, and he found that out just by . . . by touching me. And I became afraid of him. He had this way of threatening you while keeping a calm voice and a straight face."

"Fuck, Avery." Bennett jumped up and started pacing. "I want to kill that bastard."

Hearing him say that gave me the courage I needed to go on. He *did* believe me, and deep down I had always known he would. I was just too chicken to admit it. I waited for him to get over his initial shock. He took a few deep breaths and then sat back down. "I'm sorry. Please, I want to hear the rest."

"I had this great boyfriend, and we were getting serious. I wanted my first time to be with Gavin. *Not* Tim." Bennett cringed and I felt my pulse becoming more erratic. "I mean, I knew he'd be taking something I wasn't offering. He'd be stealing it from me. So technically, he wouldn't have been my *first*."

"Fucking scumbag," Bennett mumbled to himself.

"This one night, I had a feeling Tim was going to make it happen. My mom got sloppy drunk and I heard him telling her stuff about me. That I was dressing like a whore and that my boyfriend was a loser. He was setting the scene, turning my mother against me. I knew she'd never believe me over him, anyway. She was blindly in love with him."

Bennett squeezed his eyes shut, anticipating the rest.

"So I hid a pair of scissors under my mattress. When he came into my room that night, I acted like I wanted him to be there, so I could catch him off guard." I gulped in several breaths to keep my voice steady. "When he was really . . . getting into it, I reached for the scissors. I could have killed him, Bennett. And damn, I wanted to. But I told myself I was only going to scare him."

"God, Avery," he grunted. "He could have overpowered you. Used the scissors on you instead."

"I knew that going in," I said, tears burning my eyes. "But I was willing to take that risk over getting raped."

I watched as Bennett's chest moved up and down in harsh breaths. He cupped my cheeks, his eyes wide, fear coursing through them.

"I told him in a calm voice that my boyfriend had found out about us. And since Gavin's father was the mayor, he was threatening to tell him."

When Bennett's eyes locked on mine, I saw something different there. Something like admiration, or maybe respect. Maybe for the sixteen-year-old girl who had taken matters into her own hands. Who knew at that point she'd be completely on her own.

I was in awe of her, too. For being so brave—so self-possessed. It was one of the reasons I still held on to her values, her ideals, her beliefs, so fiercely now.

"I told Tim that if Gavin hadn't heard from me by midnight, he was going to tell his father everything. And that stunned the hell out of him." My tears had spilled over, and I couldn't wipe them away fast enough. "And I used that opportunity to stab him in the arm. I didn't go deep, but deep enough. And I warned him to never fucking touch me again."

My body started shaking, and Bennett pulled me onto his lap, his strong arms bracing me from behind. He covered us with the blanket and held me while I sobbed and trembled and relived that night in my memory.

Getting it out again after all of those years felt like a release.

It was liberating and terrifying all at once.

"I am so sorry that happened to you." Bennett kissed my head and whispered my name again and again, until finally there were no tears left and I sagged into his chest.

"You're so strong. So brave," he whispered. He lifted me from the couch, and my arms cradled his neck. "Let me take care of you tonight."

He carried me to bed, gently pulled back the covers, and then tucked me in. He sat near the edge and stroked my head. "I can stay until you fall asleep."

I felt safe and calm when Bennett was around, and I didn't want to be alone tonight.

When I looked up at him, I saw that he was staring at his drawing, which I'd hung on the far wall.

He brought my fingers to his lips and kissed the palm of my hand.

I lifted back the covers to invite him in. "Please, Bennett."

His eyebrows drew together. "Are you sure?"

"Yes. I want to feel you next to me again."

He stripped down to his boxers, slid in behind me, and wrapped me against his chest. "Shhh . . ." I felt warm and protected in his arms.

We didn't speak. Only listened to each other's soft breaths. I could feel his heartbeat against my back. It was a strong and steady rhythm.

"Avery?" Bennett asked. "Your plan worked, didn't it?"

"Tim left that same night," I murmured. "My mom always blamed me for him walking out."

"Your mom didn't believe you?" he asked through gritted teeth.

I shook my head, not surprised at his anger. My mother was a piece of work. Her denial sealed it for me. I knew I'd have to handle everything solo. And that it wouldn't be easy.

"What about Gavin?"

"He didn't know all of it. I didn't want him to," I said. "But it sure made our first time together uncomfortable. I just shut down on him. He didn't understand what happened. We broke up after that."

He tightened his hold on me. "You still wanted to lose your virginity so soon after all of that?"

"It's hard to explain. I didn't want to disappoint him. And I still wanted to share that with him. I thought it might help me somehow. Help me forget about Tim, too. It just didn't turn out quite the way I'd planned."

"Oh, Avery." He kissed my hair. "I hope you realize how amazing you are."

His arms were strong and unyielding and I relished his warmth as I caught my breath again.

"After that, something just snapped inside of me. I told myself that no one would have that kind of control over me again," I said, my voice gaining momentum. "I'd be in charge of my own life—including my sex life. And no guy was worth losing *myself* again."

I'd been a mess for weeks after. Skipping school and chugging Mom's beer, completely at a loss for how to gather the pieces of myself that had been scattered everywhere. But it was Adam who saved me. Along with Ella, who was going through her own grief over her brother's death. She told me she needed me as much as I needed her.

But Adam. *God*, Adam.

He knew something was up with me, and as I began to unravel right before him, I saw his confidence in me falter. There was fear in his eyes, and confusion, too. And I knew I couldn't desert him. Couldn't make him feel as alone as I'd felt. He was just a kid and desperately needed to believe in someone. And for someone to believe in *him*, too.

And I was that person for him. Always had been. Always would be. For as long as he needed me to be.

Bennett remained silent, as if considering everything I'd told him. Maybe he'd finally understand and decide to walk away. And I'd have to accept that. Even though I wasn't sure that's what I wanted anymore.

"I know it doesn't make total sense, but it's how I got through my days."

"It makes perfect sense," he said, sadness in his voice. "Thank you for telling me."

Bennett held me close until our breaths fell into a similar pattern and sleep finally consumed us.

# CHAPTER EIGHTEEN

The next morning, I was still wrapped in Bennett's arms, and it felt amazing having him in my bed again. I'd let him take care of me last night. Whether I'd admitted it or not, I'd given him a larger piece of myself. And it hadn't destroyed me or made me less of a person. In fact, it felt like a relief. It felt . . . right.

I could feel his breaths against my ear and his pulse against my back. When I turned to him, his eyes were open and he was lost in deep thought.

I hoped he wasn't thinking about what a bad idea it had been to sleep here last night. Or that he needed to get as far away from me as possible. I'd have to accept his decision if that was the case. I'd made myself vulnerable to him, but I still had a long way to go. And I wasn't sure if waiting on someone like me was the best idea. Even though I knew his attraction to me was just as palpable as mine to him.

"What are you thinking about?" I whispered.

"Honestly?" His voice was low and raspy and beyond sexy. "I was thinking I'd be scared to make love to you."

My heart thudded in my chest. "Why?"

"Well, for obvious reasons. Being my first time and all," he said. "But also because I'd be feeling all of these things, and you'd be . . ."

His breaths were coming fast and shallow.

"I'd be what?" I rasped out. "Tell me."

"You told me at the clambake that you didn't feel anything with those other guys." His breath tickled my ear, and I shivered against it. "What if you don't feel anything when you're with me, either?"

"Not possible," I said, arching my head to look him in the eye. "I'm incredibly turned on when I'm with you. I feel every kiss. Every touch. *Everything.*"

His eyes squeezed closed as his fingers brushed the back of my neck.

"I have my own fears, too, you know," I said, feeling brave.

"Like what?" He opened his eyes, and I saw a flicker of yearning inside them.

"I'm afraid you'd think—after waiting all that time—that sex with me was nothing special, after all."

"Not a chance," he whispered against my ear.

"Or that I'd get so lost in feeling all of those things . . . that I'd let my guard down."

"And that's a bad thing?"

"It leaves me wide open . . . to be taken advantage of again."

"But everyone has those fears, Avery," he said, kissing my forehead. "I understand why you have them and why you hold on to your independence so tightly. But I can't imagine ever wanting to stop caring for or protecting you."

"That's the part I don't get," I said. "I mean, you're finally free from the burden of looking after your family. Why do you like the idea of caring for someone else?"

"You make it sound like it's a chore," he said, squeezing me tight. "It would feel amazing to be needed and wanted by someone that you care deeply about."

"I don't know, Bennett. I'd say we're at a standstill."

"Or at a crossroads," he said. "Depending on how you look at it."

"Sex means different things to us," I said, playing with his bangs. "You're wound too tight and I'm wound too loose."

He kissed my shoulder. "We're more alike than you think."

"How do you mean?"

"We both have trust issues," he said. "I'd be putting faith in the person I'm having sex with, too."

"See, that's a lot of pressure," I said. "Sex for me is just about feeling good. In and out and done."

Bennett threw back his head and laughed.

He turned over and pulled me flush against him. "You know we're not just talking about sex here. We're talking about feelings, Avery. How we make each other feel when we're together."

It was true. I wasn't sure I wanted to go back to just having quickie sex after being with him. Someone who took his time, who made every single touch count. It left me overwhelmed and breathless at the same time.

I decided to go for honesty. "I love how you make me feel.

How you kiss and touch me. It makes me feel . . . special. And like I want to maul you, all at once. And that terrifies the hell out of me."

"The feeling is mutual. Especially the mauling part," he said, and I smacked him.

"Maybe we need time to build up our faith . . . in each other," he said. "Can we at least agree to try?"

"I can try, Bennett." Whoa, what was I saying here? Last night changed me more than I was willing to admit. I wanted this boy. And I was willing to compromise to get him. I was willing to put myself out there, overwhelming as it may be. "But I can't guarantee that I won't get stuck or run away sometimes."

"Just agree to always be honest with me, okay?" he said, and I nodded.

We stared into each other's eyes, and I saw my own emotions reflected back in his. Trust, hope, longing.

His lips hovered a breath away from mine and I flicked my tongue against his mouth.

He hummed in response.

He closed his mouth over mine and our tongues lingered in a slow and deliberate dance. It felt honest and pure and brand-new to kiss him again. He knotted his fingers in my hair and we stayed that way—kissing, licking, and teasing each other's lips and necks and ears.

"I'm not sure I can ever get enough of you," he murmured as he captured the skin at the hollow of my throat.

"I know the feeling," I whispered. He was lying on top of me with his bulge rubbing against my hip. I wanted badly to adjust myself so that I could feel the length of him against my underwear, which was becoming increasingly wet.

But the last time we were in this same position in my bed it had been too much for him. I didn't want him to pull away from me again.

Bennett kissed my forehead, and then my nose. He looked deeply into my eyes, and my entire body tingled in response. He thumbed the end of my T-shirt, and my breathing became shallow. "Take this off?"

I sat up and lifted the shirt over my head. I wasn't wearing a bra, and I could feel my nipples harden at his gaze. "Jesus, Avery. I'm not sure I've seen more perfect breasts." His hand brushed against my collarbone and along the top of my chest. "Is this okay?" he asked. I whimpered in response.

My stomach coiled with eagerness as he stroked his thumbs over my hard buds and then cupped my breasts. He drew one into his mouth and swirled his tongue around my nipple. I arched my back toward him, urging him on. He sucked and licked before giving my other breast the same attention.

He nudged me onto my back and then hovered above me. "I've been dreaming about how you'd taste." My breath lodged in the back of my throat.

He traced his fingers between my breasts and down to my belly.

"But if you need me to stop, just say the word." He met my eyes. "I will always stop, Avery. *Always*. Do you believe me?"

I nodded. My breaths became ragged with need.

"Do you want me to stop right now?"

"No." I exhaled a shaky breath. "Please, don't stop."

He kissed along my collarbone and then trailed his tongue down the center of my chest, stopping to flick it against my navel. "God, you smell good."

He feathered kisses against my belly and along the edges of my underwear. I squirmed and panted, almost bursting from anticipation.

I'd never had a man revere my body like this. It was overwhelming.

Bennett planted one scorching kiss over my mound and I felt his hot breath through the thin cotton material. I gripped the bedsheets and moaned.

"Damn it, Bennett," I panted. "How in the hell do you know exactly how to drive me insane?"

He trailed his tongue above my inner thigh. "I said I was a virgin, Avery. Not a *saint*."

"Or even a *monk*, apparently," I mumbled.

I felt him smile against my skin.

He thumbed the top of my underwear and dragged the material below my hip. I felt the cool breeze glide over my skin, but it did nothing to squelch the heat between my legs. Bennett licked and sucked the skin around my hip bone. "A tattoo would look sexy right here. And I'd be the only one to see it—when I did *this*."

He yanked my panties down my thighs, and I gasped.

He dropped my underwear on the floor, and then his gaze caressed the area between my legs. I suddenly felt modest at his inspection of me. But also special and extremely aroused.

"You're so beautiful, Avery."

My pulse skyrocketed when his palms slid up my calves to push apart my knees. Silky strands of his hair skimmed my thighs as he settled between my legs.

His eyes fastened on mine as his mouth lingered above me. He was watching me, wanting to see how I responded to him.

And it was the sexiest damn thing.

His hot breath prickled my skin right before I felt the broad stroke of his wet tongue.

"Oh fuck," I panted as his fingers curled around my hips.

Eyes glued to mine, he licked me again, slow and gentle, as my legs trembled beneath him.

Then he closed his lips around me and sucked hard.

My eyes rolled back in my head as I breathed out his name.

"Jesus, Avery, you taste good." I felt his deep groan vibrate against my skin, and the familiar tension of an orgasm pulsed low in my belly.

He slipped a finger inside me as he expertly used his tongue and mouth to lick and suck the tiny bundle of nerves at my epicenter.

My fingers were fisted in his hair, and I was close to losing myself.

Still, something held me back. It was so difficult to completely relinquish control. Letting go for Bennett would mean something different now. Because after last night, we'd become something different. Something real.

"I want you to trust me." Bennett's finger slid from inside of me and his other hand released hold of my thigh.

With his mouth still on me, he reached for my hands, which were now tangled in the sheets. He laced his fingers with mine and held on tight.

"Come for me, baby." Then his tongue and mouth became relentless—lapping between my slick folds and sucking with the right amount of pressure.

Pleasure and heat built to an overwhelming intensity in my body. "Oh God, Bennett, don't stop." I squeezed my eyes shut as color and light danced behind my eyelids and my whole world exploded into a million pieces.

He gripped my hands and his mouth held steady as I shivered and shook and called out his name.

Then he pulled me into his arms and stroked my hair. "Thank you."

My skin felt slick and my voice was raspy. "For what?"

"For being vulnerable in front of me."

# CHAPTER NINETEEN

Bennett and I saw each other regularly the next couple of weeks. We hung out at the corner bar for drinks, met at the campus coffee shop between classes, and ordered takeout while we studied together. We agreed not to get in the habit of sleeping in each other's beds. Though I was willing to give this trust thing a try, I wasn't ready to enfold myself in his life completely.

One thing was for certain—it was hard to leave Bennett after a marathon make-out session on my couch or at his door. I'd want to ask him to stay and fall asleep with me, but I held myself back. And I could tell he did as well.

When I had let him go down on me the other night, it was the most intense orgasm I'd ever experienced. And though I had come during sex with other men, it was just a means to an end for me. So letting go and trusting him on a whole different level—one where emotions were involved—had been intense and heady and satisfying.

But I was scared of losing myself completely in Bennett.

And signs of it were already showing. Beginning with the night of the almost-break-in at my window. Not that it was Bennett's fault. The thought of allowing someone to infiltrate my life made me feel defenseless. It was terrifying and sweet and exasperating all at the same time.

Rob had texted me twice that week, and I decided to be honest with him. I told him I'd met someone and was giving it a chance. Bennett and I never said we were exclusive, but there was an unspoken understanding there. Besides, seeing any hurt or jealousy in his eyes would have been painful.

> Rob: Is this because of that guy—your neighbor?
>
> Me: Really none of your business. Why do you ask?
>
> Rob: Could tell something's been different about you lately.
>
> Me: Guess it's just time to move on, Rob.
>
> Rob: Sure, understood. One question, though? If I had wanted more, would it have made a difference?

Whoa, what? Rob had never given me that impression. I'd thought we had a clear and mutual understanding. Part of me felt awful. He was a decent guy. Maybe he was searching for something—someone—more meaningful, too. Not that I was actually ever searching.

But I didn't want to lead him on. So I needed to be completely up front with him.

> Me: Geez Rob . . . I'm sorry. I don't know what to say. The honest truth is . . . probably not.

Rob: That's cool. Take care, Avery. You know where to find me.

I could almost hear the disappointment resonating from his words, and as I sat staring at our exchanged dialogue, I was filled with a hollow regret.

Adam and his girlfriend were coming up for the weekend. I got Saturday off work and made some casual dinner plans for us. I wasn't sure if I was ready to introduce Bennett to my family, but as the weekend drew nearer, I realized that I wanted him there.

Bennett: What time is your brother coming in?

Me: Noon. Want to grab dinner with us at that Mexican restaurant on First?

Bennett: Sounds good. See you later.

Adam and Andrea made a cute couple. The way my brother doted on her had me a bit worried until I saw that she was just as sweet on him. I drove them around the university campus, since both were considering applying there. I showed them the bookstore and the library, the admissions office, and the buildings in which most of my nursing classes were located.

We parked in the square near the campus and walked to all the little shops. The day was beautiful, the leaves were in full color, and Andrea admired how quaint the town was.

Ella met us for lunch at the campus coffee shop. They had a great selection of soups and sandwiches. She'd always loved Adam and wanted to catch up with him. She also wanted to meet his new girlfriend and give her approval.

She was almost as protective of Adam as I was. And I understood why. After what had happened to her brother, I didn't question her motives. Her love for and loyalty to Adam. It was a primitive response to the hell she and her family had been put through.

"Adam," Ella squealed. "Get over here and give me a hug."

Adam grinned and introduced her to Andrea.

"I love your hair," Andrea said, reaching out to touch Ella's waves. "I try to get mine that wavy, but it never works."

"I like her already," Ella said, nudging Adam's shoulder.

We stood in front of the coffee shop, and I saw a line forming at the counter. "Let's grab seats before they fill up."

I plopped my coat down on a chair to reserve a table in the back corner and then joined the three of them in line. Adam and Ella were busy catching up, and Andrea asked me what sandwiches were good.

"The turkey bacon one is probably my favorite, but the others are good, too," I said. "So your parents were okay with you coming up this weekend?"

"Totally," she said. "They adore Adam. He's over at our house a lot. Especially . . . if your mom has company on the weekends."

My stomach tightened with that familiar tension. "How often is that happening lately? Be honest with me."

"Maybe once a month."

At least the broad had slowed down some since I left.

"Andrea, do me a favor. Make sure to stay away on those weekends?"

I knew Adam was protective of her, but still I worried.

"Adam doesn't let me come over on weekends, actually," she said, her cheeks growing rosy. "I get why he insists."

God, I was so proud of my brother. I pulled him into a hug from behind and stood on tiptoes to kiss his cheek.

"What was that for?" he said.

"Just because I love you." I messed his hair.

He shrugged and turned back to Ella. They were discussing Ella's other brother, who was gearing up for basketball season with Adam.

"My parents were thrilled we were coming to see the campus," Andrea said. "And since they knew we were staying with you, they were cool with it."

I bit my fingernail. "Would they be cool with it if they knew I only had one air mattress for you guys to share?"

Andrea blushed a harsh shade of crimson. "You don't have to worry about us, Avery. We would never—"

"Oh gosh, Andrea, I didn't mean it like that," I said, gripping her shoulder. "I just meant . . . a good big sister would have planned that part more carefully. But I trust you guys to behave yourselves at my house."

There was that word again—trust. If they'd only known what I did back in high school. No sexcapades until college, but plenty of making out—on my terms—to rid my mind of Gavin and Tim. "I'm *so* not worried about it."

We were next up to place our orders, and I treated everybody to lunch.

I took bites of my turkey bacon sandwich while Ella talked about her psychology classes. Andrea was interested in social work as her major and also wanted to know about dorm life.

I had never experienced the dorms like Ella. I'd commuted to campus from my teeny efficiency apartment close to home so I could keep my eye on Adam. I only felt comfortable moving farther away when Adam had turned into a six-foot-two, two-hundred-pound hulking high school junior.

"Look who's here," Ella said between bites of her sandwich. "It's Avery's new boyfriend."

My head jerked around. Bennett was clear across the other side of the room with Nate and two girls. Bennett's and Nate's backs were to us, giving me a clear view of their company. The girl nearest Bennett had a pixie cut with flowery tattoos up and down both arms and a nose ring. The other girl leaned over a book close to Nate, black hair spilling over her shoulder as they talked and laughed. Bennett was having an animated conversation with tattoo girl, too. *Pretty* tattoo girl. Maybe he had more in common with her than with someone like me. A ball of jealousy lodged in my throat, and I cleared it several times.

When I turned my attention back to our table, I realized no one was speaking. Adam was staring at me, his mouth slightly ajar. "You have a boyfriend?"

"No," I said, shaking my head a little too forcefully. "Just someone I'm getting to know. I actually invited Bennett out to dinner with us tonight."

Although now I wanted to rescind my invitation, pronto.

"Bitch, you were so shooting daggers at tattoo girl just now," Ella said.

"I was *not*," I said through gritted teeth. "Besides, it's not like we're exclusive or anything. You know I wouldn't want that."

Ella twisted her bottom lip and Adam still studied me intently.

"What?" I barked at him.

"I . . . I just haven't seen you like this," he said. "In a long time."

"Like what?" I was so ready to be done with this conversation.

"Interested in a guy," he said, his voice soft and timid, like he thought I'd rip him a new one any moment now. "I was actually starting to worry that you—"

"That I *what?*"

I saw how Andrea gripped his hand now.

"That you . . ." His jaw ticked, and Andrea shook her head. "That you had more in common with Mom than you'd ever admit."

His words were like a slap in the face, and I immediately sprang up. "Screw you, Adam."

"No, sis, please listen to me," Adam pleaded. Andrea put her face in her hands.

"Sit your crazy ass down before you make a scene," Ella hissed. "Let your brother explain himself."

I sat down reluctantly, despite wanting to bolt right out the door. My heart was slamming against my chest. "Damn you, Adam. Mom and I are *nothing* alike."

"Okay, sis." Adam sighed. "All I meant was . . . you used to be different. Not so cynical. When you were with Gavin, you were happy, at least most of the time. I just . . . liked seeing you like that."

"I know, Adam. But lots of things changed after that. I'd seen too much. And I made the conscious decision to be alone.

To take care of myself," I said, reaching for his hand across the table. "I haven't been with anyone because I *chose* not to be. And Mom isn't with anyone because she chooses fucked-up men."

"She's right," Andrea said, to my surprise. His girlfriend was coming to my defense. "Adam, your sister is fiercely independent, and I admire that about her."

"Me, too," he said. "I just want her to be happy. Like we are."

"She will be," Andrea said. "When she's ready."

I was speechless. My brother and his girlfriend were having a conversation about me as if I weren't even there. I let out an exasperated breath. I knew my brother wasn't trying to be cruel. He was just worried about me. Like I was worried about him.

Ella winked. "Told you I liked that girl." Then she stood up and motioned to Andrea. "Let's go back up and get some desserts. Their cheesecake is killer here."

I knew she was just giving Adam and me privacy. But right now I was ready to throttle him.

"I'm sorry, sis," Adam said, his shoulders slumping forward.

"I know you are. Just forget about it," I said, sipping my iced tea.

Suddenly everything about how I'd chosen to spend the last few years of my life came into clear focus. Bennett told me I'd given away pieces of myself. And now Adam had accused me of being like Mom and all of her men.

And it all came crashing down on me. I wasn't giving pieces away. I was keeping them hidden. I'd only given my family and friends a small portion of myself, because I wasn't ready to give all of me. Not yet.

I should have let Adam in, told him exactly what happened with Tim. He was the one person in my life I protected the most. But he didn't know the real me. The me that was trying to become an improved version of Mom. The kind of person Grandma would have wanted her to be.

And all these years I kept telling myself I *was* better than Mom. And in many ways, I was. In huge and important ways. But not in *all* the ways that counted. Because I wasn't letting the person I loved most inside my world. Inside my heart. And I needed to change that. Right now.

"I've always had a different relationship with Mom than you did," Adam said all at once. "Mom acted like she was competing with you. Like you were more of a friend than a daughter."

I'd felt that from my mother, too. Like she was afraid I'd steal all her boyfriends or something. I just hadn't known that Adam had observed it as well.

I winced. "You noticed that, too, huh?"

"Yeah," he said. "She's not a great role model, Avery, but she's all we've got. And I get why you moved. Why you wanted to get far away from her."

"Maybe you don't know the whole story, Adam," I said, looking into his piercing eyes. Admiring how he'd turned into this handsome, smart, and strong young man.

"I think I have a good idea, sis," he mumbled, and then looked down, like he was afraid to meet my eyes. I didn't want him to feel ashamed or scared to talk to me.

I didn't want Tim to do that to us. Take that from us. I wanted us to hold our heads high. Be proud of the people we'd become.

I nudged his chin and forced him to look at me. "You do?" My heart crashed against my rib cage.

"I know it had to do with Tim," he said, meeting my eyes. "I know that after he left, not only was Mom a mess, but so were you."

So he *had* put two and two together.

"He did something to you, didn't he?" he asked, his eyes bulging with anger. "He hurt you."

"Yeah, he did," I said. "He stole something from me. My innocence. But not all of it. I was able to fight him off for good."

He looked at me in awe, his bottom lip hanging open.

Then he squeezed his eyes shut. Against the truth. And how harsh it probably seemed.

"Fuck," he said. "Mom didn't believe you, did she?"

"No, she didn't," I whispered.

"Does she now?" His mouth had curled into a grimace. "After he beat the shit out of her?"

"Yeah, she does. Guess it took her a while, huh?" I tried to keep the bitterness out of my voice. I was tired of feeling resentment. Betrayal. Anger.

"Hey, listen, little bro," I said, having the urge to cradle him in my arms, like I'd done so many times before, whenever he woke from a nightmare, or fell down on the playground. "I'm a stronger person now. He didn't break me."

Adam grabbed my hand suddenly. "Sis, you are the bravest person I've ever known. You've always been there for me. You practically raised me, taught me how to be a decent person."

My eyes filled with tears. I couldn't speak. Emotions were overflowing and spilling over the sides. Love. Gratitude. Pride.

"You showed me how to be smart, survive, take care of

myself," he said. "And I don't want you to worry about me any-more."

I shook my head. "I won't ever stop worrying."

He was my family. My heart. My home.

"I know I can always count on you. I do," he said. "But, sis, it's time."

"Time." I repeated the word. Felt it roll off my lips. "For what?"

"To live your life. Find your own happiness."

"I *am* doing that, Adam," I said, glancing around the café, the scenery coming back into focus for me. I looked every-where but at Bennett's table. Even though that happiness Adam was speaking of just might involve him.

He gave me a skeptical look. "Then prove it to me."

"How?"

"Introduce me to your new boyfriend," he said, a flicker of challenge in his eyes. "Right now. In public. Stop being a chick-enshit."

Right then Ella and Andrea came back with two plates of brownies, cookies, and cheesecake, and I breathed a sigh of relief. I was definitely a chickenshit, and now Adam was smirking at me.

I stuck out my tongue at him right before I took a bite of a brownie.

"Really, sis, you want to mess with me right now?" He lunged forward and slung his arm around my neck before I could back away.

He placed my head in a choke hold. The same move he'd used on me when we'd wrestled as kids, fighting over a televi-sion show or just messing around.

"I'll kill you," I sputtered while my fingers tried reaching under his arms to find his most ticklish spot. It had always worked when we were younger, with him dissolving into laughter.

But now he was too strong. Too grown-up. Too mature for his own good.

"Whoa! If I tried that on Avery, she'd seriously kick my ass."

I froze as the sound of Bennett's voice washed over me and swept down my back in waves. Adam released me, but not before messing my hair with his knuckles. I gave him a good punch in the arm.

"Guess brothers earn that right, though," Bennett said, and Adam looked up at him. I was too busy trying to straighten my hair. Little shit. "You must be Adam."

"Yeah." Adam reached out his hand to shake Bennett's.

"I'm Avery's friend Bennett. I've heard lots about you."

"Awesome meeting you," Adam said. "And this is my girl-friend, Andrea."

Andrea waved, and Bennett nodded in her direction.

Bennett looked down at me, and his whole face lit up when our eyes met.

Hands squeezing my shoulders, he said, "Hi."

I grinned. "Hi, yourself."

"I was just headed back to work with Lila and Jessie," he said, motioning to where Nate stood with the two girls out-side. "Nate said to say hi. I'm pretty sure he's sweet on Jessie."

Nate was standing close to Jessie, motioning to something on the sidewalk. Lila was obviously tattoo girl. I couldn't help checking her out at a closer distance. Big boobs, high cheek-bones, and skinny waist.

Bennett leaned over and whispered in my ear, "Need to borrow one of my words again?"

I elbowed him. "Nope. Not this time." My jealousy from earlier seemed so ridiculous right then. Bennett probably worked with plenty of pretty girls. But it was me that he wanted.

And damn, I wanted him. I just needed to be brave about it. Like Adam said.

"Good." He kissed my cheek, and I felt myself blush.

"See you guys for Mexican tonight?" Bennett asked, backing away from our table to head out the door.

"Cool," Adam said. "Catch you later, man."

# CHAPTER TWENTY

Bennett arrived around seven and we headed out to the Mexican restaurant. He still wore his work attire—dark-wash jeans and black fitted shirt, along with his motorcycle boots. His hair was unruly, just the way I liked it, and when I first laid eyes on him, I stifled a sigh.

We made our way down First Street, Bennett talking about the tattoo parlor and his art, Adam discussing the upcoming basketball season. I felt light, happy, and proud to have my two favorite boys spending the evening together, getting to know each other. I hoped they could each see what I admired in the other. Bennett reached for my hand.

"Can I tag along to one of your brother's games this season?" He ran his thumb along the inside of my palm, leaving me momentarily breathless.

"That would be really cool," Adam said.

I could tell Adam liked Bennett. Admired him, even. He seemed to be asking nonstop questions, and looking for college advice, too. And I guess it made sense, since Adam had never really had a positive male presence in his life. Maybe he and Bennett could become friends.

Unless Bennett and I didn't work out. Which was likely, given my fucked-up history. But I had a feeling Bennett would remain friends with him regardless.

The thought of not having Bennett in my life filled me with such melancholy that I inhaled sharply through my nose.

I needed to start being honest with myself, because it was undeniable. I was falling for Bennett Reynolds. *Fuck me.*

At the restaurant we overindulged on chips and salsa, and Bennett and I drank a whole pitcher of margaritas by ourselves. Adam asked if he could have a taste of one and I gave him a stern look.

Bennett shook his head and laughed. "You realize, Avery, that Adam has probably been around beer and weed? I mean, what were *you* doing senior year?"

"Yeah, sis." Adam smirked. "Don't worry; you know I'm responsible. But every now and again . . ."

I covered my ears with both of my hands. "Don't want to hear about it."

Bennett's mouth dropped open and he nudged my knee under the table. "I've never seen this side of you."

I made a face at him. "What side?"

"The protective, motherly side," he said. "I kind of like it."

"She can be a bigger pain in the ass than our own mother," Adam said.

I pointed an accusing finger at him. "Hey, somebody's got to be."

Adam and Andrea laughed and then started talking about

a huge homework assignment due Monday in one of their shared classes at school.

I felt Bennett staring at me, a lopsided grin plastered on his lips. "What?"

"Nothing."

He kissed my hair and then brought his mouth to my ear. "Does this mean there's a possibility you'd take care of *me* someday, too? Protect *my* heart just as fiercely?"

His words stole my breath away.

I swallowed roughly. I wanted to admit that, yes, I was beginning to feel that way about him. I didn't want to hurt him or see him harmed by anyone else, either.

"There's always a possibility." I found I couldn't meet his eyes.

He lifted my chin with his thumb. I saw my longing reflected in his gaze.

I was overwhelmed by the immediate closeness of him, and the feeling was staggering. His knee brushing mine, his breath against my hair. And in that moment I realized I didn't want to be anywhere else in the world except next to him.

My hand slid to his thigh, and he hissed through his teeth.

"What are you thinking right now, five words or less?" Bennett murmured.

My lips immediately sought out his ear. I couldn't tell him how I was losing my mind over him. Losing my fucking brain over my feelings for him. Not yet. So instead, I told him how damn much I wanted him. "I'm . . . wondering . . . how . . . you . . . taste."

"Jesus, Avery." His fingers grasped the back of my neck as his forehead angled toward mine. "Now I'm hard as a rock."

I was so turned on I gripped the armrest to get ahold of myself.

Bennett shifted away from me and adjusted himself.

"I'm going to the ladies' room," I said, standing on wobbly legs.

"I'll go with," Andrea said.

We stood side by side in front of the mirror, and I noticed my flushed cheeks.

Andrea, who was applying lip gloss, smiled at me. "You and Bennett are so cute together."

I grinned and dotted my freckles with powder.

"And I hope you don't mind my saying this, but . . . Bennett is smoking hot."

I pointed my lip gloss at her. "Hey, eyes on your own prize."

"No argument there." She sighed. "You brother is gorgeous, no doubt. I can get *so* lost in those eyes of his."

I cringed. "Not sure I can hear this."

Her cheeks reddened. "Sorry."

"No, don't apologize," I said, and turned to her. "I'm happy Adam has you."

"That means the world to me." Her face grew serious. "Don't worry. I'll take good care of him."

But I was already pretty confident that he could take care of himself.

Bennett dropped us off at my door and gave me a chaste kiss on the lips that didn't quite satisfy my craving for him. "See you tomorrow."

I got Adam and Andrea settled in the living room. They

cuddled on the couch and clicked through TV channels to find a good movie.

"Just so you know, sis, I'm gonna sleep on the couch, and Andrea's got the mattress."

"Adam," I said. "I don't care if you sleep on the same mattress. Listen, I've been there. Sometimes it's nice to sleep next to the person you care about."

My words were strangely reminiscent of Bennett saying how nice it'd been sleeping next to someone after that first night in his bed.

"We'll figure it out," Adam said, a bit flustered. "So, um, I really like Bennett."

"I'm glad. What do you like about him?" I was curious what my brother saw in him. Were they the same things I saw?

"He's cool, mature, and a decent guy." Adam ticked off Bennett's qualities on his fingers as he spoke. "And I can tell he adores you, sis. Do . . . do you feel the same?"

"I . . . I might." Suddenly I wanted to see Bennett right that instant. To show him how much I craved his company. How much I cared. Maybe even reveal what was deeply hidden—my longing, my doubts, how his nearness was overpowering because it filled up the hollow places inside of me.

"Which reminds me," I mumbled. "I . . . I'll be right back. I forgot to tell Bennett something."

I flew out the door before they could see how flushed I'd become.

I needed to hold him. Kiss him. Taste him. I was nearly blinded by my desire for him.

When Bennett pulled open his door, he seemed bowled over to see me. "What are you—"

Before he could get the words out, my lips were on his. I walked him backward into his apartment, shut the door with my foot, and forced him hard against the wall.

"Avery," he moaned into my mouth.

Yanking his shirt over his head, I saw goose bumps swell across his skin.

I licked and sucked his neck before dragging my tongue down his chest. I stopped to flick against each of his nipples and watched how they hardened in response.

Bennett knocked his head against the wall. "Jesus."

I felt powerful in ways I hadn't experienced before. And it was a major turn-on.

When I continued down Bennett's stomach, his breaths shot out fast and hard.

I kissed along the path of the tornado on his rib cage, and his stomach trembled in my wake.

Then I trailed my tongue along his hip bone, turning him to continue on to his back. I was determined to get a decent look at his hourglass tattoo.

I studied it, caressing it with my fingers. It was outlined in black, with the sand inside a burnt orange hue. The hourglass itself was misshaped—almost like it was melted—just like the one in his drawing.

"Tell me about this one."

He was trying hard to control his breathing. "Always been interested in the concept of bending time."

I slid my hands along his waistline while he panted.

"There's a saying that goes like this: The hourglass freezes in moments of sorrow. Races along in moments of bliss." He spun and pulled me to my feet. Cupping my cheeks, he gazed into my eyes. "The very concept of time is a demand. That you own it, savor it, mean it. Before you waste it . . . or it wastes *you*."

Then he fused his mouth to mine, his kiss so intense, it was as if I were unraveling from the inside. Like he was siphoning my breaths out of my body.

He broke the kiss, and we stood gasping against each other. "That's totally hot," I mumbled.

He reached around my waist. "*You're* totally hot."

My fingers inched to his waistband, and I fastened my eyes on his. "I want my mouth on you."

He sucked in a harsh breath.

"I want to taste every part of you. Will you let me?"

"Holy shit, Avery. When you put it like that . . ."

His eyes turned dark with want, and I felt the tickle of need between my legs.

But tonight was all about him.

I worked to unbutton his jeans, then tugged them down, and he kicked them off his legs.

His cotton boxers were molded to his shape, and I could see the anticipation bulging beneath them. My fingers stroked him through the fabric, and his head rolled back with a shudder.

When I pulled them off, he stood stark naked before me. Never had I seen anyone as breathtaking in my life. "God, you're amazing. I could look at you all day *long*."

He yanked my face to his, and his tongue lapped against mine in a deep and powerful kiss.

I felt him hard and taut against my stomach as I walked him backward to the couch. I positioned myself on my knees between his legs and stared into his hooded eyes. He was devastatingly handsome.

"I can't believe you're here," he whispered. His hand snaked to my neck, and he freed my hair from its ponytail. My blond locks fell around my shoulders like a curtain, and he twirled the ends with his fingers. "You're like a dream."

As my fingers traveled up his thighs to fasten around him, his shaft involuntarily twitched in expectation. "I want you to come inside my mouth."

"Fuck, baby." I watched his lips tremble as I dragged my tongue up the length of him.

When I swirled my tongue around the head, he closed his eyes and groaned.

Inch by inch I took him into my mouth until I felt him hit the back of my throat.

I thrust in and out in a steady rhythm, my fingers low on his shaft.

"Oh God, Avery." He fisted my hair in his fingers, careful not to press too hard.

"Mmmm . . . you taste good." When I closed my lips around his tip, his breaths became frantic, and I knew he was close.

"I've never swallowed for a guy before." I looked into his eyes. "You'd be my first."

I plunged my mouth down the length of him, and that was the tipping point.

He cried out as warm, salty liquid shot past my lips and I lapped up every single drop.

He let out a deep groan that made the hairs stand on the

back of my neck. "Baby, that . . . no one's ever . . . *that* was incredible."

He pulled me onto his lap and I straddled him.

I held him against me until his breaths became slow and steady.

# CHAPTER TWENTY-ONE

Ella, Rachel, and I were at the coffee shop between classes. I had a shift soon and needed some sustenance. And some girl time.

I'd received a text from Bennett that morning saying that he had a class and would be heading to work after. Since that night I'd come up to his place, things seemed different between us. Cozier, sweeter, more personal—despite us not directly discussing it.

"So, when are we rescheduling our road trip?" Ella asked before taking a huge bite of her blueberry muffin.

"I've already asked for two Saturdays off in as little as two months," I said. "I'm pretty sure I won't be granted another one for awhile."

"Let's try again after the holidays," Rachel said, and then shot Ella an evil look. "And no boy plans messing it up."

"Right, asshead," Ella said. "So, Avery, what's happening with the police case? Are they any closer to finding the intruder?"

"They said there'd been plenty of break-ins around the area. But so far, no leads," I said, and then took a bite of my bagel. "He must be in hiding, because the detective said they haven't had another report since that night at my building."

"Maybe Bennett spooked him that night," Ella said. "He got a good look *and* caught him in the act."

"True. I don't think he'll return, but if he does, I'll be ready for him."

I had been channeling all of my kickboxing energy into imagining that intruder. I felt stronger, readier, should anything happen again.

Except that's what I thought prior to it happening, too. I was imagining someone like Tim, though. Someone that I *knew*. Not a complete stranger.

"Whoa, you badass," Rachel said. "Don't be practicing any of those moves on me."

"You and I could stand to learn a few of those moves," Ella said, paging through her psychology book, prepping for the test she had in an hour.

"Speaking of *intruders*," Rachel said a bit too loudly for my taste. "What about Virgin Boy?"

I cringed. "What about him?"

"Have you broken him down yet—finally slept with him?" She batted her eyelashes at me. "Wasn't that your ultimate plan?"

"Don't be a dick. Of course it wasn't."

"Oh c'mon. You could have bet me some cold hard cash, because I knew you'd weaken his resolve, have him begging you for sex. Is he at least well-hung?"

Rachel could be ridiculous. Sometimes it was best not to

even argue the point with her. She always got in the last word, and usually it was hilarious.

Unless it involved something personal and someone you cared about.

I decided to just let it go. Let her have her fun.

"Yeah, sure, Rachel. His package is perfect and we've had some good sexy-time."

"I knew Virgin Boy would come through for you. I bet he begs for it all the time now. Be sure to send him my way next."

She tried to high-five me but I just shook my head.

I heard a muffled gasp from Ella. When I looked up, her lower jaw hung open and her eyes were focused on something behind me. I turned to see the blur of a red baseball cap and Bennett storming out the door. I could only see a side view, but his lips were drawn tight, his eyes narrowed.

"Fuck." My ass was suddenly glued to my seat.

"Go after him, dickhead," Ella hissed at me.

Her words unstuck me. I jolted up and raced for the door. I looked both up and down the street but he was nowhere in sight.

I dragged myself back to my seat, my stomach bunched into a hard ball.

"Shit, was that Virgin Boy?" Rachel squealed. "Did he hear our conversation?"

Ella looked at me with a mixture of sadness and frustration in her eyes.

"Was he standing behind me for long?" I groaned and slumped forward.

"Probably long enough to hear everything," she said. "He looked . . . hurt, Avery."

"Who the fuck cares?" Rachel said. "You got what you wanted from him, right?"

"Wrong, Rachel. I've been . . . lying to you. And to myself." I felt the prickle of tears behind my eyes. "I really like him, Rachel. *Like* him, like him."

She remained silent, probably shocked by my revelation. Stunned, because for as long as I'd known her, I'd never uttered anything remotely close to those words.

I pulled out my phone and typed a message with shaky fingers.

**It's not how it sounded.**

No response.

**Please, let me explain.**

Again, no response.

My shoulders sagged.

Ella was studying me, words I probably didn't want to hear hanging from her lips.

"Just say it already." I pushed away the plate of my half-eaten bagel a little too roughly. "I know I fucked up, okay?"

"Maybe it's time you told Bennett how you really feel about him."

"What if I don't know yet?"

"You *know*, dill weed," she said, slapping her hand on the table. "You're just afraid to admit it out loud. Is it worth losing him over?"

"Wait, what?" Rachel said, clueing in to the seriousness of our conversation. "Was the sex that good?"

"There hasn't even been any sex yet." I stood up and gathered my stuff to leave. "Just lots of build-up."

"Maybe *that's* it, then," Rachel said. "Maybe the sexual frustration is messing with your head."

I rolled my eyes and walked out the door. I got what Rachel was saying. There was some seriously strong sexual frustration between us. But that wasn't all I craved from Bennett.

Sure, I wanted him. I wanted *all* of him.

His love of poetry. His integrity. His quiet grace.

"Avery, wait." I stopped at the corner of the street and turned to face Rachel.

"What's up?" I kept my voice steady, but I was in no mood for her jokes or sarcasm.

"Listen, I'm sorry," she said, her cheeks a bit flushed. "Ella told me I was being a dickwad."

"It's cool." I wasn't sure if Rachel was actually capable of having a heart-to-heart, so I figured if she was big enough to apologize, I'd leave it at that.

"I know what that's like, you know," she said, gripping my arm. "To feel that way about somebody."

"I know you do, but you never talk about it."

"That's because it hurts too much." She bit her lip. I'd never seen her look that vulnerable before. "And I made a lot of mistakes."

"Got it," I said. "We all have, Rach. So if you ever want to talk . . ."

"Okay, enough of this touchy-feely shit," she said, making

a wrap-it-up signal with her finger. She backed away from me to cross the street to her car. "If you want that nice piece of ass, then go after him."

All I could do was shake my head and laugh.

I texted Bennett one last time on my way to work.

**I hope you're willing to talk to me after my shift. Can I come by?**

Still no response. I almost threw my phone at the ground, smashing it into a thousand pieces.

I arrived at work fifteen minutes before shift change. Passing the security desk in the lobby, I showed my badge and gave a small wave to Robert, our security guard on duty.

Lillian was behind the nurses' station jotting down notes. She looked up. "Morning, Avery."

"It's almost lunchtime, actually." I took a deep breath and tried to remove the snotty attitude from my voice. It wasn't her fault I was a major fuckup. "What's been happening around here?"

"Mr. Meyers in 121 passed away last night. A new resident will fill his bed tomorrow." She paused to write something down and to let that news sink in. Mr. Meyers had been a very ill and immobile patient. We'd had to change his position regularly to keep ahead of his bedsores. I knew it was only a matter of time, but it was sad nonetheless. "And Mrs. Jackson had another TIA last night. She's weak and exhausted today."

My chest tightened. "Has her family been in to see her this morning?"

"Not yet."

I locked my grief away in a dark corner of my heart. It was

the only way to get through this day. It was a useful skill I'd developed and had always been good at it—especially at my job.

I prepped a catheter for Mrs. Alvinia, found a bedpan for Ms. Wilson, who'd just buzzed the desk, and opened new sponges for Mr. Lewis's bath.

When I finally made it to Mrs. Jackson's room, her back was turned, but her eyes were open. Her gaze was fixed on the giant maple tree outside her window, which had lost most of its leaves.

Her skin looked dry and scaly, and I figured she could use a gentle massage to help her loosen her limbs. One of her hands was curled into a rigid ball from the stroke, and that was the one I worked on regularly.

Grabbing some therapeutic lotion from the cart, I squirted it into my hand.

I smoothed my fingers over her course black hair, and her eyes found mine. "Okay if I massage you for a bit?"

Her head moved slightly, and I took that as affirmation. I tried to dislodge the ache from my gut upon seeing her vacant eyes. I knew she was in some pain, but there was little to do except give her meds and bring some comfort.

I rubbed her hand using a circular motion, and her fingers unclenched. She closed her eyes, relief crossing her face. I was thankful I could provide her some form of respite. A stroke was debilitating on the body, especially when muscle and motor activity were affected.

"Thank you." Her voice sounded weak and broken. It was tough to see her that way. This, added to hurting Bennett's feelings that morning, made me feel lost and weepy. But I needed to hold it together.

"You're very welcome."

Without any prompting, she began talking about her life, much like she'd done in the past. But this time felt different.

Patients sometimes reminisced like that at the end stage of their lives, so hearing her ramble on made my throat close up.

"Marrying Mr. Jackson was the best decision I've ever made. He brought children into my life and taught me about love. I'm so grateful for that man. Despite all our hardships, it was magic to share my life with him."

"Well, aren't you talkative this afternoon?" I kept my voice light and normal, trying to engage her in our regular banter. "What brought all of that on?"

"I'm not dense, you know. I know my time is coming, maybe sooner than later." Her voice was ragged from the effort. But I knew better than to tell her to save her breath. She'd only put me in my place. "I want to make sure the people I deeply care for know exactly how I feel. I've already laid down my roots; now I'm just cultivating them. Hoping the seeds carry into the wind and spread."

I kept my tears at bay. Mrs. Jackson's message was one for me as well. And there was talk of those damn roots again.

Before I left her room, I made sure to whisper in her ear how much she meant to me and had influenced my life. *Just in case.*

After my shift, I went straight up the elevator in my building to the fifth floor, sick with worry that I had ruined something special. I knocked on Bennett's door, but he didn't answer, and the apartment sounded empty.

So I went home, showered, and changed into pajamas. I drank a glass of white wine and then went to bed.

I pulled out my phone one last time.

Please talk to me, Bennett. I'm sick about this.

Finally there was a response, and I wondered where exactly he was, if he wasn't at home. I held my breath as I read it.

Bennett: I just . . . need time.

That hurt. But I replied right away.

Me: We promised to be honest with each other when we wanted to run away, remember? I just need to know what you're thinking.

Bennett: Fine. I'm thinking that maybe this was all some conquest for you. Some joke. Bag the virgin. Laugh it up with your friends.

Me: Damn it, that's NOT TRUE. My friend Rachel is a piece of work. She's crude and a huge player. Sometimes it's not worth it to have a real conversation with her. So instead, I just agreed with her and let it go.

Bennett: See, that's just the thing. I wasn't worth the effort for you to set her straight. You didn't protect my principles, my reputation, my heart, Avery.

Me: No, Bennett. I'm sorry, that's not at all how it was meant.

And his last message nearly broke me.

Bennett: I believe you're sorry. I do. And I accept your apology. But I still need time. To think it all through. To figure out what I really want.

. . .

t had been two days since that text conversation and I was miserable. I didn't know what to do. Bennett obviously meant something to me, and I missed him terribly.

I was the one always running from him. Never would I have thought he'd run from me. And I had been an idiot that day with Rachel. I was too afraid to say what I really felt. That I was falling for this amazing guy. I was immature and stupid. And I guess losing him would be a lesson learned.

All along I was protecting my own heart, never considering that I needed to defend his as well.

I changed into my sports bra and shorts for kickboxing class, despite wanting to just lie on my couch all day and sulk.

I shut my door behind me, listening for the latch to catch. When I turned, I nearly plunged right into Rebecca and Bennett, who were coming in the front entrance.

My stomach was in my throat.

"Hi, Avery," Rebecca said in a way-too-cheery voice. I couldn't get the words to form on my lips, so I just nodded.

Bennett worried his lip between his teeth. I knew he saw the pain and sadness in my eyes . . . which is probably what prompted him to actually speak to me. "Rebecca has an appointment with the guidance department. So I agreed to get her there and show her around."

"Before I make any decision to come here," she said, "I need to see how many of my credits will actually transfer."

"Good plan," I said, wanting to get the hell away from her as soon as possible. "I need to get to the gym. Good luck, Rebecca."

Rebecca started walking to the bank of elevators, but

Bennett turned and gripped my forearm. The air was so thick between us I almost choked on the fumes.

My heart flapped and fluttered and strained against my chest.

Would Rebecca try to move in on him? Would he *let* her today?

"No," he said, meeting my eyes. "Never."

Had I said that out loud?

Or was he just reading my mind?

"I . . . I . . . what?"

"I know what you're thinking." He released his grip, and my muscle quivered from the contact.

I still couldn't get any damn words out. "I wasn't . . ."

"I wouldn't do that, Avery. Even if I'm still ticked and unsure about things." He jammed his hands in his pockets and then clenched his jaw. "Because all day, every day, you're still stuck in my head—in my every *damn* thought."

He stormed away, and my breath whooshed right out of me.

He met Rebecca at the opening elevator door and then stepped inside with her.

And still I stood there, his words washing over me like a salve.

I received a text from him the next day.

Bennett: Everything's gone to shit with my family. Mom and Henry got in a fight and he walked out. I'm going home for the weekend. Just wanted you to know where I'd be.

Me: ☹ I'm sorry. I'm here if you need me.

But he must not have needed me. Because I didn't hear from him again.

# CHAPTER TWENTY-TWO

By the end of the weekend I'd decided on a plan. I wasn't sure what was happening with Bennett's family and whether it meant he'd have to be spending a lot of time there, or even move back home.

But I knew that I wanted to be there for him *and* fight for him.

What punctuated this truth more than anything was the phone call I received from my mother asking me to go to the hearing with her. She was going to follow through with the restraining order and wanted my support.

If she could start getting her act together, so could I.

I called Raw Ink and scheduled back-to-back consult and tattoo appointments with Bennett. Under a different name. I'd decided on exactly the kind of tattoo I wanted on my hip, and only he could ink it.

And maybe while I was there, he'd actually talk to me.

I fidgeted nervously in the lobby until I heard the deep timbre of his voice in the hallway. When Bennett saw me, he stopped dead in his tracks. He looked around for his scheduled appointment, but I was the only one sitting there.

"So, um, you're *Michael*?"

"Yep, Avery Michaels. Pleased to meet you." I worked to keep my lips in a neat, straight line. "Your, um, receptionist might have gotten my name wrong."

A ghost of a lopsided grin splayed across his cheeks, and he looked back at Holly, who was on the phone behind the front desk.

"Avery, what are you doing here?"

"I came to get a tattoo, of course."

We walked to his room in silence, and he closed the door behind us. He sat down at the same table we'd used last month with Ella. He pulled out his sketch pad and was acting the consummate professional, except for his knee jiggling a mile a minute. And I wasn't much better. I had all but crumpled the rock band flyer I'd picked up in the lobby.

"So." He kept his eyes on the table. "Where do you want this tattoo?"

"On my hip."

He inhaled sharply through his nose. "Seriously, Avery? It was only a suggestion that night."

"One that I liked. A lot." I tried catching his eye, but he wasn't going for it. "So will you do it?"

He stole a glance at me. "What kind do you want?"

"Like a lopsided heart that looks like it's planted in roots. The kind of roots that grow beneath a tree. Thick and gnarly."

His fingers immediately traveled across the sketch pad. The heart he drew was irregularly shaped and crooked, kind

226

of like all that stuff in the middle of his painting back home. When he started on the roots, he said, "What does it mean?"

"It means that my heart is ready . . . to lay down roots," I said. "I suppose it's always been ready. It just needed something . . . to finally believe in."

He arched an eyebrow at me.

"See, it's because of a certain beautiful boy who's recently come into my life." We shared a long, unblinking look that lit all the dark corners of my heart. "He made me feel things. Incredible things. And now I know what I want—what I need—and no matter what happens, I'll always have him to thank for that."

He didn't say anything—just breathed in and out of his mouth, his eyes softening.

So I kept talking. "That's what Mrs. Jackson calls it, anyway. Laying down roots."

"Mrs. Jackson?" he asked. "You've talked to her about . . . that guy?"

"Yeah, a whole bunch. She always knew from the beginning, way before I did, that this boy was changing my life," I said. "And she's always spouting off about love and roots and making sure people know how you feel before they leave you . . . for good."

I sprang from my seat, because my own words haunted me. I checked out the art on his wall to escape his probing eyes. "The tattoo also reminds me of this awesome poem."

"What poem?"

"That same boy introduced me to modern poetry," I said, still too chicken to meet his eyes. "Anyway, I'd been searching the Internet the last couple of days and this one poem I found kind of knocked me over the head."

"How does it go?"

"Well, it's called 'Forget Me Not.'" I fastened my eyes on him now, despite my shaking fingers. "Let's see. 'I tried to forget, but you grew roots around my rib cage, and sprouted flowers just below my collarbone.'"

He seemed entranced by the words. So I continued. "'All day I pluck their petals. But I have not yet ascertained whether you . . . *love* me or *not*.'"

He squeezed his eyes closed and shifted in his seat.

Taking a deep breath, he returned to the drawing, his jaw locked tight.

He looked handsome as his fingers skated across the page, trying to capture the essence of what I wanted based on my confession and the words of the poem.

When he finished, I leaned over his shoulder to get a better look. I heard him holding his breath. I took the opportunity to take a whiff of his hair. I missed that smell.

His sketch was stunning, and I was certain it was the one. That *he* was the one. But he needed to be sure about me, too, and he could only decide that on his own.

"It's amazing. Perfect."

"Cool," he said. "Did you want to wait in the lobby for me while I get set up?"

"Can . . . can I wait in here? I won't bother you." I just needed to be near him.

He nodded and got busy copying his drawing to transfer paper. I answered e-mails on my phone and looked through his portfolio, all the while thinking about how much I liked being around him again.

"It's ready," he said, standing up and moving toward me. "I need to transfer this to your skin now."

I pulled my jeans over my hips, and then tugged my underwear down, making sure not to expose myself. Although I still felt his gaze press in on me like a wall of heat.

Wearing the lacy red underwear might have been an unfair advantage. But I was desperate to know if he was still affected by me. If the red lacy set reminded him of that one day in the laundry room, when he first started flirting with me.

He knelt in front of me, hands trembling. He sucked in a harsh breath, as if to gather himself, and then set to work rubbing the transfer onto my skin.

Feeling his fingers on my skin made all my blood pool to the area between my legs.

He was meticulous and precise and finally stood to grab the hand mirror. "How does it look?"

When I saw it on my hip, I felt a winging in my chest. Like the tattoo represented everything special to me, Mrs. Jackson included. Bennett's fingers created this magic that would now become a permanent part of me. "I love it."

"Great. Let's get started," he said, moving away. "Since it's going on your hip, I need you to lie here."

He walked to the black padded table against the wall, and I followed. Hopping up, I settled in. I stared at the ceiling while he fiddled with his instruments and dye.

"You sure you're ready for this? The hip is a sensitive area of the body, so it'll feel slightly different than the one behind your ear."

"I'll be okay. I'm in good hands."

He wheeled the stool closer, and I tried to concentrate on the music piping through his iPod. It was soft and rhythmic, and I breathed in deep and meaningful breaths to calm my jangling nerves.

For the next hour I'd be at Bennett's mercy. Once the stinging precision of the needle began its journey, I'd be stationary and helpless. Fear gripped my stomach, and I almost shot up and raced out of the room.

But I squashed it down. This was the same fear that had immobilized me for the better part of four years, and it was time to work through it. This was Bennett, the man I wanted in my life. The man I had fallen hard for.

He made me feel safe and protected. Being with him hadn't made me disappear or became anything less. Maybe we *could* fold into each other's lives without compromising who we were.

I'd just have to trust that. Trust *him*. And get him to trust *me*.

I felt my shoulders unraveling, the tension evaporating, calm flowing through me. He wouldn't hurt me. In fact, he was good at taking care of me. And because of him, I'd become a different version of myself. A better version of myself.

I studied his lips, his skin, his hair, the way his eyes were intense and focused.

"Avery, you're going to have to stop that." He was looking down, loading the machine with a needle.

"Stop what?"

"Looking at me like that."

"Are you saying, Mr. Reynolds, that you haven't had chicks all hot for you in here?" A smile quirked my lips. "Especially when you're about to touch an intimate place on their body?"

"Usually, there's terror in their eyes," he said, finally meeting my gaze. "But yes, once or twice that's happened. But those times didn't matter."

"Why not?"

"Because, Avery, they weren't *you*."

I inhaled a lungful of air. "Bennett—"

"Let's just get through this, okay? I need to be professional here." His eyes were so dark they were almost black. "I'm giving you a tattoo. I'm not thinking about how I want to trace my mouth over every damn part of your body, including your lips. Nope, never even crossed my mind. So, let's get started."

He fired up the machine, and it blotted out the moan I stifled in the back of my throat. We were silent after that. I was intent on staring at the ceiling while he concentrated on his design.

When his fingers braced my lower belly, I nearly whimpered, but bit down on my lip instead. I hoped he didn't notice how my nipples hardened at his touch.

His face hovered over my navel as he pulled my skin taut. I could smell him. Coconut, sun, and beach.

Then the needle went in. It stung, and my hand fisted the edge of the table. But the burn was familiar, and I knew I'd become adjusted to the cadence of the machine soon enough.

"So, what's happening at home, Bennett?"

"My mom's a wreck. She's realizing what a fuckup she's been. But I told her the only way to get Henry back is to prove she's made some changes."

I couldn't help thinking his words were a message for me, too.

"I think Henry's willing to try again," Bennett said. "But he needs to know she's serious."

Again, a double message.

"She needs to start holding up her end of the relationship. Show him that she wants him and . . . *loves* him."

"You know, Bennett, when you lose something you didn't even realize you needed in your life, it's a hard lesson," I said, both for his mother and for me. "There's regret and sorrow. All you want is that person back so you can show them how you feel."

The needle had stopped moving, and Bennett's eyes were latched on to mine, so penetrating and full of need that it felt more intimate than having his lips on me.

He wiped away excess ink with a wet paper towel. "I'm finished with the outline. The shading shouldn't take long." His voice was raspy and gruff, sending a shiver through me.

Suddenly, I wanted to lie there for two hours more. I liked having him call the shots, be in control. I'd been holding on to all the pieces of myself with a death grip for so long that to release some of them was liberating.

"Anyway, I'm heading home right after my shift tonight," he said. "Taylor needs my help, and Henry's coming by—we're going to have, like, a family meeting."

"Will you be staying there?" I tried not to sound disappointed about him not being around. Even when he wasn't talking to me this past week, at least I had still known he was there—somewhere.

"I'm not sure. At least overnight, since I'm not scheduled tomorrow."

When he finished, he helped me off the table and retrieved the mirror.

His artwork gripped my heart so forcefully that it leapt out of my chest and fell to his feet. Begged him to hold her. Keep her. Take the largest piece of her.

My skin pebbled with goose bumps, and my eyes watered. I was so thankful he'd created this masterpiece on my skin. No matter what happened, I'd always be grateful.

"Hey," he said, his hands reaching for my shoulders. "Why are you crying?"

"Because you created exactly what I wanted. It's beautiful." I sniffled, leaning my forehead against his shoulder. "And even if you decide you . . . you don't want me, I'll always have *this* . . . this masterpiece you created for me."

"Avery, look at me." He pushed his fingers through my hair. "I was hurt. I don't ever want to be some joke. I want to be real. For *this* to be real. For both of us."

"It's more real than anything's been in my whole life."

"That's all I needed to hear." His fingers traced my jawline, and his kiss was soft and fluttery against my lips.

I closed my eyes and reveled in it.

The phone buzzed from his desk.

"Bennett," Holly's voice chirped through the intercom. "Your last appointment's here."

He cradled me in his arms. "Let's get you cleaned up."

# CHAPTER TWENTY-THREE

I followed Bennett's care instructions to the letter the next couple of days. Don't wear tight clothing, keep the tattoo moist using over-the-counter medicine, and expose it to air as much as possible.

The heart had scabbed over and was healing nicely. I couldn't stop admiring it every chance I got, and even allowed Mrs. Jackson a peek at work.

She continued to recover from her latest ministroke and was becoming more animated every day. "Girl, I'm proud of you. That boy is going to have some fun with you and that tattoo."

"Mrs. Jackson, you're making me blush."

"Stop playing. You don't blush. You just can't wait to get home to him tonight."

It was true. Bennett had kept in touch with me from home the last couple of days. They'd had a family meeting, Henry and his mother had made up, and he was willing to stick around and raise his girls.

Until the next big fight. His mom was as much a work in

235

progress as mine. Mom had been different on the phone with me since the restraining order ordeal. She was more honest, less critical, and maybe even a bit scared of getting involved with another guy like Tim. But that didn't stop her from trolling the bars every weekend.

I encouraged her to change all the locks in case Tim still had a spare key, and she agreed to call a locksmith before the hearing next week. She even agreed to sign up for a local self-defense class. But I had a feeling she wouldn't follow through with it. *Baby steps.*

Bennett had gotten home that morning while I was at work and said he'd be stopping over at my apartment after his last tattoo appointment to check on his handiwork. I had a pharmacology test to study for, so I brought my textbook to work to get a head start during my lunch. Waiting for him now felt like that first time I saw him. Butterflies were battering the sides out of my stomach, and I was nervous I'd say or do the wrong thing to mess it all up again.

But when I let him inside, all of my nervousness flowed out of me and was replaced by excitement. He was stunning and sexy, and I knew I wanted him in my life.

I just hoped he felt the same way.

"God, I missed you," he said, his gaze caressing me with such tenderness.

I focused on the curve of his jaw, the angle of his cheekbones, and the devotion stirring behind his russet eyes. There was apprehension hidden there as well and that only made me want him more.

This boy had gathered the pieces of my heart that had been

scattered in the wind and tucked them in the safe pocket of his hand. And now it was time to treat his heart with the same gentleness.

"Avery, I want . . ." He closed the distance between us. "I *need* to touch you."

He cupped my cheeks and brought his lips to mine. His kiss was slow, hesitant, delicious.

And wholly intoxicating.

When I opened my eyes, he brushed a stray hair from my cheek and gazed at me in adoration. My hands tangled in his curls, and I drew his mouth toward me again. The feel of my tongue stroking hungrily against his made him hum with desire.

His hands became more insistent as he tugged my hair out of its ponytail and trailed his thumbs along my neck, making me shiver to my very core.

His fingers explored my waist and back before finally landing on the buttons of my shirt. One by one he unfastened them as his lips whispered against my collarbone and the tops of my breasts. He peeled my shirt from my shoulders, along with my bra straps, and then licked and nipped the tender skin there.

After removing my bra, he swirled his tongue around my hardened peak while I clutched at fistfuls of his shirt. When he moved to my other breast, he bit down lightly, and my knees buckled beneath me. He grabbed my waist and pulled me to him. "I've got you, baby."

His lips found mine, and he moved us backward into my bedroom. "I need to check on my masterpiece." When he nudged me back on the bed, my fever for him continued to build, ready to consume me.

He pulled my leggings down to my knees and then slid them off my legs. I reached for him to remove his shirt, and he lifted it over his head. I marveled at his smooth chest and tight stomach.

He gently shifted my underwear down my hips, and then pulled back for a look at his handiwork. "Damn, that's sexy."

He reached for my hands, tugging them above my head, and lacing them through his fingers. Then he kissed me again, this time long and deep. His desire was like an undercurrent humming through him and transferring to me.

"Avery, I have this overwhelming need . . . to be inside of you." I melted into the covers, my body becoming liquid. "Will you let me?"

I knew what he was asking without him saying the exact words.

He wanted me to be his first. He was giving me his body.

I was desperate to feel him inside of me. I wanted him so badly it ached.

But part of me still worried whether I'd be able to be everything he needed me to be. Everything good enough for him.

"God, Bennett." My voice was shaky, my breathing shallow. "Are you sure?"

"I'm sure, baby," he whispered. "I want you. I want you to be mine."

I yanked his head down in a frantic kiss, trying to convey everything I was feeling in that moment. He was putting his faith in me, and I wanted to cherish it. Nurture it. Worship it.

I leaned back as he unbuttoned his jeans and slipped out of them, along with his boxers. He was naked before me and I couldn't help but appreciate the view. His sturdy shoulders and his strapping arms were contrasted by his delicate hip bones that led down to all that was divinely him.

He grabbed hold of my ankles and tugged them gently to the edge of the bed. Then he positioned himself over me. I gasped as he flicked his tongue along the length of my torso and dipped below my navel, careful not to touch my tattoo, which would still be tender for a few more days.

I tried reaching out my hand to touch his chest, but he backed away.

"No," he said. "You. *All of you.* Your creamy skin, your perfect breasts, your taste, your smell. Your *heart.*"

Then his hands were on my knees, nudging them apart, and his gaze fastened on the area between my legs. He swept kisses along the inside of my thighs and watched as my breaths grew desperate.

His tongue dipped down and tasted me, and I moaned and tensed beneath his mouth.

He softly parted me with his thumbs and swept his tongue over me, and then inside of me, as I whimpered and squirmed, practically coming unglued.

My back arched off the bed as I reached for him, begging him with my eyes.

I wanted him inside of me right that very instant.

But it needed to be on his terms, not mine.

He looked at me with such need, such want, and such affection. I knew what this meant to him. He had told me that he was waiting for love, and though he hadn't uttered those precise words, his eyes conveyed everything.

I was bursting with emotion for him, and I hoped it was reflected in my eyes as well.

"Avery, I didn't exactly plan this. Do you have a condom?"

I motioned to my bedside table, almost embarrassed that I was so prepared.

He removed the foil wrapper and then fumbled with the condom. I took it from his fingers, unrolled it, and pulled it over his taut skin. He was so hard and ready, trembling with need.

I slid my body up the bed to my pillows, reaching for his hand, asking him to join me.

He crawled up to me and then crushed his lips into mine. "I want you so damn bad," he growled.

He positioned himself between my legs, and I was panting from anticipation.

His eyes pressed into mine with a silent question.

He was asking my permission—making sure I wanted this, too.

"Yes, please," I moaned. "All of you. *Only you.*"

And then he urged his tip inside of me, and I shuddered against the feel of it. He kept his eyes locked on mine as he pushed in deeper and deeper, filling me completely. His mouth fell open in heavy breaths. "Jesus, Avery, you feel fucking incredible."

I was overcome with the emotion of him being nestled inside me. It felt different than anything I'd ever experienced, and my eyes became glassy and full from the pure wonder of it.

It may have been his first time. But in a way, it was *my* first time, too.

He rocked his hips gently against me, sliding almost all the way out and then driving himself back in. "Fuck, baby, I'm so deep."

The feeling was indescribable, and a familiar tension pulsed low in my belly.

I wrapped my legs around his waist and rocked against him in a slow and seductive rhythm. He leaned down and claimed my mouth in a profound and meaningful kiss.

"You're so warm, Avery. God, *so* warm."

His thumb came up and found my sweet spot, and he drove me to my breaking point.

I came with a violent shudder all around him.

He became still, relishing the feel of me tightening and pulsing against him, complete and utter awe in his eyes.

"Oh God, Avery." He thrust himself back inside, the tempo controlled and deliberate. "You . . . I . . . Jesus, this is unbelievable."

Watching him get his release was a thing of pure beauty. His lips open, his eyes unfocused, his chest shuddering from pleasure.

He collapsed on top of me, raining warm kisses on my lips, my jaw, and my neck.

"You're fucking beautiful," he whispered against my ear.

I tightened my grasp around his neck.

"Don't move. Not yet," I mumbled. "I want to feel you just like this."

We laid that way until our breaths slowed and our limbs were less fluid.

Before he fell asleep that night, Bennett mumbled my name over and over.

I felt my heart unfurling, smoothing out, blossoming—into an unblemished kind of love.

# CHAPTER TWENTY-FOUR

woke in Bennett's arms the next morning, and it just felt right. Making love to him had been sensual, emotional, and incredible.

When my alarm blared, we immediately jumped into hurry mode. We each had an early class and work. Then Bennett had a night out with his coworkers.

He flew out the door with a kiss and the promise of texting me later. I thought of nothing else all day long. Just the feel of his skin against mine, and how different my orgasm had felt than it had those other times.

I wanted to ask him how his first time had been, but I didn't want to embarrass him or make him feel juvenile. All I could go on was the way his eyes had searched mine and the noises that had tumbled out of his beautiful mouth.

Though I was certain how I felt about Bennett, I hadn't said it that night.

And neither had he. But maybe I'd be brave enough to say it sometime soon.

Mrs. Jackson noticed the change in me right away, and I blushed the entire time she asked about Bennett. "You be sure to cherish that boy, you hear me?"

Her vitals were erratic that day, and even as I encouraged her to eat more from her tray than just the chicken broth, I squashed down the feeling that another stroke was imminent.

I was exhausted by bedtime and fell straight into my sheets. Just as I was drifting off, I received a text from Bennett. I knew he was at a local bar with his coworkers, and my heart leapt at seeing his message flash across the screen.

Bennett: How was the rest of your day?

Me: Exhausting. Already in bed.

Bennett: Mmm . . . sleep sounds good. Our night is just getting started.

Me: You can text on your way home if you want. Have fun with your friends.

Bennett: I'll let you sleep and bother you tomorrow instead. Good night, baby.

I stared at the screen and tried to read between the lines. All day long, I had gotten the distinct impression that Bennett was holding himself back. All of his texts had fallen just short of mushy.

Like he didn't want me to feel smothered just because he had given himself to me.

Like he didn't want me to run away.

Little did he know, I wasn't about to go anywhere.

And I planned on showing him that—tomorrow.

The following day at work, I stood at the nurses' station, finishing my note on Mrs. Jackson—about how she was flushed and restless all day; even her husband had commented on it just ten minutes ago—when security buzzed me from the lobby.

"Ms. Michaels, there's a package here for you," Robert said. "It's signed for and sitting on the counter. Come down when you're free."

A package? Usually packages for the unit came filled with medical equipment, but this one sounded personal. I headed down, curiosity getting the best of me. When I rounded the corner I saw it, along with Robert's giant grin. It was a large bouquet of flowers.

Robert handed them to me. "Someone must be smitten with you, Ms. Michaels."

My cheeks burned as I walked my package to a nearby table in the visitors' section, unable to wait any longer. The bouquet was a mixture of red, orange, and pink Gerbera daisies. The colors were striking and lush, and they were easily one of my favorite flowers.

Right away I noticed that one of the flowers had lost nearly all of its petals—only one clung on for dear life. There was a note attached to the stem.

I removed the note and carefully unfolded it, noticing Bennett's initial at the bottom before scanning back up to read it.

*A.*
*Yes, I do. No question about it.*

A smile burst from my lips. I knew without question that Bennett was referring to the "Forget Me Not" poem that I'd recited to him before he gave me my tattoo. "I have not yet ascertained whether you *love* me or *not*."

He was telling me in his own way that he loved me. My heart leapt straight out of my chest, performed a classic dive-bomb, and ran the half mile back home to find him.

Below his admission of love, he had written more.

*I hope you feel the same.*

He wanted to know if I loved him, too. And I did. Oh, I did.

*Can I see you tonight?*
*B.*
*P.S. And as for the other night . . . there are no words,*
*Avery. No words.*

I couldn't contain my grin.

When I realized I was still in the nearly empty lobby, I headed back to my unit to pack up, give my report, and head home.

But before I did, I was going to march straight into Mrs. Jackson's room to show her that I finally got my flowers, and then tease her about showing up Mr. Jackson's bouquet today.

As soon as I stepped through the automatic double doors, I noticed that the front desk was empty. And then I heard the low hum. The one that signified a code blue in the unit. It meant the code blue team was gathered in the room of the resident who was experiencing distress.

I'd been through my share of code blues, but this time felt different. I couldn't get my feet unstuck from the floor. I gripped the flower vase so it wouldn't slip through my fingers and crash into a million little shards.

Like my heart was doing right now.

I knew with every fiber of my being who the resident having trouble was. And damn it, she'd waited until I was out of the unit to leave without saying good-bye.

That thought alone drove me to action. No way was she going to die while I was off duty. I hastily placed the flowers on the desk and headed toward her room. My footsteps were hollow and tinny against the cold linoleum floor, echoing the beats of my plunging heart.

But as I neared her door, the code blue team of nurses and doctors were already headed out, heads hanging low.

And I knew she was already gone.

My fingers splayed against the wall as I tried to keep all the pieces of myself together. I had never cried for a resident before, outside of my first month, when I was new and green.

But this was no ordinary resident. She meant something more to me. Much more.

My feet were like lead as Lillian rounded the corner from Mrs. Jackson's room. "I think this was the big one. Took her immediately. They called time of death already."

I shut my eyes against her words and then felt her cold fingers on my arm. "I'm sorry."

I waited until the space had cleared before I gathered enough courage to step inside. There were certain procedures that needed to be followed after a death, and a nurse was left in the room to carry them out.

When I rounded the white curtain to her bed, it felt surreal to see her so lifeless. So spiritless. So still.

Her eyes were closed, her arms tucked beneath the sheets, already in prep mode. Her face was free of worry and pain. Almost peaceful. Almost.

I noticed a person slumped in a chair, clutching a bouquet of tulips. *Mr. Jackson.* I'd forgotten he was still here. He must have alerted them to the emergency.

I sat down beside him in the cream plastic chair, and he took a deep, shuddering breath.

At first I didn't know what to say to him. What could I possibly articulate when the woman he had spent his life with was lying dead before him?

"She loved you fiercely, you know." My voice sounded vacant and small. "She . . . she was the best kind of person. I'm grateful to have known her."

A sob escaped his lips, and it reverberated in my chest, creating a gaping hole.

"I don't know what I'm going to do without her."

The air whooshed right out of me.

Was this the flip side of love?

You created a life with someone—shared your whole heart, your whole soul—and then one day, they left you. It was a harsh and brutal kind of reality.

And I wasn't convinced it was worth it.

To open yourself up to someone, only to be left with a cavernous wound.

Mr. Jackson cleared his throat and looked at his wife. His eyes were red, his brown skin splotchy, but his voice was strong. "But I wouldn't take back one day of our forty years together. Not one damn day. Do you hear me, Louise?"

He was no longer talking to me, and I was glued to my seat, entranced by his words. "You made my life worth living. You made it *matter*. You made it infinitely better." His voice cracked on those last words, and he tucked his head into his hand.

I waited next to him as he sobbed into his fingers and then wiped his cheeks with a Kleenex. The nurse cleared the room, allowing for privacy. She patted my shoulder on her way out.

Mr. Jackson stood up and inched toward his wife. Placing the tulips on the pillow above her, he kissed her forehead. "I know I'll see you again. I have to believe that. God wouldn't be that cruel, to take you from me without the hope of our reunion."

I pinched my eyes closed as a tear escaped.

I already knew what it felt like to be without Bennett. But that paled in comparison to what Mr. Jackson was going through. And now I'd be without Mrs. Jackson, too. Coming to work would be difficult for a long damn time, like having a cloud hovering over my head, raining sadness over me.

But I could hear her voice in my head, urging me to move on, to live my life, to stop being so damn sad.

Just then Mr. and Mrs. Jackson's children burst into the room and gathered around their father.

Tears and hugs, grief and love.

All combined in a circle of limbs and heads and hearts.

# CHAPTER TWENTY-FIVE

Backing out of Mrs. Jackson's room, I recited my own silent and painful good-bye.

I gathered my flowers and coat and walked home in a numb fog.

I considered Mr. Jackson's words. Making a life with someone was all-encompassing.

You either took a chance or put up road blocks.

Whichever way, you were taking a risk, gambling with fate.

Toying with your own happiness.

My phone buzzed with a text.

Ella: What's new?

Me: Mrs. Jackson died today. I can't believe she's gone. On my way home now.

Ella: I'm so sorry. I'll meet you at your place.

Ella came bearing Chinese food. She let me cry on her

shoulder over a bottle of wine. She knew how fond I'd grown of Mrs. Jackson and how the lady had slowly infiltrated my life. Mrs. Jackson made me question my ideals, as if she were a reflection of the person I hoped to become, despite my upbringing, my hardened heart, and my meaningless flings.

We ate ice cream and watched bad TV, and I told her everything.

About my tattoo, making up with Bennett, making love, *feeling* love.

And it felt good. To let someone in.

"For whatever it's worth, I'm proud of you, bitch," Ella said, throwing away our empty food containers.

"For what?" I asked before taking the final sip from my wineglass.

"I've known you a long-ass time," she said, topping off our glasses and then sitting back down. "Your life can be divided into a before and after period."

I kept my mouth shut, reflecting on her words.

"The Avery *before* Tim was fun, optimistic even, despite your mother not really acting like much of a parent most of the time. Even after your grandma died, you still seemed to have hope about the future."

I did. I missed my grandma desperately, but she made me want something better for myself.

"The Avery *after* Tim was hardened, broken, and closed off. And I got it. God, I *so* got it." She adjusted herself on the couch in order to face me better. "Despite all of that, you still tried to have some fun. It's just . . . the fun was different."

"Different how?"

"Like you were just filling a need, taking care of business."

I nodded because she was right. So right. About all of it. I had just been going through the motions, except when it came to school, my job, and Adam.

"First," I said, "I hate that you just marked my life with that bastard's name."

"Why *not* say his name out loud?" she asked. "You want him to remain anonymous? Let's *out* that asshole! Tim! Tim! Tim! The fucking bastard!"

I laughed while taking another sip and almost choked on my wine.

"Second," I said, after clearing my throat several times, "*your* life could be marked by a before and after, too, my dear bitch-ass friend."

Ella's eyes darkened at the reminder of her brother's death, and I grabbed for her hand.

"But shit, I admire how you handled it, Ella. I wish I'd been more like you. You got help and never changed who you were," I said. "I mean, *I* saw how you were different, because I've known you for so long, but you didn't let it . . . take you down."

"I love you, asshead." Ella grabbed me for a tight hug. "Thank you for finally letting me in. Promise you won't shut me out again. Or Bennett. Or anybody."

She was right. I had closed myself off in ways even I hadn't realized.

"Promise," I said, but still I hoped I could hold up my end of the bargain.

Besides, if I *hadn't* promised, Mrs. Jackson might've kicked my ass the next time she got ahold of me.

When I next looked at the time it was already nine o'clock. I realized Bennett would've been home for a couple of hours by now.

And I had never called him.

I never responded to his flowers and note.

I never invited him over.

Looked like I fucked up again.

I put my head in my hands, my brain abuzz with worry.

All at once there was a knock on my door. My stomach bunched into a hard ball. I was afraid it was Bennett coming over to give me a piece of his mind.

To tell me I'd hurt him again.

Ella answered the door and let him inside. My heart strained against my rib cage. I wanted to race into his arms and push him away at the same time. My emotions were all over the map.

I wanted him so badly that it terrified the hell out of me.

"Hey." He stood in front of me, and my fingers tangled in the afghan draped across my legs. I couldn't look at him. If I saw his eyes I'd find hurt, pain, anger.

But if I looked deeply enough, I'd also find love. The flip side of fear, Mrs. Jackson had said.

Bennett knelt down and lifted my chin with his thumb.

My gaze slid up to meet his. His eyes were soft and concerned, not angry.

"Bennett, I'm sorry, I . . ."

"I'm here to relieve Ella," he said. "She called and told me what happened. We agreed to do a shift change at nine o'clock."

I stared at Ella, confusion in my eyes.

"That's right, dill weed," Ella said, her voice smug. "Now make room for him and let him feed you some more ice cream."

I looked between Bennett and Ella, my heart swelling tenfold.

She grabbed her coat, kissed my cheek, and headed for the door. "You're in good hands now." And then she was gone.

Bennett immediately wrapped me up in a hug. "I'm so sorry you lost your friend. I want to be here for you tonight."

I was so relieved that he wasn't mad or hurt.

He wasn't pushing me to think or talk about anything that happened today or yesterday.

He understood that I was grieving and left it at that.

"Bennett, I wanted to call you, tell you those flowers were amazing, and invite you over."

"Shhhh . . ." he said, wrapping us in the blanket. "We have plenty of time to talk about all of that. For now, let's just be together."

We lay on the couch, staring into each other's eyes, saying nothing and everything all at once.

I told him stories about Mrs. Jackson, and how she was a pain in the ass, but also pushed me to be a better person. Kind of like what Bennett had been doing. Without him even realizing it. He was just being him. Loving me purely. Easily. Incredibly.

Later, we retreated to my bedroom to watch bad reality TV, and he held me all night.

Before we drifted off to sleep, he whispered in my ear, "Avery, I want us to work through the sad and hard parts together. To always find our way back to each other."

. . .

The next morning I woke with the initial shock and sting of losing someone.

But underneath the surface of my raw emotions were the underpinnings of truth.

Of love. Of friendship. Of hope.

As I lay awake in Bennett's arms and listened to his soft breaths, my eyes focused in on his drawing across the room. I considered his bedtime confession and wondered if in fact we *had* weeded through all that baggage in our paths and finally found a way to each other.

We both had class that morning, but agreed to meet back at my place in the afternoon. Neither of us was scheduled to work, and we wanted desperately to spend the day together.

I called my supervisor to ask if she'd heard about any of the funeral arrangements for Mrs. Jackson and whether I could have the time off to attend. She assured me that I could.

Before we hung up, she said, "You know, every one of us has had a Mrs. Jackson in our lives. A person we've grown close to, despite trying not to. And it's a good thing. In fact, it's a necessary part of life. It means we're human, Avery."

Bennett and I went out for a late lunch and then tooled around the local art museum together. He showed me his favorite artists and helped me appreciate some of their earlier works.

It was comforting to be with him. To do normal things with him. To start folding him into my life.

We made love that night on my terms. I was on top, and it was fast and frantic, soft and sexy, and everything in between. Afterward, we lay wrapped up in each other's arms.

"I'm not sure I'll ever tire of this," Bennett said, still

winded. His hand skated over my breasts, to my stomach, to my thighs, making me quiver with need again.

And for the first time in years, I felt a flicker of joy.

Incandescent. Radiating inside me and through me.

His fingers reached for my face, and he kissed me slow and melting, his tongue tangling with mine in a way that felt so private. So profound. So right.

# CHAPTER TWENTY-SIX

Bennett and I were inseparable the following week. He attended Mrs. Jackson's funeral service with me, politely introducing himself and shaking family members' hands.

Her daughter, Star, seemed to know more about me than I thought she had, which comforted me. It cemented the idea in place that Mrs. Jackson was as fond of me as I was of her.

At the wake, she whispered, "Bennett seems like a good man. Momma would have liked him."

Bennett surprised me by bringing a bouquet of daisies to the cemetery. We stood with Mrs. Jackson's family as everyone departed, throwing the long stems onto her casket, one by one.

Work that week had been tough. A new resident had already taken Mrs. Jackson's bed, as if trying to wipe clean the memory of her. But she'd always be with me.

Her kind and wise words. Her confidence and biting humor.

The new resident was a crotchety old man named Mr. Smith, and I snickered every time he barked an order as I crossed into the room. I figured Mrs. Jackson would get a kick out of it, too.

*You're trying to make me miss you, aren't you?*

And then Bennett drove with me to Mom's court hearing. He asked if he could tag along, and at first I wasn't sure how I felt about that. It was as if he were inserting himself into my past and all its ugly secrets.

He had taken the morning off work and said he wanted to come to the courthouse for moral support—that he'd wait in the car or the lobby for me.

He knew there was the possibility that Tim would be there. The defendant had the right to attend the hearing. If he didn't show, he'd still be served the paperwork.

As we pulled into my mother's driveway, my palms became slick on the steering wheel. Adam was at school, Bennett would be meeting Mom for the first time, and my queasy stomach refused to cooperate.

I'd already met Bennett's family, and we definitely shared similar backgrounds. But I was afraid he'd uncover just how fucked-up my reality was once he met my mother.

Mom was chain-smoking at the kitchen table when we stepped inside. Her fingers were shaking, and shadows had formed below her eyes, alerting me that this decision had taken its toll.

"Mom, this is Bennett." I refrained from saying that he was my boyfriend. I was just getting used to that idea. But she knew the deal. I had never brought any guys around before.

"It's nice to finally meet you, Ms. Michaels." Bennett cleared his throat and gave a small smile.

"You, too." I could see Mom checking him out, her gaze wandering up and down his body as I clenched my teeth.

He was half her age and still she thought she could act that way. She needed to stop thinking I was her competition, and after today I'd damn well let her know it.

But for now, before this hearing, I'd let it go.

"Ready, Mom?"

Bennett had been teetering in the doorway, hands deep in his front pockets, and he looked relieved that her scrutiny of him would be ending.

"As ready as I'll ever be." As she stood up, I realized she was wearing a modest blue dress, and I was thankful that none of her cleavage was showing. "It'll be hard to face him if he shows up."

"Hard for both of us, Mom."

Bennett squeezed my hand as we headed out the door.

Bennett drove my car and dropped us off at the front entrance of the courthouse. Said he'd park and join us in the hall.

Mom exited the backseat and started to head inside. She had retained one of her lawyer exes to help her through the proceedings and was meeting him before the hearing. She had been with Lance for a few months a couple of years ago, and even got a used car out of the deal. Too bad he'd been married at the time. I wondered how she'd be paying him this time.

As my hand reached for the door handle, Bennett pulled me into a kiss. It was sweet and reassuring, but still warmed my belly, despite the enormity of the situation.

"Good luck, baby," he whispered in my ear. "You were strong back then, and you're even tougher now."

My stomach flipped somersaults all the way up the stone courthouse stairs. It was an old historical building in the center of town, and I'd visited once with Gavin when he met his father there about excessive parking tickets. Gavin was always leaving his car at empty meters across town, and it had finally caught up to him. Like Tim, Gavin also had a little of that overconfidence gene in him, being the mayor's son. I couldn't totally blame him for it. It was just how he was raised.

But from what I could gather about Tim, his boldness was all DNA, and being on the police force had only helped bolster that inflated opinion of himself.

Mom had already checked in and was meeting with her lawyer friend, who was dressed sharply in a shiny black suit and red tie. I sat down beside her on the cold wooden bench and looked around, hoping not to lock eyes with Tim. I was dressed in simple black pants and a blouse, with flat shoes. If he showed up, I wanted him to know I was a grown-ass woman, not the scared teen he'd known four years ago.

The place overflowed with people like us, waiting for their cases to go before the judge, and I figured we were in for a long morning.

When it was finally our turn, I was thankful that we had gone to the police station and filed the report the day after Tim assaulted Mom. The pictures of her bruises were on file, and Lance assured us it would be a clear case in our favor.

With my permission, Mom had also disclosed that Tim had assaulted me years ago, but Lance was confident that extraneous evidence to Mom's case would probably be unnecessary.

He had been right.

The judge fairly quickly granted a permanent restraining order, good for five years.

Bennett was waiting in the lobby as we exited the wooden doors, and I told him the news.

His jaw remained locked. "Was *he* in there with you?"

I shook my head. Tim had never shown his face, and I breathed a sigh of relief, despite the small part of me that wanted to see the bastard. Over the years, I had built him up in my mind to be a monster. I had only been sixteen, and I figured he might look quite different to me now.

Mom had to wait at the courthouse for an official copy of the document to keep in her possession should she ever need to call the police. She assured me that Lance would drive her home after they had gone to lunch to celebrate.

I *bet* they'd celebrate.

"I wanted to make sure we called a locksmith before I left today, Mom." Of course she hadn't done it yet. How could she still be so oblivious about her own safety?

She looked down, biting her lip. "Oh, um, Lance said he knew a good locksmith and would make the call for me."

I sighed. *Here we go again. Eager for a man to call all the shots.*

But maybe I couldn't blame her. Wasn't she just hoping for someone to take care of her heart, too? I thought back to Bennett's tattoo poem and the idea of disappearing for love. I just hoped she got it right someday.

Bennett had left to pull the car around, so I stepped outside and walked toward the side street to make the pickup easier for him. The turnaround in front of the courthouse was jam-packed with cars.

As I stood on the corner waiting, I felt the hairs rise on the back of my neck. Maybe it was his heavy breaths or the way he cleared his throat, but I sensed him there before I even laid eyes on him.

His voice was one forever etched in my nightmares. "You look the same as you always did."

My heart thundered in my chest as I turned around to face him. Tim looked smaller somehow, less imposing. His hair was graying and he had a heavier beard. I realized it was *me* who had grown up, and *he* was the one who'd stayed exactly the same.

He stepped closer, and I could feel his emotions rolling off of him—excitement, arrogance, desire. I tried not to shudder.

Instead I found my voice. "So do you, Tim. Like a child predator. An abuser of women. You *disgust* me."

His top lip curled, and I took a step back, not wanting him to see me flinch.

"So what happened, you too much of a wimp-ass to show up at your own hearing?"

"My lawyer advised me that it wouldn't matter whether I showed or not. Your mother had a strong enough case against me."

"So then why are you here?"

"On the off chance that *you'd* be here and I could finally lay my eyes on you."

My stomach rolled and lurched as his gaze became hooded.

"I've missed you, Avery."

Had we not been on a crowded street corner I might have turned and fled. I was that certain he would have tried to take me down right then and there and finally have his way with me.

But not before I put up a damn good fight. I balled my fists and stood my ground.

"Your mother might have a restraining order against me," he said, leaning over. So close. *Too close.* "But you don't. No reason I can't get as close to you as I want."

Holy fuck. He was threatening me. Saying he'd come after me. Find me.

My mind drew a blank and all I saw were swirls of black and gray behind my eyelids as terror slowly consumed me.

I heard a grunt and a car door slam. "Avery?"

Tim backed away and then crossed the street in a rush.

Bennett grabbed hold of my shoulders and lightly shook me. "Avery, look at me. Who was that?"

"What?" My mind was hazy with fear and disbelief.

"Who the fuck was that, Avery?"

"T . . . Tim," I mumbled. "That was Tim."

Bennett's eyes widened right before he turned and raced across the street to follow him.

What the hell was he doing?

"Hey!" he yelled, and I spotted Tim, who was halfway down the block, freeze in place.

I had never seen Bennett so full of rage. It scared the shit out of me. It was enough to get my legs moving again. I crossed the street to chase after him.

Bennett was still yelling, his hands flying in the air, and Tim just stood there, a menacing smirk hanging from his lips.

"You motherfucker." Bennett inched closer to him. "You will never lay another hand on her, you hear me?"

Then I saw Bennett's fist clench and his arm fly forward as it crushed against Tim's jaw.

"Bennett, no! Wait!" I was terrified of what Tim would be capable of.

Tim yanked Bennett's legs out from under him, and suddenly they were both on the ground wrestling and landing punches. Bennett definitely had the height, weight, and raw emotion. But Tim thought he was cunning and invincible, and I knew that was a deadly combination.

"Bennett, stop. Let him go. We can handle this another way." In fact, I was marching straight back into that courthouse and filing my own restraining order.

The sound of my voice momentarily immobilized Bennett, giving Tim the upper hand. He knelt over Bennett, his fist crashing into his stomach.

Blood was smeared on Tim's face and on Bennett's shirt and hands. I couldn't tell whether it was coming from Tim's nose or Bennett's cheek.

Bennett looked so defenseless lying on the ground, and something snapped in the very center of me. This asshole was not going to hurt the person I loved.

Using all the focus I could muster, I turned sideways and rotated my knee, making sure the upper part of my foot would make contact. A growl escaped my lips right before I landed a perfectly hard roundhouse kick to Tim's back. I heard a crack and he went down, groaning.

Kickboxing classes had finally paid off.

"Get up, please." I pulled Bennett to a sitting position and whispered to him, "Let Tim leave, trust me. I'll handle this legally."

Tim was already on his knees, and Bennett and I backed away to allow him room. An audience had formed across the street, and I was sure the cops would be there any moment to arrest them both. No question Tim would file assault charges against Bennett and we'd be in a world of trouble.

Tim stood up and limped a couple steps backward. I was hoping I'd cracked a rib or two. But he'd never give me the satisfaction of showing it.

"Get the fuck out of my sight, Tim. Before the cops come," I snarled. I wanted him to believe I was letting this go. Otherwise, he'd figure out a new way to hurt us. "He won't touch you again."

His face was emotionless except for the tick in his jaw. We watched as he hobbled down the street and around the corner, only looking back once.

# CHAPTER TWENTY-SEVEN

My body sagged against Bennett and he folded me into his arms.

"Oh my God, are you okay?" I asked. I was so relieved that he hadn't come away limping. "You shouldn't have gone after him like that."

"Avery, listen to me." His breath was heavy as he held me close. "I recognize him."

I pulled back to look at him. "What do you mean?"

"It was him," he said, eyes wide. "He tried breaking into your window that night. I'm sure of it."

I stumbled as my legs gave way, and Bennett scooped me into his arms.

Tim was going to rape me that night. And Bennett had saved me.

Bennett deposited me in the passenger seat of my car as I panted for air. He used my phone to call my mom.

She and Lance rushed outside and Bennett explained what

had transpired. Mom sat down hard on the curb and put her head in her hands.

Lance advised me to file a restraining order and police report immediately. I didn't dispute him.

Then he was on his cell phone, calling in a favor to a judge. He also called his contact at the police station.

While he was on hold he flipped the phone away from his mouth. "Bennett, you were smart not to say anything in front of Tim about the break-in."

Bennett nodded. He had used good judgment even in a state of rage.

"If he had known you recognized him, he might have fled. But I'm confident he'll be picked up fairly quickly and charged. His case had already been flagged by the mayor," Lance said, looking at me.

I felt gratitude to Gavin for helping me in that small way, when he didn't even have to.

"As long as you're willing to identify him in a lineup?" Lance asked.

"Of course," Bennett said.

"How do we know he won't run now?" Mom asked, her eyes laced with fear.

"I guess there's still that possibility," I said finally. "But I made it seem like we didn't want any more trouble. Just hope he bought it."

Mom knelt in front of me and grabbed my hands. "I'm so sorry, baby. About everything."

I had finally gotten my apology, on a street corner, in the middle of all of this chaos. The relief I felt overwhelmed my senses, and I couldn't control the tears leaking from my eyes.

Or stop my hands from shaking as my mother grasped them in hers. "I know you are, Mom."

Lance accompanied us to file the reports and used his contacts to expedite the order. The detective on the case said they had Tim's home and work addresses and that he was bound to show up one place or the other today. Mom also provided the names of some local bars he frequented, which was helpful, but made me roll my eyes.

After all was said and done, Bennett drove us home. Blood was still caked to his hair and shirt. But other than the bruise forming above his cheekbone, he only admitted to feeling sore. He wouldn't even let me drive.

I was so thankful that he wasn't more hurt. And I prayed the whole way home that Tim would be picked up soon. Lance assured us that our local police department was on alert and would increase security on our street.

I was pretty sure I'd only feel safe if I moved out of my building, but in the meantime, I needed to take one day at a time. One hour at a time.

It felt like I'd never rid Tim from my life. And now Bennett was undeniably involved. What a huge-ass mess.

Bennett parked in the back lot and we headed inside.

"Let's get your stuff. You're staying with me tonight, and every night, until I know it's safe," Bennett said. I didn't argue the point. I knew he was right. He'd also called our landlord on the way home and alerted him of the situation.

While I was in my room gathering clean clothes, I avoided looking at that same window that Tim had attempted to break through. I figured my life would look starkly different right then had Bennett not come home when he did that night.

I shut off my bedroom light and was headed toward the living room when I got a call from Lance. I put him on speakerphone.

"They've got him," he said, out of breath. I sank down on the edge of the couch. "Snatched him at his job. Boss said he had gotten there late because of some fractured ribs."

Bennett kissed my forehead, and I couldn't help allowing a small smile.

"Oh my God." I laid my head back against the cushions, relief coursing through me. "Thank you for all of your help, Lance."

"Wait, Avery, there's more."

Bennett stopped pacing and looked at me, concern in his eyes.

"O . . . kay." I braced my fist to my knee.

"There was a warrant out for his arrest in another county . . . for attempted rape."

Bennett was immediately next to me, rubbing my shoulders while I inhaled a sharp lungful of air.

"You . . . you're kidding."

I guess I had always known in the back of my mind that I couldn't have been the only one. Someone else out there had told. They were braver than I was. And in that moment I said a silent thank-you to whoever that girl was.

I hoped against hope that she had had the support and trust and love that I had never had.

Until now.

"There's still a chance he could get out on bail," Lance said as reality slammed back into me. "But if these charges stick, he'll be going away for a long time."

I couldn't stop the fat trails of tears coursing down my face. "Thank you again for everything, Lance."

"You're very welcome. If we got another bastard off the street, then I've done my job."

I sat up and took a deep breath. "Is Mom there with you?"

"Um, yeah," he said, awkwardly. I pictured him at our kitchen table, Mom already whipping up dinner, like she'd done for him a couple years ago. "Yeah, she is."

"Can you put her on the phone for a minute?"

"Of course."

"Oh, and, Lance? One more thing." I stood up and stared out the window at the street lamps flashing on. "Treat my momma right."

I looked back at Bennett, shocked by my own declaration.

But he got it. He understood why I'd said it.

A ghost of a smile touched his lips, and he winked.

# CHAPTER TWENTY-EIGHT

After I chatted with my mom for five minutes more and asked her to have Adam call me, Bennett and I went up to the fifth floor.

He wanted me with him, and I needed to be there, too. My apartment just didn't feel right, for tonight. It was filled with coiled shadows, whispered threats, and murky recollections.

I'd rather work through all of those emotions in the daytime, when I could recall all the brighter and sweeter memories I'd created in my first-floor unit.

I placed my overnight bag in his room while he thirstily guzzled a tall glass of water in his kitchen. He looked exhausted and worn, and I had the strong urge to take care of him.

"Let's go," I said. "I'm putting you in the shower."

We both undressed and stood beneath the stream of hot water. I carefully shampooed the blood out of Bennett's hair, checking for any other injuries. Then I washed his body, delicately stroking the washcloth around the bruise that had formed on his rib cage.

"I can't believe you did that for me," I said.

I was talking about several things at once. The potential break-in. The fight with Tim. Driving to court with me in the first place that morning.

"Nobody's going to harm one hair on your precious head, if I have anything to do with it," he said. "Although you certainly kicked the shit out of Tim. He didn't know *what* hit him."

I smiled and leaned my head into his chest, feeling the water wash down my back as he rinsed shampoo from my hair.

"I want you in my life for a very long time," Bennett said, lifting my face with his hands. "Avery, I lo—"

I sealed my mouth over his before he could get the words out. He hadn't told me he loved me since that note with the flowers. Maybe he'd been waiting for me to say it back. Maybe he didn't want to overwhelm or rush me.

But I didn't need to hear the words fall from his lips right then. I already knew how he felt. He had already showed me *plenty* today.

Our kiss turned passionate—all lips and tongue and slick bodies. His hardness bumped against my stomach, sending a shock wave through me.

I reached down, stroked him lightly, and felt him throb between my fingers.

"Let me take care of you." I knelt down and flicked my tongue against his skin.

"God, Avery," he groaned.

Just as my lips were sealing around his tip, he reached for

my arms and pulled me up. His eyes were dark—so dark—with need.

"I want to feel connected to you," he growled against my lips. "I need to be inside you. *Right now.*"

His gruff voice sent a path of gooseflesh between my thighs. I reached for one of the condoms that he now stored in his bathroom drawer and helped wrap it over his taut skin.

He lifted me up as if I weighed nothing at all. Like he didn't have any bruised ribs. I wrapped my legs around his waist, and he pinned me against the shower wall.

He thrust into me, whipping all lucid thought out of my head. It was just him and me in our own little perfect bubble.

And it felt so amazingly right, when everything that had happened that day felt so infuriatingly wrong.

His grip tightened on my thighs as he nestled himself deeper. My head fell back against the cool tiles, and I moaned out his name.

"Baby," he whispered, and then gave me a slow and molten kiss that stole my breath away. All of my muscles went liquid, and I was thankful that he was holding me up.

When he moved against me, it wasn't with the hungry need I'd anticipated, given his haste to make love. It was with a maddening fluidity that made me shudder against him.

A yearning flickered inside my chest and radiated outward. Nothing in the world mattered except the drugging rhythm of his body and the soothing murmur of his voice.

A cry wrenched from my throat and my muscles jerked as he pushed me higher against the wall and drove himself in more deeply.

My pleasure turned into a raging inferno as my breath caught and my mouth fell open. "Oh God, Bennett. Yes."

We both came fast and hard, like we had poured all of the turmoil and chaos of the day into each other.

Afterward, we lay on his bed kissing, wrapped in nothing more than his soft and warm sheets.

I didn't know what was going to happen after today. There was uncertainty and confusion and a good amount of fear.

But at that moment I was so glad to be enveloped in the arms of this beautiful man who I cared for unfathomably.

Who would never make me feel unsafe or invisible.

Who would protect my heart and my body.

If only I'd let him.

I broke out of a kiss to catch my breath and traced my fingers over his swollen cheek.

Then my lips found his ear. "Ask me what I'm feeling right now."

"In five words or less?" he said, a smile quirking his lips.

I kissed his forehead. "Of course."

He cleared his throat. "Ms. Michaels, please tell me what you're feeling this very instant in five words or less. And no cheating."

I sat up and straddled him, my lips close to his, our eyes locked in one long, unblinking look.

"Fierce . . . intense . . . toe-curling . . . *love*."

And then I poured all of those words into a kiss, leaving him panting and breathless.

Making sure he felt all of my truths to the very depths of his heart.

And in all the spaces between.

# ACKNOWLEDGMENTS

First, I need to thank my agent, Sara Megibow, whose business savvy, professionalism, support, and positive attitude makes me realize how lucky I am to have her in my corner.

To the entire Penguin team, and especially to my editor, Jesse Feldman, who not only read my book and instantly loved it—but also immediately *got* it. Got the story. Got me. And through amazing edits, made the book better.

To K. M. Walton, for showing me the ropes and then lighting the path for me to follow behind. You are by far one of the most compassionate and generous human beings I have ever known.

To Stina Lindenblatt, for your daily and multilayered doses of humor and reality. For being my cheerleader and becoming a trusted friend. You make the perfect "work spouse."

To Alina, Deb, Lindsay, Lydia, Elaine, Lola, Kate, and Stina, for reading this book, believing in it, and cheering me on.

To the following authors who were so generous with advice and support of my debut: Roni Loren, Julianna Stone,

Rachel Harris, Monica Murphy, Lauren Blakely, and A. L. Jackson.

To the amazing poet Anna Peters, who so graciously allowed me to use her poem "Forget Me Not." Without question, it inspired me and helped deepen the romance between Avery and Bennett.

To my family in Ohio (Alina, Elaine, Terri, Dwayne, Michelle, Marcus, Nick, Donny, Christa), in Florida (Joan and George aka "Mom and Dad"), and in Michigan (Connie, Paul, Bryan, Stacie, Niki, Scott, Lisa, and Larry) for all of your love, help, and support.

To my friends: Denise, Deb, Sussan (also known as my besties for life), I love you gals to pieces. To Dani, Amy, Katie, Monica, Janice, and Melissa. Where would I be without all of your smiles, shoulders, and bottles of wine?

To Alina—what can I say about a sister who is also a best friend? You are that bright and steady star in the sky that I always gravitate toward. Don't know what I'd do without you.

To my Twitter, Blogger, and Facebook communities. Writing doesn't feel so solitary when you have a sense of kinship online.

To the readers who picked up this book and took a chance. And to the book reviewers out there. So much gratitude.

This has been such an exciting and crazy-busy time in my life. A dream come true. I hope to God I didn't forget to thank anybody. Please know how much I appreciate all of you.

And last, to Greg and Evan. You are my whole world and I adore you unquestionably. You make me want to be a better human being. Thank you for showing me what unconditional love and romance are all about.

Photo by Elaine M. Johnson

**Christina Lee** lives outside of Cleveland with her husband and son—her two favorite guys. She's addicted to lip gloss and salted caramel everything. Reading has always been her favorite pastime, so creating imaginary worlds has become a dream job. She also owns her own jewelry business, where she hand-stamps meaningful words or letters onto silver for her customers. She loves to hear from her readers.

CONNECT ONLINE

christinalee.net

Read on for a sneak peek from the second book in
Christina Lee's Between Breaths series,

*BEFORE YOU BREAK*

Available wherever e-books are sold and
coming in paperback from New American Library in October.

..........................................................................................

# ELLA

This was so embarrassing. I was sick to my stomach but thankful that I hadn't actually puked my brains out. Nothing like blowing chunks in front of one of Joel's frat buddies.

"I'm okay," I said, the words like cotton in my mouth. My head was pounding like a steel drum band. "Th-thanks for asking."

Then I felt the heat of Quinn's body and heard his soft voice near my ear. "Ella, you need to cover up in case some drunk-ass busts in here and sees you."

*Like him?* Except he didn't seem drunk at all. He sounded . . . concerned.

I tried shrugging my shoulders but I wasn't even sure if they'd moved. Before I had time to register my next thought, I felt his rough hands tug down my T-shirt. And then he took a quick step back, like he was afraid I'd think he was fondling me or something.

I laid my cheek against the toilet seat, praying nothing gross was stuck to it, while the room spun around me. Somehow I didn't even care. I just needed my stomach to stop sloshing around and my brain to stop feeling like sludge.

Why the hell had I downed that last shot and then chased it back with a beer?

Oh yeah, because my boyfriend was an asshole and had made me feel like I wasn't even in the room. Maybe it was time I started being more truthful with myself *and* with Joel. Tell him how he made me feel and how he needed to cut that crap out. I didn't know why I'd let things that bothered me go for so long.

"I'll wet a washcloth," Quinn said. I heard the faucet turn on and a vanity drawer slide open. "Might make you feel better."

Before I could protest, Quinn clunked down on the tile behind me, and passed me the wet towel. My hand reached back but I had trouble grasping it; I was that squeamish. Instead, a low groan came out of my mouth.

"I'm gonna help you." His voice was low and raspy, and right then and there I wished this strange meeting were under different circumstances. That I could actually lift my head and look at him. Figure out what he might be thinking. Discover the true color of his eyes. Were they green or copper or a mix of both? Had he thrown on his university ball cap again or was his russet hair a mess of tangles?

I was pretty sure I didn't need anyone babying me, especially not mysterious Quinn. But I supposed it could have been worse. Jimmy, who always partied hard, might have tried to cop a feel alone in here with me. I didn't get that impression from Quinn. He was handsome and broody. It always seemed like he had a lot on his mind. Like he was pretty serious about baseball and school. And not about girls or partying.

"Okay?" he whispered. He was waiting on permission to touch me again. And, God, I appreciated that about him.

"Yeah," I said, another wave of nausea rolling over me. I swallowed the warm bile in the back of my throat and squeezed my eyes shut.

I felt Quinn's hot fingers lift up my hair and then smooth it from my shoulders. I attempted to hold in a shiver. His heat mixed with my clammy skin made my stomach do weird flips. Next, I felt the cool cloth against the nape of my neck and I let out a deep sigh. It soothed and cooled my skin.

"If you raise your head, I can wipe your forehead, too."

"N-not sure if I can yet." I swallowed back my nausea.

I felt his breath against my cheek. "Let me do it."

Why did this suddenly feel too damned intimate? I prayed that I smelled halfway decent and that my makeup was still intact and not beneath my eyes. I'd never been this up close and personal with Quinn and I felt like he could see all of my flaws. Hell, he'd already seen my ass. I wasn't petite like my two best girls. I had curves. Curves that Joel used to appreciate.

The question was, why did I care?

Quinn was only being nice and I was in no state to think it through more clearly. "Okay."

His large and rough palm slipped beneath my cheek and gently lifted my head. He swiped the cool cloth over my forehead and then down the sides of my face.

"Hmmmm . . . so good." I sounded ridiculous, but I couldn't help it. It was nice being taken care of, even if it was by a virtual stranger. A cute, mysterious stranger.

"Can you sit up yet?" he asked, sounding a little breathless. "I can help you back to Joel's room if you want."

I shook my head a little too forcefully, causing me to pitch forward and dry-heave again. I was suddenly glad I hadn't eaten any dinner. It might have ended up in Quinn's lap.

"Shoot." I lay down with my cheek against the cool tile floor. I could feel my T-shirt rising above my hips again, but again, I just didn't care. Besides, he'd already seen it all. "I'm just going to stay here for a while."

I listened to him inhale a lungful of air and then release it quickly. "Um, okay. I'm gonna bolt."

I heard him stand and mutter, *"Fucking Joel,"* under his breath. "But I don't like the idea of you being in here all night. I'm gonna check on you again in a little bit."

"Wh-why wouldn't you want me in here?" I asked. "What's the big deal? I'll be fine."

"Ella, your shirt's riding up again." I heard him struggling for words. "You're in a house full of horny drunk guys and you can't stand up long enough to lock the door behind me."

*Crap. I hadn't thought of it like that.*

"But everyone knows me," I said, with some effort. "I'm Joel's girlfriend."

"Sure." He took a deep breath like he was contemplating saying something else. And then I heard him pace once, then twice. "No offense, Ella, but Joel doesn't exactly give the guys the impression that you're off-limits. Not like Brian does with

286

Tracey. Not like I'd do . . ." Breathe in. Breathe out. "Never mind."

His words stung. But I wanted him to tell me more. To say everything. "No, don't stop. Finish what you were going to say."

"No, I'd better not." I heard his hollow steps on the tile floor. "I should go."

"Wait. Don't go yet." What was I even saying? "Can you . . . can you wet that washcloth again?"

Why would I want Quinn to stay if I hardly even knew him? And why did he make me feel so protected, more than Joel ever did?

"Sure," Quinn said, and then swore under his breath. "But, Ella, you've got to pull your shirt down."

My eyes flew open. He sounded like he was struggling to keep himself together. To not have naughty thoughts about me. A strange emotion jammed in my chest. I was affecting have-nothing-to-do-with-girls Quinn? I'll admit, I was curious about his answers when the guys were grilling him at the poker table. Why *was* he never with any girls?

My hands struggled with my T-shirt. "Is that better?"

I was asking him to look at my ass again? Brilliant.

He let out a shaky breath. "Yeah, better."

I heard him run the faucet and then sit back down. "Ready?"

"Yes, please."

He shifted my hair over my shoulder again and then I shivered against the coolness of the cloth. "Hmmm . . . feels nice."

I felt Quinn's fingers shaking and I wondered what the hell was wrong with him.

"Quinn . . ." I rasped out. He didn't answer me, just remained silent, but I could hear his harsh breaths, like it was taking some effort to contain them. Had I done something to upset him? Did he wish he hadn't stayed?

"I'm sorry. I probably shouldn't have asked you to stay. I just . . ." I struggled to get my thoughts out. "You can leave now. I'll be okay. You sound—"

"No, I'm cool," he said, and his fingers relaxed against my neck. We stayed quiet for another couple of minutes; the only sound was our breath. It was a comfortable silence and I was glad to not be alone. He dabbed at my forehead and cheeks and then put the cloth back on my neck.

I wanted so badly to continue our conversation from before but I didn't know him or his moods. Would he get mad if I pushed him about it?

"Quinn. Would you mind . . . if I asked you to finish what you were saying . . . um . . . before?"

"I shouldn't have talked about Joel like that," he said in a rush.

"Things haven't been right between Joel and me for weeks. And I'm sure it shows," I said, swallowing several times. "I guess I keep hoping we can work it out, make it what it once was."

"Which was what?" he mumbled.

"What do you mean?"

"I mean, what made it special?" His voice was low, soft. "What did you guys have . . . that's now lost?"

There was no sarcasm in his voice. Only sincerity. Honesty. Curiosity.

It made me wonder how many relationships he'd been in.

Made me want to lift my head and see whether there was any emotion in his eyes. But I didn't want to risk puking on him.

All I had to go by was the sound of his voice.

# QUINN

"I don't know," she said, like she was thinking it through out loud. "Maybe it just felt like something more."

And then she went still, so I waited for her to finish her thought. I wanted to tell her that maybe Joel was the kind of guy who only made girls feel like there was something more, but I didn't want to hurt her feelings.

It's not like I knew anyway—I wasn't inside Joel's head. Maybe he'd kept her around as long as he had because they had something special together. Maybe he thought he'd try to take it to the next level. More serious than he'd ever been with other girls.

Except he sure had a hell of a way of showing it.

What the fuck was I still doing in this bathroom with Joel's girl? I was going to get my ass beaten. But, shit, someone needed to be in here, protecting her. Taking care of her. Having a middle-of-the-night conversation with her.

And more. So much more.

She was only wearing a T-shirt and skimpy pink underwear. No bra. And her damn sexy voice telling me how good the wet washcloth felt against her skin almost made me come unglued.

And those legs. Strong and shapely. They could wrap

around my waist so easily. With that dragonfly tattoo on her ankle that I wanted to know more about.

For a brief moment I imagined Ella being stone-cold sober, begging me to kiss her, to touch her, and to be inside her.

She'd have to be sober for me to touch her. She'd also have to ditch Joel. No way would I get myself involved in something like that again. Keeping things on the down-low wasn't all it was cracked up to be. It hurt people. Even *killed* them. And you paid for that shit.

You paid every single day for that shit.

*Fuck.* I couldn't even believe I was entertaining thoughts like that about this girl.

Someone else's girl.

And then Ella started talking again. Her voice was soft and breathy. Like fingernails raking through my hair and then down my back.

I needed to cut that crap out.

Damn, I should've been glad she couldn't see my raging hard-on.

"You know that feeling at the beginning of a relationship with someone?" she asked. "When you're excited to talk to them, see them, and spend time with them? And you absolutely know the feeling is mutual? At least, at first?"

"Yeah, I do," I said, thinking about the couple of girls I'd dated over the years.

"Is that what you were hinting at before . . . before you stopped yourself?" She rolled her head to the other side and her hand came up to rub her temple. I reached over to do it for her before my fingers fell short. I needed to stop touching her before I started liking it too much.

"Maybe. I just think . . ." I rushed my fingers through my hair. "If you're going to be with somebody, then *really* be with them, you know? And if you have doubts or change your mind, don't string them along. Talk to them about it."

"Is that what you think Joel is doing—stringing me along?" She sounded hurt, like a wounded animal. And I didn't want to be the one to make her feel that way.

"Hell if I know," I said. "That's for you guys to figure out. I just know it should be him in here, not me. And maybe . . . maybe you should tell him that."

"How would *you* do things differently? If you were with . . . a girl." She seemed hesitant to ask me. *Shit.* Did *she* wonder if I was gay, too?

Or maybe she just felt she was overstepping bounds.

If anyone had disregarded boundaries tonight, it was me. I hoped she'd stop asking me questions about Joel. Joel was *not* Sebastian. I just wished I'd had the courage to speak up to Sebastian sooner.

Before I ruined his life. His family's life. My life.

"First, I'd make sure the girl was *worth* it," I said, trying to hide the bitterness in my voice. It wasn't totally Amber's fault. I was just a weak-ass fool.

"What do you mean?" She sounded so sleepy. Good thing, because that was the extent of the talking I was willing to do about any of that.

"How about I tell you another time and you try to close your eyes for a bit?"

She mumbled something else and then all I heard was her soft breaths.

Before I knew it, my eyes drifted closed as well.

I jerked awake a while later. My neck was stiff from falling asleep against the wall and my legs felt tight and tense.

Ella had somehow managed to prop her head against my leg. And shit if my hand wasn't tangled in the back of her hair. It was soft and shiny, even though it looked like a long, knotted mess in some spots.

*What the fuck?* Anyone could have walked in here and seen us. And I hoped to hell no one had. Or used their phone to take a photo or some other shit.

I carefully moved her head off my leg and then sprang to my knees. I should have done this an hour ago and been asleep in my own bed by now. I lifted Ella into my arms and then carried her to Joel's room. My forearm was beneath her ass, but I ignored the feel of her skin against mine.

The house was so quiet, I doubted anyone was up. I breathed a sigh of relief.

Ella shifted in her sleep and draped her arm around my neck. Her head was against my lips and hell if I didn't take a quick whiff of her hair. And damn if she didn't smell like almond shampoo.

Joel didn't stir when we inched inside the room. I slid her down next to him and got the hell out of Dodge.